Book Cover by R.A. Rex Draco
Illustrations by R.A. Rex Draco

I0693223

TURBO SUITS 1

The Red Star

By R.A. Rex Draco

THE DRAGONFLY

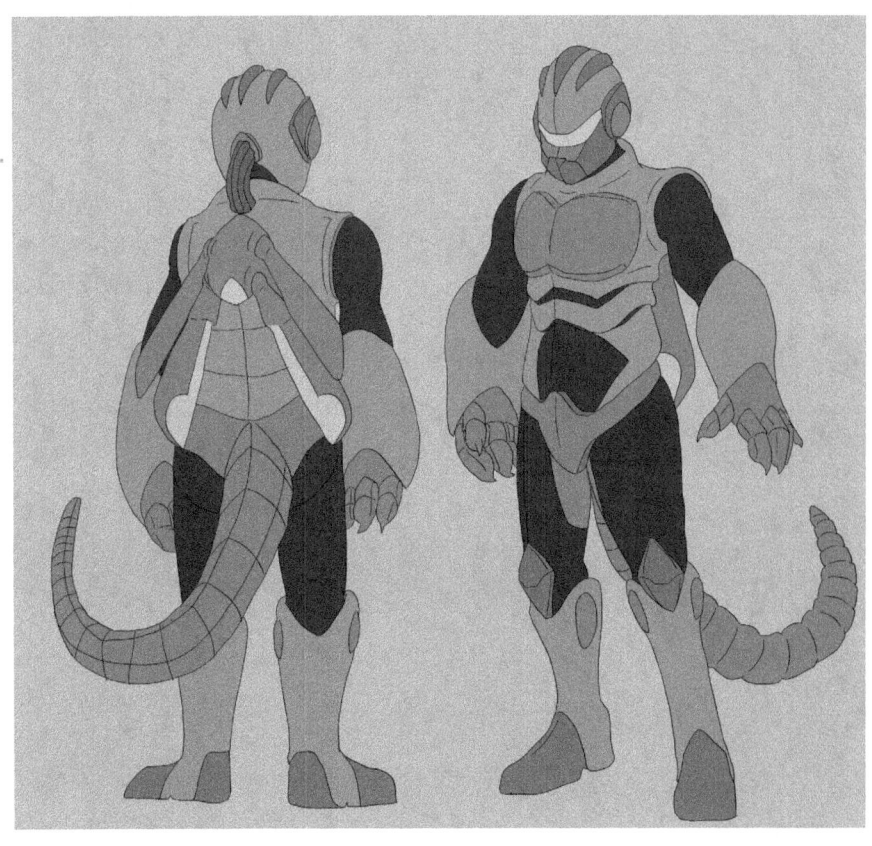

CONTENT WARNING

Classism
Death
Misogyny
Racism
Violence & Blood

CONTENTS

CHAPTER ONE

A Waking Nightmare

"I had never seen anything like it before, and never since.

It was unnatural seeing the world beyond my stonewall grave. We had lived underground for so many generations that the idea of the sun had become a myth. It had turned to dust, consumed by the endless dark... At least that was what our history lessons spoke to as the reason for our migration below the surface. The scriptures read the event with a magnanimous flair so grand it is difficult to discern the truth from the moral quandary.

'The light was like a fire, but it burned white and turned my skin black. I felt it: true fear. I had to get away, my heart unable to still in my chest. It had been a foolish idea to come to the surface. None belonged here on the Ifriti's land and so we returned below the red soils where we stole away to return to the womb of the world.'

The nightmare that I had every night would once again grip my heart.

Despite this idea of labor until death, I wished to escape. The punishment, were I caught, would be far worse than the years I suffered in imprisonment, so I ran. I looked up as the shards of Ifriti fell from the skies: which had been so thusly consumed by the glaring flames. Their shapes were amorphous, outlines distorted by the heavenfires. They were here for my judgment. Massive angels with wings of steel and eyes of black. I couldn't fight, not alone, but I knew they were all dead because I couldn't keep my promise. The angels of steel turned their gnashing claws to me: palms glowing like the tail end of a subterranean lurker. I ran, but my body felt chained. I could hear the metal of their cold talons as they scraped against the ground, but I couldn't let it hold me down. I pushed ahead toward the only place that had not yet been consumed by fire. All around me everything was burning.

Steel spires were melted in on themselves while the crimson tongues of the flames turned to ash the bodies of any caught in the crossfire of the angel's retribution. I ran through rubble and scattered ancient remnants, indescribable pieces of a past I had never before seen. Just how did our ancestors live in a wasteland barren of trees and abundant with stone and steel?

I could hear it grinding its claws against the walls. It was like acid falling into my ears: dripping and burning with every touch. No matter how far I ran it seemed I was trapped, another victim of circumstance. Ducking beneath what appeared to be a building swallowed by the shifting red soils: I awaited the inevitable, lavishing in the momentary reprieve. By now I understood where my impulses brought me, but to face a death like this seemed to far outweigh the wrongs I was unjustly accused of. I was innocent. I just wanted to live free! But now I was going to die: cornered and burned to cinders.

I could hear the hiss of the angel's mechanical wings, the shallow cry as it exhaled in an inhuman tenor. Then it began to pound against my shelter. All that stood between me and this Angel of Death was a piece of sheet metal, centuries old and malleable from the intense heat. Before I knew it: it was beginning to bend *under the force of its pursuit."*

Bang.

Bang!

The banging continued ringing until it wrapped around the head.

"Lights out scumbags!" The bellowing call of a deep, scraping voice cut through the haunting silence of the halls of the prison.

The shouting man had a grizzled face, twisted by scars that pulled the left half of his features into a disfiguring pinch. The corner of his lip was upturned in a sneer which was a permanent feature thanks to the scarring. His drifting gaze crawled along the predesignated route and his brows would deeply furrow, posture shifting to present a pristine state of health despite his malformations which were caused by a consuming disease.

At a glance it was difficult to discern just how old the man was as his skin had become wrinkled and twisted by his calloused flesh. His neck was wrinkled, in some places discolored patches of skin had become so taut that in those spots it drew swirls of flesh forcing it to sag in others places.

The pallid, off-grey color that painted his skin had been the result of the aforementioned invasive sickness that permeated his cells since birth; he was considered to be the senior of the facility he kept watch over. He was its warden and caretaker. Despite his emaciated form, and his bones seemingly rattling with every step: the man presented enough strength to repeatedly hammer away at the bars of the cell doors with a baton, knuckles white from his unrelenting grip. His orders were absolute and his authority over those housed was unshakeable. But those exhausted and twisted by illness were in no rush to act on the demands of the warden. The lights maintained their luminosity, the faint red gleam twisting around corridors of dilapidated stone and rusting metal stood as a sign that there was some life and a will of defiance towards their fate.

The metal bars that barricaded individual rooms had been designed to control the flow of bodies like chattel through the peeling husk of a prison. Moss that covered walls sweat regularly with the putrid scent of mold and would irritate exposed skin just on passing, often leaving prisoners' lesions to inflame with puss.

The defiance soon faded as the luminous, red hues which painted the walls of the small, stone rooms began to dim and shut off. One by one the bodies that were housed in these cramped quarters lost the strength and will to ignore the commands. Once the lights had gone out a solid darkness filled the voids within the enclosed spaces and could little be penetrated with the naked eye. Nothing remained lit save for the faint lights which hung from the hall ceilings that allowed guards to maintain their patrols, not that it was necessary. Many of these men were dying and could no longer fight for freedom.

What lights still remained occasionally flickered at what limited energy resources were allowed to be divested to the prison. Their needs were discounted as their crimes left them naught but slaves, wards of the state. The walls were soaked with a festering rot and what stone remained secured in its mortar was painted with bioluminescent lichen that rooted in the channels of grout. The gunk was ever growing, filling cracks that had expanded out like a network of wires, only coming in to center upon a pillar engraved with old letters and words no longer legible by the greater population. Many were able to read, but the script no longer held meaning as the building had been abandoned by its former occupants generations ago and reclaimed as a prison for the sick and dying. Plants that preferred the wet and humid environment of the prison grew without prejudice. Many gave off a pale, blue glow and were regularly tended to by inmates who had lost their minds to their illness and sought to care for something other than themselves.

At least they knew the plants would survive.

Every few paces the open cells of prisoners could be peered into. The sparsest of amenities was provided: a bed, a seat, and a washing basin. There were no true doors to keep the criminals trapped as walls were too corroded to support a level structure. That, though, did not matter as most of the inmates lived in a persistent state of undernourishment or declared too sick to escape their poorly secured holds.

In one of the cramped rooms rest an inseparable pair of prisoners who lived what was left of their waking hours together. A crooked bunk sat pushed up in the corner of the room, askew from a crumbling window frame which had been lazily barred by some rusting pipes crossed and bound with ferrous wire, inches thick. There was a space between the pipes that would allow one to gaze into the yard where prisoners would be put to work daily. The western wall, where the toilet would normally sit, was naught but an exposed pipe in the ground, the mouth of which was caked in rust and festering with mold and lichen. Much of the wall had crumbled away leaving behind its foundation of metal rods.

A man was laid on his side on the top bunk. "Klaus..." He called.

With dull, green hair and pallid skin the man looked years beyond his age, the sickness having eaten away any remnants of youth they may have had.

The prison's uniform was limited. Tattered cloths of pale browns served as sparse covering for their daily work in the fields of mud and stone. Shoes were for those who could afford to partake in the prison's economy: the buying and selling of contraband. If the soles of the man's feet were any indication: he wasn't the sort to play into the backwards economy that divided and sold rations, smoking herbs, and clothing. It was too much of a hassle and the soles of his feet were already stained with a permanent red hue that came from a lifetime of working on sanctioned farms filled plot to plot with the underground's deep, red soil.

Strands of his dull green hair hung over his face, arms folded behind his head as he lazily swayed a raised knee: his other leg dangling off the side of his top bunk, swinging in the air. Old scars drew lines that blossomed out from behind his neck: tracing a trail of intricate roads along his pale skin before they vanished into the valley of his shoulder blades.

The man had gotten no response from his cellmate who was his younger brother. The man had got imprisoned with him simply because they had been together. "Klaus, he's comin'." The man warned again, his brother standing across the way at the small window.

"In a minute Eric..." But it was never just a minute.

CHAPTER TWO

A Bizarre Religion

The man on the bed didn't have much patience for dealing with the warden's insistence, but he couldn't force his brother to make his life easier by abandoning the only piece of joy they had left in this rotting hellhole. That window had become an escape for Klaus who, when in his cell, stood there for hours with his arms hanging out. Their cell was below ground level and allowed the prisoner to reach out and place his hands on the only bit of land they could reach. Eric felt a sense of annoyance, or maybe it was helplessness, when the Warden walked down the halls and knew that they too would get so sick, that one day they wouldn't have the strength to even dream of being out there. Maybe that was why the bastard had not taken away Klaus' window.

The Warden would be glad to squeeze any ounce of joy that the twins would find. Klaus in particular had been feeding a Dogfish that had burrowed beneath the mud nearby. It was still small enough that the Warden hadn't caught wind of it. Dogfish often laid their eggs in muddy soils where they would hatch and eventually find a Pigwar. These were one of the many strange creatures brought from the brink of extinction with old technology. A symbiotic animal the Dogfish fry latched to a Pigwar's body where they worked to survive together. It was a bit poetic considering their own desires. They wanted to escape this place and work together to survive in this harsh world.

Eric had lived in the prison for about six years of what was left of his short life with his brother. Eric had always fancied himself a mischievous sort who often troubled authority figures, but as a red-foot he lived his life under the thumb of authority that he had not thought to fight until he was no longer able to. Red-foot was the spiteful term for people who worked out in the farms where they could not afford the most basic of needs like shoes and, as such, the soles of their feet were permanently stained red from the nutrient-rich soils that they tended. They were the lowest of low, and adding to the fact that they were men: put them at the bottom of a chain of a hierarchy that would compare them to livestock. In their society it has long come to pass that women have become empowered due to history railing against the primitive structures in the brain that made men inferior. This along with increased religious rhetoric that men were the reason the Ifriti had burned the surface of their world caused men to fall away as leaders.

There hadn't been a major conflict in a thousand years since they lost power, which the ruling parliament known as the Sisters, would use as proof of their unquestionable guidance. But Eric wasn't born in a world where he had any connection to these acts of blasphemy. He was born a second class citizen due simply to his gender, but now he was not even that. The moment he became a prisoner was when he lost all his standing as a living being. Eric turned his green-hued eyes toward his brother who had been staring out the window, waiting for the lights of the city to peek over the horizon.

Beyond the stellar lights of radiant blue lit up every day

at this hour. There wasn't much else to see as the sky above was naught but stone and steel as their life underground has long hid them away from the star filled skies that littered the religious texts with symbology and power. In this place, this world: everyone lived underground. Above them was a ceiling of solid mantle. They sat about 500km below the surface of their planet, which had long since become uninhabitable after the Ifriti rained their world with the tears of the sun.

They had adapted to their underground lives. Low light vision and an organ that housed an extra sensor for light allowed them to feel around much like their burrowing ancestors of presurface eras. It gave them a distinct advantage living where no light penetrated. It wasn't until they had rediscovered the use of bioluminescent plants that they had once thought to have gone extinct during the War of the Sun, as it has come to be known in history books. The plants had gone into hibernation in the post war environment, deep underground, only to resurface about the time their population's numbers began to decline.

The plants were kept in lamps and held in a liquid that encouraged a type of suspended animation. The temperature of the liquid was changed to alter their states of luminosity: cold to keep them asleep and warmth to wake them up. They were woken up during more active hours to maintain productivity among cities and farms. The system was strung together through a network of wires which were braided and fed through interconnected pipe shafts that ran through generators. The activation and deactivation of these generators would pump power, generating the heat the plants required to rouse from their temporary hibernation. Since

Amaroxians were unable to withstand, and in some cases even see, the infrared spectrum the plants made a perfect medium. The liquid was a nitrogen rich fluid that slowed or completely stopped the active decay and aging of the organic matter.

There was a point in the past that the fluid, known only as Jule Vapor, was used to treat Mugenes. It was made of abundant elements, and if necessary could be safely synthesized: but when used in conjunction with the virus it was shown to speed up the infections. There were some rumors that Jule Vapor ended up mutating subjects. It had become a conspiracy popular among citizens of the Southern hemisphere who accused the Northern states of kidnapping throngs of Southern citizens to use in their experiments, while the North accused the South of the very same. It had become weaponized propaganda and nearly ended in conflict when the daughter of an important political figure had disappeared under mysterious circumstances.

It was the first time whispers of a group known as the Red Rebels came into the Amaroxian consciousness. There are some who say the group fights against the Military complex of the Northern sphere, while others say they are against the South's willingness to augment their bodies until there wasn't a piece of organic matter left. Whatever the case the Daughters had caught wind of the situation and quickly shut down all work with Jule Vapor, banning the use of the fluid beyond use in the electrical sector's work.

Klaus was a childish sort to always look forward to these sorts of things so he never missed a chance to watch the "stars" over the city light up. Klaus never showed a sense of responsibility, but Eric knew that Klaus had always been the harder worker of the two, more than Eric cared to admit. Many found it intriguing how different their personalities were as twins, but twins were ever rarely born outside of female pairs to really document the behavioral differences in males.

That aside it was quite strange to call the lights 'stars'. As a people they have not seen a star filled sky in over ten thousand years. Even old texts that described the sky lights were just pictures printed in books that have little context to just how bright they were. Their stars were the lights that glittered across the domes of the capital. Capital cities were some of the brightest places on Amaroxia. Many say one felt safest in the heart of the cities where darkness could not reach.

"Erick, look! They're on!" When Klaus looked back Eric felt like he was staring into a mirror. It was the face of someone he wished he could be like. "Isn't it amazing?" A wide smile painted the youthful will of a carefree spirit, one of which Eric wished to share.

Eric leaned over to peer through the narrow window. "Yeah, it's really nice." Though he said that, he didn't feel the same excitement as his brother. He felt empty.

Klaus smiled and turned back to the vision of stars that speckled the ceiling above. "Yeah." The soft tone made Eric feel that Klaus maybe understood his lackluster feeling towards the starlit sky and what it meant. "You know..." Klaus walked toward their bunk and pushed to his tiptoes to reach the height of Eric's bunk. "You should smile more -- mph!" Eric pressed his hand to his brother's face, smothering the words before they could form.

"I don't want to hear that from you." Eric complained while making an uncomfortable face. "You sound like mom when you say things like that. It's creepy." Though his words were harsh, the upward glance and forced frown were enough to show Klaus that he did not find it as disarming as Eric showed.

It was nice to have memories of the outside world once in a while.

CHAPTER THREE

The Warden's Face

Klaus grinned and slipped into his bunk below Eric's just as the warden and two armed guards walked by. The twins were resting in their beds, suspiciously rolled on their sides with their backs to the cell's twisted gate. The warden was an older man with a scaled patch of skin over his right eye where his eyelid had once been. It had been eaten away by the disease and replaced with a hard fold in order to replicate the delicate skin. Instead of blinking, the man had to roll his eyes up in order to lubricate it.

Much of the prison was home to the sick and dying, many of which were used in experiments at local facilities to help promote scientific and military advancement in the name of the Sisters. Prisoners no longer had rights and were, in turn, property to the colonies that spread across the underground realm. A decline in the population was in part due to a terrifying disease that affected both men and women, though primarily incubated in the male body, eating it away at a grossly increased rate. Cells mutated rapidly: so much so that the body could not keep up and eventually would calcify and become like stone. It had come from off planet, by way of a trade in goods with an alien peoples.

They had traded for a type of organic ore that could be grown and manufactured into a strong metal. No one had any idea that the metal would not only spur the industrial growth of the declining economy, but it would also destroy its people entirely.

Of course Klaus and Eric were still much too young to have known anything about the disease other than that everyone was born with it due to contact with an alien race. After the War of the Sun the planet had tried to rebuild its economy and would trade with outsiders via an ancient elevator built by their ancestors to descend and ascend between the underground and surface. A shy hundred years and a planet full of Amaroxians, turned into a few underground colonies that struggled to survive and the elevator sealed, the world becoming total isolationists.

The warden sneered at the pictures of tranquility the two displayed in mock defiance of his presence. Raising his arm he would rapidly hit against the metal of the bars with his baton, causing the rest of the prisoners to writhe and moan in pain. An Amaroxian's sense of hearing was nearly six times that of other races. In every sense, Amaroxians were similar to Earthlings, beyond the difference that allowed them to live on a world with over less than half Earth's gravity.

This meant Amaroxians were heavier in their build to maintain contact with the surface: a reduced mass and pneumatized bones which allowed for increased body mass without negative results. Their skin was pale, almost translucent with hyper flexible, and hyperextending joints. Their skin was tough, hardened in the way a reptile's would be, making it sandpapery to the touch, but retaining features that could easily be mistaken for an Earthling's delicate skin. Amaroxians once lived as long as Earthlings as well, but that too has since been lost to the disease. A life underground made such things as astrology and astronomy worthless, along with their isolationist society making contact and education of other races the bare minimum, if only to avoid them. Their world, Amaroxia came from a mashup of old languages used to describe the world before the War of the Sun.

The twins snapped their hands to their ears and rolled over to face the door. "You shitty old man, that hurts!" Eric complained loudly, in order to shout over the incessant banging.

Klaus remained silent as a pained expression marred his features, but he otherwise maintained a passive energy.

"Ho hooo," The warden always fancied himself superior, but of all of them he suffered the most handicaps from the disease, which has been aptly named: Mugenes. "You filthy am'lo twins 'sleep already?"

He didn't like the twins, but they always caused him more trouble than he felt they were worth. To him prisoners were just animals who couldn't abide by the basic laws of society. They didn't have to do much as men save to remain submissive to the peaceful rule of the Sisters and all their needs would be provided for them. Am'lo was a term to describe a wild and untamed animal, left over from pre-War language.

Amaroxia's language has shifted many times over the years as their ancient math and science languages had interfered with their home languages. Over time the Amaroxian tongue had settled to what it is today, though the Northern and Southern hemispheres had their own dialects that came as a result of the Southern Hemisphere's use of Botanical language.

There was no such thing as a wild animal on Amaroxia. Most animals lived among or with the Amaroxians, so all of them did their best to get along well. There were, what were called, feral logators, which were a type of massive, burrowing driger that violently consumed any living creature in the underground. Logators were killed on sight, or used in experimentation due to their longevity and hearty natures. The creatures were called Amaroxian Logators, or am'lo for short. Prisoners were often called am'lo due to their inability to follow the general rules and expectations for living with others.

There were some animals that were considered domesticated, but they were often work animals that were used on farms or by emergency services to help find people who have been caught in cave-ins, which were a common problem in the underground society. The most well known of domestic animal in Amaroxia was the Red Wolf, though it was not related to the quadrupedal predators found on Earth or other Earth-like planets. It was some sort of reptilian offshoot that was closely related to Dragons.

Eric smiled. "I was having such a wonderful dream..." he began, below him Klaus nodding with a smile. Eric's expression became dark as his brows flattened and his head lowered, shoulders slumping. "You weren't there..." Klaus shook his head only to jump when the warden slammed his fist against the wall.

Eric was stubborn when it came to dealing with the arrogant warden so found it difficult not to bark back. It often made Klaus worry, but the older male (by three minutes) had a pride that was unshakeable even in their current state. Eric hadn't always been such a foul-mouthed sort. He used to take orders well. There were some things even an obedient slave wouldn't do.

Eric often defied convention when it came to a man's position in society and was a brilliant liar when it came to his own feelings. He knew he should keep his head down and listen and for many years he had done just that. Klaus was a bit more honest and would smile or cry when happy or hurt, but he easily pushed away from confrontational events that his brother stirred with the warden.

For Klaus it hadn't always been that way between them. Klaus had always been the one to brute force his way through situations but since they ended up here the man felt he lost his spine when they were stripped from their mother's skirt. Eric found his bravado and would stand up against the Warden's unjust, abusive ways.

Klaus would often find himself silently begging Eric not to prod the warden any more, for both their sakes. But the silence would not quell Eric's temper this evening. It was not until Klaus quietly murmured a name that Eric's tense form seemed to settle. His harsh glare remained on the warden before it dissipated and his eyes lowered to his lap.

"That's okay." The warden smirked, the sort of twisted grin that made an uneasy feeling inside. It was like watching a snake eat itself.

The man leaned forward and rested his arm against the

bars of their cell. His warm smile made the hairs on the backs of their necks stand on end. "You're going to be visiting your *favorite* doctor tomorrow." He stressed the word, grinding his lips over the term knowing it would cause them to react.

Eric all but fumbled from the top bunk as he shot forward and onto his knees. If not for Klaus sitting up and letting Eric use his thighs as a stepping stool to the ground, both panicking men would have likely been a pile of bodies on the floor. Klaus moved to stand beside Eric who rushed the gates, grabbing the bars with ferocity, despite his physical ailments. The warden leaned back, the smile still on his face.

The quack, as Eric fondly called them. Because of their unusual condition they were pincushions for the local Science Laboratory down the hills. At first the Military division showed interest due to their health, but it seems they had a request from their science division to use them like a pair of lab rats.

CHAPTER FOUR

Not Just An Animal

"You bastard, we aren't going back to that nut-job's lab!" Eric was a willful sort especially when it came to being experimented on, yet there was not much he could do to stop it. As men they didn't have choices, and prisoners even less.

If he had to make the choice he would rather stay here and deal with Warden Haut's shit than listen to that mad scientist spout their chaotic rhetoric. It had only been a few days since they arrived in the prison when they were first approached by Haut with the news that they would be so fondly looked after by the Porvin Science Division. Since this was their first time in the Porvin Zone they had never heard of the Science division out there and had only assumed there were just a stretch of prisons lined up for the Daughters to dump the sick and dying.

"You serve no good in society anymore, so be glad yer being given this chance to make something of your worthless lives." While the warden hated the pair, he was still a man. And as a man he prided himself in mindlessly serving the autonomous matriarchies of the colonies. "It's best for everyone that you just quietly give up your lives. I hear they're pretty intrigued with how slow your mutations are taking hold. At yer age you should be already missin' an eye, or your tongues." The warden's smirk pushed up his permanently lidded eye, only further accenting the patch of false skin over it.

The warden had lost his right eye's use at around fifteen years of age so much of it was bionic, the lid having no functionality left was also replaced. He was born with Class B Mugenes. He had been born without a lung and his entire gastrointestinal tract was all but gone. He had to be fitted with artificial, bionic intestines.

He lost his eye and the use of his left arm at fifteen. The warden would be a Class S infection in a few short years. While he had no use in society at this age and level of infection, he still fought to find use in the prisons, corralling sick and dying prisoners that couldn't fight back. He clung to his duty fervently because once he was unable to continue he knew he would be at death's door.

It was the main Laboratory under Red Shield's control here in the Porvin Zone that focused on biological research and as such they needed specimens so the Provin Detention Center was a perfect source of bodies. Of course the laboratory wasn't here that long and was built a month after the prisons became full. One wouldn't think it so easy to fill a prison with such a high mortality rate on the planet, but they managed.

For some it seemed more like a place to hold spare bodies they could use for experimentation as it was illegal to use citizens as test subjects for anything from experimental medical procedures to vaccines. That was especially important with the Mugenes virus which was an inescapable fact of Amaroxian life for the past hundred years. They made sure to have enough stock of varied states of infection to test possible cures. The closest anyone has ever come to a cure was a painkiller that diminished the pain the virus produced in the body and slowed its growth enough to study it at length.

The infections affected people differently. While the naturally stable genome of men was consumed more rapidly than the constantly changing genome of their female counterparts, there were still some who suffered at a much slower pace. The average life expectancy for a male Amaroxian was thirty. The warden was twenty-four and was already losing mobility as is skin calcified over his bones. There are individuals who live to fifty years of age, but those individuals receive regular injections of the serum, meaning that only the rich or those with roles in the government complex could access the medicine. The poor, the laborour, and anyone else outside of these classes found themselves with the short end of the stick.

The infections affected people differently. While the naturally stable genome of men was consumed more rapidly than the constantly changing genome of their female counterparts, there were still some who suffered at a much slower pace. The average life expectancy for a male Amaroxian was thirty. The warden was twenty-four and was already losing mobility as is skin calcified over his bones.

Eric and Klaus were born on a farm part of a manufacturing colony. They were more highly susceptible to the illness being so close to industrial production of the ore. No one knows at what level of infection the pair were born at. The doctor they were currently seeing suspected they were born Mugenes free, but such a thing had only ever occurred for those in the role of Sisters. It had been quite the declaration, one that had lost the doctor their accreditation with the Capital.

At the age of seventeen the twins were at a Class C infection level, which meant their geroiid organs, a small organ found in the forehead which normally helped Amaroxians sense their environment, were rendered useless. But this did not happen. Their lungs and stomachs also remained untouched which, by the time an infection rose to a C Class: much of the function in the digestive tract would slow or halt entirely.

Klaus would move to stand behind Erick, resting his hand on his brother's shoulder as a frown painted his solemn features. "That isn't fair warden..." Klaus rarely voiced disagreement, which sent the warden momentarily aback, face stretching as he looked to Klaus with a disapproving expression.

Eric knew his brother hated going to the laboratories. The doctor's assistant scared Klaus for some reason. She was a paraplegic with a Class A infection, so one would think her hardly a threat. But she still had a mean swing and meaner temper. She'd hurl a piece of computer equipment at you without thinking twice about you or the expensive lab gear.

Eric didn't get along with either of them, but he primarily held his distrust for the doctor in charge as it was her fault they had to go to the labs and had been forcibly enrolled in the government program.

It wasn't going to save her reputation and he felt it as a step backwards to any attempt to find a cure for this disease.

For prisoners they were sent to one of two places: a lab or a plantation where am'lo were put to work in highly toxic industrial waste management. They were cheaper labor than the foreign work bought from the Andrium Colonies on the southern hemisphere of the planet's core.

The government program made them, essentially, lab animals for the mad scientist and her government funded research. All because of what was between their legs.

The warden scoffed, finally finding his spine, his will having tapered off for a moment when Klaus trained his gaze on him. "Too damn bad, life ain't fair. You'll just have to be ready tomorrow. She'll be sending someone special ta pick you up. She says it's a big day for you two lil' shits." He laughed out. "Least yer makin' use of ya'selves before you rot in the Void."

Eric had been staring at the warden with a hard glare this entire time, but his gaze wasn't as strong as Klaus' had been. If nothing else the warden felt more empowered tearing Eric down. Eric's hands squeezed around the metal bars, gripping until one could see the blood pumping through his veins beneath his near-translucent skin. Klaus moved to drop his hand from his brother's shoulder, feeling the imminent meltdown.

Eric tried to rattle the bars like a snake baring his fangs, but Eric's were dull, venom empty. "Yeah, well at least I'll be rotting in the Void and not a piece of art for the Sister's shitty garden ya friggin' gargoyle." Eric bit out.

Klaus' heart dropped as it was too late to stop his brother's verbal assault. When one reached a Class S Infection, they were also known as Gargoyles due to their haunting expressions of pain as their bodies completely shut down after full body calcification.

The warden began to fume, his officers unable to fully stifle their laughter. "Fine!" Smoke was almost blowing out of his now-red face. "You shits can go to the labs 'morrow with sand to eat!" He bit back and stomped off.

The two guards looked to each other with troubled expressions before hurrying after the warden.

"Erick..." Klaus gently reprimanded.

He knew Eric couldn't help his temper when it came to the warden, at least not lately. The warden got sicker with each passing day. He was at the end of his life and he spent it making inmates miserable. It wouldn't be long until a new warden would be sent, but until then everyone suffered the warden's high and mighty attitude and his aggressions.

He would disrupt prisoners when they slept, or kept their rations from them and forced them to work the fields on empty stomachs. Eric and Klaus may have been born with disadvantageous lots, but at least they were able to survive on their own wit and skill. But here in the warden's prison they were am'lo, creatures unworthy of his mercy and care.

CHAPTER FIVE

A Desolate Struggle

Eric knew he couldn't always bark when he hadn't any bite to back it up, but if there was one thing he couldn't stand was people in power mistreating the people they should be taking care of. They weren't weak and sick like the other prisoners. If they wanted they could escape, but they were too far from the capital to truly escape anywhere. They were surrounded by scattered military-owned scientific compounds and badlands. The closest city was Sluumin, but even that was far into the wastes with the only usable Tunnel leading from there to the Capital.

The only official way into Sluumin was through a military convoy, but there were many whispers in the prisons of Harvesters, who shepherded the sick between the capital and poverty stricken wastes for cheap labour. It was a place to live that was not in the prisons or stranded out in the Industrial Colonies shoveling toxic waste until you died of the noxious fumes before you could ever turn to stone. There was a sanctuary deep beneath the clay walls of Sluumin, but it was only a rumor, quickly squashed by military presence.

With lights out the prison had become a tomb. The industrial machines that the prisoners were forced to work on day in and day out were shut down for the night, putting an end to the dragging, scraping vibrations that rattled through the collapsing prison walls all throughout the day.

Due to the Planet's unstable deliverance of power to far off sectors: the use of power was heavily restricted for industrial machines not only to conserve, but to reduce the toxic fumes that would condense in the air. As an underground society the gasses had few places to escape through the mantle. Much of the planet's power was diverted to pumps that expelled the toxic gasses from the core and the rest powered Amaroxian municipalities, so it was an unsustainable endeavor and a strain when both were active at all hours of the day.

Amaroxia was split into sectors. Each sector had its own generator and backup generator which was connected to the main system located in the Capital which was at the center of the sector divisions. Farms were disconnected from these systems and relied on their own ingenuity. They were provided with bio-lamps and kits to build a makeshift generator on any geothermal vents found on their land, but the kits themselves were expensive and often ate into half a farmer's credits for the season, as most of their credits went back into necessities and power just didn't seem to be one.

According to Amaroxian laws power was not necessary for survival, or even being comfortable as it has been determined an adult Amaroxian can survive comfortably with sufficient food and water. This may have been the measured statistics, but any farmer could tell you that power helped a great deal and reduced the hours spent idle when they could be productive. True generators were massive and were paid for by the Capital's taxes. Each city in a sector, particularly newly built cities, would end up with increased tax to pay off the generators provided by the Capital for an upward of fifty years. It didn't seem a long time for most civilized societies, but seeing as the Amaroxian lifespan was cut laughably short from the Mugenes virus, coupled with low populations: there was no city to date that has yet to complete their payment program.

Without the rumble of machines or the grating hum of power all was silent save for the choking coughs from those suffering in their cells. The Mugenes disease was terrifying -- and there was not one person on the planet born without the affliction. Their days were cut short by the ravaging plight with no cure discovered even with almost a hundred years of scientific research. The night was always a solemn reminder of what little time each person had left. The night was an obstacle and it seemed an easy enough hurdle -- until the coughing stopped.

The twins had settled in their bunks. On the top bunk Eric lay staring at the mold encrusted ceiling, his hands crossed over his chest as he contemplated on the number of years they spent here, and how many more they had left in this dying society. They ran against a clock that seemed to speed up and slow down on a whim.

His fingers snaked back through his hair, eyes pinching closed as he felt the frustration of the warden's words and actions -- or perhaps it was his own ineptitudes and weakness that grated on his nerves. He carried the guilt of believing he had doomed his brother and himself to this hell, burdening himself as the cause for their current predicament.

"Hey Klaus..." Eric could feel his brother awake beneath his bunk. It wasn't hard to notice what Klaus was thinking most of the time, or know how he felt despite his usually expressionless features. "The world doesn't need us."

Eric had always thought it was a normal feeling to have with a brother, a twin -- one you have lived with since before birth: but the theories from their doctor had him fretting that they perhaps were a mutation among the disease that was an aberration rather than a blessing in this cruel world.

It made them a target for their scalpels.

"Let's escape together." Eric expressed, hands coming to rest on his stomach as he finally collected his thoughts.

Klaus, on his bunk below, looked up toward the underside of Eric's bed. His head tilted slightly as he blinked. "Really?" The whisper of hope touched his voice made Eric's heart ache. "We'll go back home right?" But they were from Agris, which was all the way across the hemisphere... The trip on foot was nigh impossible. "Go back to mum."

But how could Eric deny such an innocent and gentle whim from his brother? "Yeah..." Eric rolled to his side, letting his arm dangle over the edge of his bed. He waited until he felt Klaus' fingers wrapped around his own. "We'll kick the warden's ass on the way out." He promised.

Amaroxia had no rivers or seas: just mountains, valleys and immeasurable trenches that made travel long and difficult. Most major tunnels and means of rapid transportation were tightly controlled by the military as Amaroxia was a stratocracy based on a matriarchal rule. Traversing the badlands, which was any road and tunnel not guarded by the military, was a dangerous task.

Not only because of the unstable land that shook and fell apart underfoot, but the undeniable fact that there lived many creatures that Amaroxians denied existed; they were the types of creatures that the people had no word for. They lived with amiable, passive animals that did as they needed. These creatures were rumored to be far worse than am'lo drigers.

"Erick…" Klaus tugged at his hand. "I'm here too, I'll fight the battles you can't." Klaus' voice was soft, but there was a conviction to his words. He had felt the hesitation in his brother's tentative grip. "And we'll go far, farther than anyone."

"Right. Let's go to sleep Klaus." Eric didn't want to admit it, but he was scared -- scared that his nightmare was something more than just the feverish madness of a dying body.

With a rumbling clank and shuddering hiss the industrial machines started back up come the morning, hailing the start of work hours. One would have little indication it was morning in the way many creatures would have perceived. Light beneath the surface of Amaroxia simply did not exist. Instead of a sunrise generators turned up the dim red lights that filled every hall, crevasse, tunnel and chamber that had been occupied by the people. It was never a gentle waking.

The violence of the machines churning to life provided a stark reminder of the urgency that filled their lives. They were on borrowed time and they all knew it. One had to hand it to the Amaroxians though. Instead of collapsing into anarchy, or slipping into the obsessive, nihilistic thoughts that accompanied the end of days – they turned to science and the military. Political correctness became everyone's peaceful solution. Violence was meaningless in a world where a virus that shortened the lifespan by over half was an inescapable fact that haunted every aspect of society: from its laws to its religion.

Eric felt his heart thunder in his chest as the taste of metal and dirt filled the air. He noticed a difference in the taste since he had arrived at the prison. The air here was filthy. The metal particles were so dense they cut the back of the throat when you breathed, making the work at the prisons dangerous as a stray spark could light the air on fire or one could simply not wake, suffocated when perforated lungs rupture in the middle of the night. Eric's eyes felt heavy but he would eventually crack them open, only to see the cold wall of his cell. Some days he would forget where he was and that he was no longer at home.

CHAPTER SIX

Hard Knock Half-Life

The waking hours were always the hardest to push through. As much as the pair protested their daily lives: they worked harder than anyone else out there and without a whisper to one another. They were used to the backbreaking labor and it gave them a sense of home as well as a way to forget the present.

Men were gathered in the fields and pitted against the environment. The prison sat on land that was dry. Plants refused to grow on it while jagged stones sat scattered around, jutting out of the ground. There was nothing to harvest, nothing to nurture, yet they were forced to tend soils to allow for the dried out minerals to be aerated. Prisoners were made to clear old metal fields, places they mined for natural and unnatural resources found on Amaroxia. Their work would allow new fields to be eventually terraformed. A new field often took several months to prepare, so in the cycle of new and old prisoners the one field could be constantly worked until the government made use of it.

Eric's eyes would snap open as his cell doors were slammed wide by the guards. From outside they banged their batons against the walls with enough force to wake the many dead that slept among the living. No matter how much Eric was wrapped around in his thin sheets, he'd always managed to find himself sans a blanket and his twin pressed up against his back.

It wasn't that Eric minded it, but he didn't like to admit to himself that he couldn't sleep alone. Neither of them could. They were born together, and he romanced the idea they would die together. His fists clenched at the thought of dying in this prison. It only made him more determined to escape. The idea trailed off his chest followed by an annoyed huff. He swung back his elbow to push Klaus away and out of bed, but the man was difficult to rouse in the early hours of the work day. Eric took no pity when Klaus whined about wanting five more minutes of slumber to accumulate lost hours from work. Neither brother looked forward to the day, but they could not stall for time much longer as the guards would eventually turn hoses on them.

The elder of the two would arch his back, feeling his bones pop and complain with sore knots at his movement. He reached his hand back to shove at Klaus' face, peeling the lazy wart off him as the younger tried to desperately cling to his sibling's torso.

"We don't have time for this." Eric complained, recalling what awaited them this day.

Knowing what was to come did not make his body feel any less awake, let alone willing to work.

It was pointless work, he knew. He used to like a hard day's work, but with these fields one would never see a stone grow from its confines again. Just by touching it he could tell it had been completely drained of all its nutrients. It's been recycled too much.

But it was not as if they had a choice. They may not have worked for pay, or made to work to succeed, but at least they had something to occupy their minds for the day. Back home they produced the planet's main source of organic metal, Eomite. Eomite was rock that grew and could be planted in nutrient rich fields. This stone was everything for Amaroxia as it produced energy, it could be made into food and was a strong building material.

Eric and Klaus lived with their mother back on farmland. Farmland, as it was called, was owned by the government. The large plots of land were often settled every 600 square meters and ranged anywhere from barren, red soil to arid, ashen dirt. Boulders with bioluminescent Agarical fungi were planted every few miles to provide sufficient light and tangible markers for every three meters. This is where those born of the working class slaved away from birth until death. It was the only skill they afforded. They could not usually read, they could not afford to go to the education facilities in the city as compensation provided to farmers from the government was usually in the form of rations and enough to trade for clothing and equipment. It was risky to send a child to an education facility. They were highly competitive and one risked losing the family's limited funds.

Anything produced on the farms went directly to the Colonies and, in return, you were given goods equal to your production rate which was dictated in Parliament during the first colonial settlements underground as a way of reducing waste and managing resources. Machines were sent to help with farming, and materials for repairing the mills' machinery. They even sent food rations, enough for the working families to survive with. There was little luxury, something of which they could only find on the days off. Hunting and mud fishing were among the more leisurely events a low-class family was permitted to do on the government plots.

The imprisoned workers were quick to hop from their bunks at the cacophony roused by the guards' growing impatience. Sick or not a schedule had to be kept in order to maintain the status quo. Amaroxia was also called the Red Clock, because everything in the day could be measured: from the waste disposal hours to the crying of babes. Klaus and Eric were hooted and hollered at to get dressed, so they had no choice but to ready themselves for work lest find themselves further under the ire of the Warden's temper.

The clothing they were given was simple, colorless sleeveless tops and a pair of faded, blue shorts, which were loose and stopped just above their knees, giving protection to their exposed skin, while keeping their legs free to move about the deep, sucking muds of the fields. A red sash was given to them to keep their heads and necks cool when forced to excavate crystal caverns, super heated caves that grew organic crystal stone.

Day did not come to Amaroxia as it did for other worlds, not anymore. Not only was the entirety of their culture a subterranean one, where the peoples had come to live their hourly cycles devoid of solar light, but one's whose religion told the history of the death of their world's sun. That was not to say that there weren't other forms of illumination or warmth, such as bioluminescent phytoplankton, mosses, or geothermal geysers. The skin of what was once a diverse species had become dull and colorless, somewhat translucent in the void of the planet's belly.

Their color vision had deteriorated over the course of thousands of years. Senses such as hearing took precedence over taste, smell over touch which left them with diminished feeling on the surface of their pale flesh. There was also the natural pull of the planet's core that created a centralized magnetic direction that always let the tunnel dwellers never find retreat in the Abyss. The Abyss was a place in Amaroxia that had nothing. It had no sense of up or down. It was a place forbidden where even criminals were remiss to flee to. There was no life in the Abyss. It was a blackhole.

But was prison any different from the Abyss? The Void?

They were not provided much in the way of protective clothing to work in the fields. The laborers' bare feet scraped against the stone-filled soils which became bruised and bloodied by the jagged stones. They had no shovels nor anything that could constitute as a tool, but years of being raised on what was a veritable rock farm: the twin's feet had become hardened and inked red by the nutrient rich soils and their hands capable of gripping surfaces with the ease of a mite.

Ushered out like cattle they ended up in a line-up of prisoners, two by two, many of which suffered from various stages of the Mugenes mutation. Coughing and sluggish steps kept the guards on duty, trying to keep time or else the prison lost money, because that was all prisoners were for the land. It was given to wardens who could scrape up what little resources the deadland could be squeezed for. Grants were given to them to support their efforts and so long as they reaped profits the government would pay. They were a resource and a valuable one, too valuable to pass out pardons and free dying men...

"Erick." Klaus kept pace behind his brother, his voice held under his breath.

Eric looked up, following Klaus' gaze. Up ahead one of the prisoners had collapsed. He was a Class C and the disease had taken his geroiid and infected much of his lungs. He was thrown into a coughing fit before crumbling to the ground. It sounded like a wet rag being stuffed into the engine of a machine. It sputtered until it just -- stopped. Eric turned his head away from the man and continued to walk. They never knew how quick the disease would mutate. It was never the same. Eric gripped his arm, hugging it to his chest as he squeezed his eyes shut. It never got easier to see.

CHAPTER SEVEN

Line In The Sand

Klaus placed his hand on Eric's shoulder, the tight pull of Eric's muscles obvious beneath his palm. The guards grabbed the collapsed man's shirt to pull him to his feet. Some of the prisoners had stepped back and turned away to return to their march. It had not been clear what the others had seen, but when the limp man's figure was turned around as he was escorted off the field his back was visible and there was no denying the sickening sight as his shirt was wrinkled up from the guards' harsh treatment. The fallen prisoner's back looked calloused, rough. It was discolored and thick knots ran along the line of his spine.

Eric rolled his shoulder out of Klaus' grip as he moved to turn away, putting distance between himself and the dead man walking. "There's nothing we can do." Eric's voice was shaky, though it was little more than a whisper exhaled from his chest.

The disease had likely reached the man's spine and would soon have him crippled.

The disease had likely reached the man's spine and would soon have him crippled. As bones calcified they became fused and as a result the body could no longer move. Here in the Northern Hemisphere there was a strong distrust of prosthetics and many opted out of replacing damaged parts, but those were those who strictly adhered to the religion. For others it was, once again, something tied to wealth. No one was going to give a prisoner a new spine. And those who did have replaced parts were, more often than not, government workers who could afford the obscene cost of the complicated medical procedures.

Even if a labourer were to save for half his life, from birth, he still wouldn't have made enough to even replace a finger bone, let alone tracts of intestine or an intricate system such as the spinal chord. Here in the prisons you were the spare parts. When you died your blood went to the hospitals. Your organs shipped off as needed and what was left wasn't even given to the scavengers. It was scooped up by the scientists for testing.

The prisoner would no longer be able to work meaning his use as a labor resource was gone – but now he was free game for the scientists to use as a lab rat until his death. Resources changed hands quickly, and it didn't matter who you went to, or what happened to you. A person's usefulness to society was not diminished by death.

Eric had often heard Criers speak resentfully of those who looked to abandon their world for solitude and death in the Abyss. Criers were cults who denounced the Sun's Scriptures in lieu for the totality and light that remained deep in the Abyss. The Abyss, according to Criers, set one free, not to his death.

Sometimes Eric felt that such a place was judged without anyone ever knowing it. Had anyone ever been there? There were many rumors that circled around the Abyss, but the story that most captured Eric's imagination was the rumor of a paradise out of the reach of the government where none ruled and all were provided for. It was a lawless zone that had no gender. Everyone was equal. Though it was hard to believe such a place stayed out of the Sister's control for so long.

It was fair to argue that they did not have the desire to explore it, because they certainly had the technology. Within a few feet of the Abyss it was said that all magnetic pull stopped, and any bioluminescent plants taken near its entrance withered upon crossing the threshold, leaving Amaroxians essentially blind in the darkness.

Maybe a place where no man could reach was a Paradise.

Though sometimes it was a strange concept everyone had access to technology, so even cultists had no excuse to have not explored it. Even now the most advanced pieces of technology afforded to the common man were small pads filled with digital information, connected to a single server that sat at the center of Amaroxia's Capital with unfiltered information passing through the systems, constantly updating residents on activity within the Citadel.

There were still stories of machines that could fly and swim over vast expanses, but they were mere myths now. Amaroxians had naught but whimsical tales of vast, unexplorable swells of deep water and infinite skies.

With the line of men broken by the unexpected loss of a comrade the rest of the day became that much longer, and they had yet to be marched out into the fields to start work. Eric did what he could to avoid his thoughts surrounding the ever present reality of a looming death. Despair thickly laced the air of the dilapidated, stone walls of the prison with a sorrow that was palatable.

The grounds hadn't always been a prison. The land had been bought by the current Warden's family and had a purpose prior to its current use, long forgotten by its incarcerated inhabitants. It had been a story passed down from inmate to inmate, a means of diminishing the land's hold over them. From its design one could guess it had once been a mill, where Eomite was ground to produce food. Eric had lived in a place like this once. If he were free, could he find home again? It felt so far now. Traveling on foot made it seem an impossible dream to return to.

There was once a way people could locate each other on the surface with the use of a type of self triangulating map, but down below they were forced to live using this inborn sensory location due to an abundant metal in Amaroxia called Khromus, which prevented most machines from seeing very far. The metal was sometimes known as Krons because of its use in many time keeping devices. Khromus was plentiful and was practical in its uses in what was a primarily digital society.

Khromus could be grown when planted in fields and were settled in old fields where Goryanium once grew. Goraynium was an organic metal that was grown in the soils of Amaroxia. It was a foreign, parasitic metal that was hastily imported into the planet. Goraynium is the primary source of the Mugenes Virus and because of their strict standards of trading the ore had been put under strict control, but their world was eventually isolated from the surface entirely. Unfortunately it had been too late to stop its spread.

These days there is not a single child born without the

Mugenes Virus. The planet was a ticking time bomb on the path to death, which only made the Sister's rule all the more powerful. They kept society running at a pace which kept the world from falling to pieces, for many believed there was a chance to save themselves from the inevitable end.

In the search of a new, renewable resource Goraynium was discovered off-world through trades. Negotiations with an alien race, many just called Vims, helped the government to secure a steady supply of the bumper crop for their world. The Vims called themselves by another name unpronounceable by the Amaroxian tongue, not that it mattered anymore. It was a metal that could grow more rapidly than Eomite and produced a chemical known as sekosterid necessary for much of the functions in the Amaroxian body, so it was a valuable resource that replaced many types of primary crops at Farms.

Goraynium produced over ten times the amount of sekosterids than Eomites, but unlike Eomite it produced high levels of infrared radiation in the refining process. For an Amaroxian, even a minute level of white light radiation was highly toxic. It produced hardening of the skin and third-degree burns. But the infrared rays were harder for Amaroxians to detect and eventually led to the development of the Virus, though only in name as Mugenes was a genetic disease. Amaroxians typically lived under conditions of chemiluminescence which produced no radiation, and had no ill effects on their constitutions.

"Erick, Klaus!" the Warden's voice carried through the silence, breaking the solemn air, causing many to wince at the harsh shout.

Eyes would try to avoid the man as he stalked passed. When the twins were called everyone was at risk of the warden's temper. The old, scar covered man marched with purpose, the brothers busy with their work, trying to ignore the inevitable confrontation. With two armed guards he came to a stop a few feet from the siblings.

The guards could hardly be considered a threat with medical masks over their faces and dingy uniforms that were barely kept together at the seams. Their only means of defense from the feeble prisoners were batons. It was plenty against weak willed men, but that was little defense against the feral beasts that roved the edges of the barren wastes.

The man would turn his good eye towards the body they had dragged out of the lines. They were still breathing, but barely. "Get the shovels, I don't want this rotting on my land." He wanted them to bury the man before he had finished dying.

CHAPTER EIGHT

Selling Broken Goods

It was a task no one cared to partake in but some say suffocation was a mercy to the hardening process. The act of burying the dead was also viewed as an archaic ritual, but in the wastes, due to lack of surveillance, it was an absurdly common practice. Burying your dead whilst living underground risked causing cave-ins, but it also put what little ground water they had at risk, not that it mattered to the Warden.

The twins were unceremoniously shoved towards a field just west of the main yard, a wheeled barrow carrying the corpse-to-be. The body was pushed along by the brothers, the guards carrying their shovels along for the task. They needed to babysit the two because the warden didn't trust them, but on a personal level the masked men wouldn't have felt right making the two do this on their own. The prisoner was still a man and deserved a bit more dignity in death than he was allowed in life.

The western field had once been a scientific research facility, but it was abandoned over a century ago after it was met with disaster. A controlled explosion testing the stability of Goraynium as a kinetic energy source brought to light the volatility of the ore, making many of the facilities handling it in the capital to hire off-colony farms to start manufacturing it. It was this action in the line of many that created a breeding ground for the catalyst of the ore's eventual hazards. Perhaps had the people a better understanding of the mineral it would not have become such a pervasive cancer.

They arrived at an open space free of debris and hadn't already been dug. The dead of the prison were often buried here. When they died they too would be out in this field so they made sure to find their comrade a good plot. With the shovels being thrust into their hands they felt as if they had no choice but to start digging.

"This isn't right, and you know it." Eric glared at the guards who could do nothing but shrug.

The one moved to shove Eric ahead. "We don't have much of a choice. The Warden will bury us sooner if we argue." Even though the Warden was at a higher stage of infection it had not meant he became weaker.

If nothing else the mutations increased an Amaroxian's strength. Despite the unrelenting pain and the maddening maladies that came with the Mugenes there were numerous benefits that, sadly, could not outweigh its presence. Aside from the elevated physical prowess there was also a startling set of alterations that strengthened the eyes that reduced light sensitivity. Another queer change was the body's vitality and physical defenses. The calcification hardened a layer of dermis which made it difficult to pierce. It was a problematic change nearer the final stages of the disease as it was harder for doctors to retrieve blood samples. With additional vitality one would find their stamina nigh exhaustible.

Strength, vitality, and loss of light sensitivity were immeasurable benefits, but with the body slowly turning into stone and bones fusing together along with nausea, vertigo, and gastrointestinal disruptions as well as reproductive deficits: the faster they could find a cure for Mugenes the sooner they would be able to break this cycle of death perpetuated by a mistake made a thousand years prior.

The loose ground was a risk to anyone digging. The guards dragged the prisoner in not long after the twins began pushing the soils aside. The inmate was still breathing, but it was labored and sporadic. His lungs were hardening. His body was graciously tossed against the topsoils. The guards made sure to stand a good distance away so if the unstable soils decided to collapse they would be safe.

Eric stared at the ground, the head of his shovel stabbing into the hard earth. "Maybe if we kept digging...we could escape in another way." The consideration was morbid and caused the guards to take another step back.

For Amaroxians, who lived underground, a ceiling of hard mantle over them, the only way out was further down. They had once lived on the surface. Remnants of the journey from above ground to below still exist today. The sky elevator, or Worm's Spine: extended from the center of the capital over 500km to the ceiling. The surface is uninhabitable due to the white fire that consumed the land, turning it into charred desert. It was an event simply known as the War of the Sun. It is believed a war raged by man had called down the Ifriti from the sun to wipe out Amaroxians.

Klaus considered his brother's words with a heavy sigh. He leaned against his shovel feeling his thoughts crawling over the ones he shared with his brother.

Yes. Underground would be good. But there was no escape from what they had done. They would always know.

Klaus stood up, resting his hand on the neck of his shovel as he sighed. "It'll be dark here soon." The man looked over as he rested his chin against the top of his red-stained hand, which lay atop the head of the shovel. "It's too cold."

Amaroxians saw with heat, ultraviolets. The world below them is said to be so cold that you become blind. The magnetic force is so distressing that one cannot recall up from down. Eric looked to Klaus, his green eyes focusing on his sibling as his gaze narrowed and lip turned up in a half-sneer. Sometimes he was troubled by the idea of a world below them, but at the same time it seemed more a freedom than here. Being lost in an all encompassing void... it sounded perfect.

No sickness, no beasts, nothing...

Eric smacked his tongue over his lips. "It would be wonderful." He chuckled as the hole was deepened.

The two dug with hopes of seeing a glimpse of that world. Eric seemed the most enthusiastic about the idea. "Down there you'll never see or hear people. Just peace."

Klaus became unnerved as Eric's digging became frantic. The younger twin reached out his hand, moving to press it against his brother's back. Their bare feet dug against the red soils, sinking against the soft surface they had disturbed.

Eric's manic focus was becoming intense, but before it reached an apex --

"I got a grand surprise for you boys!" The sound of the warden's voice cut through the air, eliciting a shiver from all those present.

He sounded happy, almost glad of something. It was disturbing, considering they knew the man only took pleasure in the misery of others. The twins looked up as the warden walked forward from where he had been standing. The man was grinning, lips pulled ear to ear as he stared off into the open field of stone and dirt. There was nothing for miles, at least not until you got to the other facility built a distance out, which wasn't visible beyond the cliff.

It was also a scientific compound, built a decade after the Warden's family had purchased this land. Back then the radiation causing the Mugenes virus was not as invasive and speedily progressive as it was today so scientists took to experimenting on prisoners to discover a way to eliminate it. Only a scant few years later the Warden's family's land became a prison.

"Oh?" Eric's words stabbed the empty air with an audible snap. "Do tell, I am **so** excited to hear this news." A dry wit scraped between teeth and tongue, his only weapon against the shortsighted warden.

In the other field prisoners worked under the watchful eyes of the armed guards. Coughing, snorting, moaning and groaning created a cacophony that was, in a way, relieving.

So long as people were alive enough to suffer they were alive, weren't they?

A dark smirk drew itself upon the features of the warden, who found Eric's distress satisfying. "Well," the man leaned forward as the words drawled between his lips. "It is my pleasure to announce you'll be headin' to see the doc a lot more often now. In fact you're getting transferred over to that facility." He stood, pointing out beyond the cliff. "I sold you." He stated flatly, arms crossing over his chest in smug pride.

Jaws dropped. The guards looked to each other before looking to the Warden. They motioned their hands, shocked by his decision. These were their prisoners after all, their responsibility.

It was bad enough the twins had to go to the quack doctor's lab every few days, but now they were their property?!

No! Sold? Prisoners belonged to the colony, not one single individual. They were property, sure, less than people, but too they were a public property that could neither be sold or bought. This act alone was one of greed and selfishness that men were branded against. It was men like him that gave them all a bad name.

CHAPTER NINE

A Monstrous Beast

Eric threw his shovel to the ground, stomping his foot, digging it into the soil "What?!" He shouted before moving to charge the scar-faced man, but Klaus held him back. "What gives you that right?!" Eric struggled in his brother's grip, voice cracking as he shouted at the top of his lungs, voice carrying down the hills.

The warden offered a pleased, almost twisted grin as the tip of his tongue poked out to brush his dry, scarred lips. He put his hands to his hips as his head shook in amusement.

"You boys actually think you got a choice? This'll get you out of here and it'll make sure I get the Vox sooner." The guards beside him looked to one another, their brows furrowing as their masks covered the lower half of their face.

Eric's body stiffened as his form became slack in Klaus' grip. The twins looked to the Warden, horror painting their faces as they realized. Klaus silently shook his head, Eric's weak struggle wrenching him from the man's slacked grip. The elder twin parted his jaws as he struggled to form words.

Vox was a medicine produced by the city. It was an addictive nerve numbing agent that not only slowed mutation, but it made the pain just... stop. Mugenes was extremely painful. Its deforming growths would press into the nerves, twist bones, and irritate flesh. Sometimes the pain became a dull throb in the back of the mind, other times it stirred a madness in an individual that forced medical officers to end their lives as those troubled few ended up rampaging from the sheer agony. It was a rare fate, but nevertheless the most horrifying side effect of the mutation.

Vox was a rare substance derived from a chemical compound, whose main bonds were found in rarity in the atmosphere. This meant it was controlled by the Sisters. The deal the Warden was making was -- selfish, dastardly. There were prisoners, civilians, sicker than him... younger with more years on their clock.

The Warden had not a shred of remorse as he continued to talk, despite the accusing gazes. "She'll be sending a military attaché to pick you two mongrels up in the morning." He spoke with a tone of finality.

The twins had gone to the facility twice a week to see Doctor Newberry. Due to their physical retardation of the viral infection they had become valuable research for the Medical Research Field as a whole. The only reason the visits were so few was because the MRF had limited funding and needed to focus on research which the Capital designated in importance through a standard generated by the SOLAS computer systems which measured the overall needs of the world through calculations of census data. The head doctor could also only stand Eric two days of the week.

The agreement still had the Warden making money and there were fees required to take inmates from their designated prisons for military or scientific research as the facilities were also restricted by governmental procedures. The certain types of labour required of prisoners was deemed more important as they provided terraforming labour that machines could not do. The Warden was essentially renting them out to the lab.

But now? Everything he was doing was what was wrong with the world and why men were looked at with hatred and disgrace. He was almost gone, the Warden. Vox was the last thing he needed, he deserved.

The Warden smirked. "Oh, don't worry. With all the money I'm earnin' from selling your sorry asses to science, I can afford to have your friends dig out the rest of their own graves! Hahaha!"

His laughter was like a leaky pipe rattling wetly as the rust crusted metal whined with every flush of water. Everything about this man was vile. Could he even be considered Amaroxian anymore with such twisted values of self? And what values could a people have that treated their prisoners as sub-humanoid?

His laughter would be drowned out by the low rumble of an all terrain vehicle rushing down the rocky path from below the cliff. A rough road had been carved out by prisoners past to make it easier for the two facilities to maintain their connectedness. The ground shook beneath the twins' bare feet. It was the trumpet of their impending doom.

The ATV was not a new concept in the universe: but underground it was designed to withstand both the atmospheric pressure of the deep world and the harrowing dangers of the feral beasts it was known to house. Drigers were dangerous creatures that ate stone, often creating landslides and cave-ins with their voracious appetites. They were known to alter entire chambers, which were pockets within Amaroxia's mantle that the people could inhabit so having them changed or even completely collapsed limited the occupancy of a colony which could be up to ten or more chambers connected. Due to their inability to be domesticated many Amaroxians believed the creatures to be avatars of the Void as they had not been present underground until the Mugenes surfaced.

The well armored vehicle had to fend against Driger that were known to inhabit the less traveled tunnels between cities. Drigers could see heat due to their contest with other Drigers for territory and nothing gave off more heat than the hydraulic systems of the machines that, to Driger, gave off the same heat and sounds of others of their kind. While Drigers fed off soil and stone that did not stop them from occasionally consuming the odd traveler or two.

The vehicle came to a stop just a few feet from the group. At either side the doors popped open. A metal claw wrapped around the outer edge of the door before a fully metallic beast slunk from its confines, breaking into the open air with clicks and whirs. Black-steel boots crunched the trodden ground with a wet thump as the soles dug deeply into the drying muds. By all accounts the mechanical beast looked like a monster with spikes protruding from its shoulder and head as well as wisps of steam billowed from its joints. A haunting effigy that only roused at the witching hour to spirit away souls of the damned. But to Amaroxians it was a much more practical entity.

It was a Turbo Suit.

Over 200lbs of metal wrapped around the frame of a person. Steel pauldrons over the shoulders, with black thermal fabric stretched over the limbs regulating the heat produced by the suit of armor. A bodice of tempered metal weighed the chest down, causing its user to have a distinct hunch which was counterbalanced by the metal groundbreaker, or dorsal fin, on the back. The fins not only acted as a counter balance but were also where excess electronic wiring was housed to maximize the system's output.

The spikes that protruded from the shoulders had a brass, almost rusted hue to them while the visorless helm of the outfit covered the head in entirety, electronic modules over the ears to assist the hearing and visual sensors and an array of external vents to compensate for the heat produced by the armors most basic functions. A hiss of hot steam would occasionally escape the breaks between the joints. The black thermal suit was all that stood between the sensitive skin and the third degree burns that could be produced by the overheated frame.

A whirring noise crackled from the helm of the suit. By the wires that hung from the modules that sat over the ears, it was clear that this was a T1 model. They were prone to overheating and were known to short out when the exposed coolant wires would drastically shift in pressure and disrupt the cooling systems. There had been stories of suits becoming unusable after their users were welded into the interface that layered the inside of the exoskeleton.

The twins were in awe at being witness to a first generation Suit first hand. They had never seen a T1 up close, but why was it here? By its brass and obsidian design it was clearly a Military suit. The Science Division had a distinct silver and jade brand leaving the Medical sector to raise their distinct gold and ruby combination.

"What is this?!" Eric demanded, only to receive no answer from the Warden.

The suit-wearer gave off a smug air and that alone was enough to tell the elder twin it wasn't good. Eric could feel Klaus gripping his forearm, their bodies tensing as the machine marched to the front of the vehicle and stared them down.

Even though they couldn't see the pilot's face: they knew that he was looking down on them, callously. This was the first time they've seen the General bring someone else along. Could it be because he suspected their desire to run? Or perhaps he had a job to do? Suits were useful for many things. Aside from physical labour they were used by the Military in extermination ops that sent soldiers into the wilds to destroy Driger nests and eliminate pockets of dangerous foreigners that sometimes squatted in abandoned tunnels.

CHAPTER TEN

Bane Of My Existence

The Military had originally designed the suits for combat, but that was before they lived in the Underground. Below the crust they proved to create more problems than they were worth. The limited space risked cave-ins with their high powered weapons. The suits were like a second skin that was worn over a person's body to expand their already present strengths and reduce their weaknesses. The suits required a heavy amount of mental prowess to use.

A receptor would connect to the base of the skull and use the electromagnetic energy released from the Geroiid. The problem was, because the machine was so labor intensive, it would create migraines and symptoms of nausea and motion sickness. And those were the less extreme cases. It was rumored that many more died from their Geroiid's simply overloading and frying in their owner's skulls, though that was the rumor. The idea had been rejected outright by direct orders.

Honestly a lot of workers were hopeful this could be used in a field. It was an exciting day when they were revealed during the testing stages, but as quickly as they became a symbol of the Military's progress, they faded away as a failure to their overachieving incompetence driven by a selfish need to reach the surface we were shunned from. It was a sign to many of us that the return to the surface would never come.

But they had little time to be in awe before the man standing beside the Unit spoke.

"Bring them."

General Timothy Honchberg. He was the head of the Porvin Red Shield Military Post and the one who carted the twins to and from the prison to the laboratory. He was interested in the experiments being conducted by the Hurvor labs, so had an interest in them that the pair felt they could live better without, maybe even live longer.

-

-

-

The twins were led to the second basement of the Hurvor Laboratory. The building was named after the first male doctor to receive the Copper Cross, for his discovery of the Mugenes rRNA sequence that allowed the development of the V-1 O2Xe, or the Vox vaccine. It was the only laboratory in the Porvin zone that did not concentrate on Military Research for the development of Turbo Suit technology. Though, that did not mean they didn't conduct such work, for it was the only way to receive government grants. The main building was a twenty minute ride from the prison. The building itself was made of silver steel resting upon solid, red stone. Each floor housed space where doctors and biologists worked tirelessly to break the secret of Mugenes.

The top floor was called the Sumerin Department. Criminals that came in and out were checked in here by young grul from the neighboring district of Sluumin, part of the eastern Porvin zone. After the Conyard Incident, records were no longer kept within easy public access, so the Hurvor Facility kept its record halls in the third basement, deep below the underground. The first and second basements were Research and Development, led by different heads of department.

Elizabeth Newberry. She was the current head of the Newberry Family, some of the top researchers of the Mugenes infection. She had short, blonde colored hair and silver eyes. Her figure was thin, but still healthy. Eric felt her most important asset was lacking, as her hands were far too smooth for someone who 'works' as hard as she claims. Oh but her chest was always pleasantly present for the twins' gaze. It was about the only good thing about her. She was infected, but it was very low. She had lost both her lungs, so a machine does her breathing for her, while her Geroiid is known to misfire, likely causing her to lose concentration at random times or over process for times not yet here.

"Eric, stop staring, you pervert!"

That mouth of hers made her unattractive. Eric shrugged at her sharp glare and turned his head away as he settled his hands on their hips.

"You'll have to forgive me, I'm just an animal after all." He thinks his words flustered her.

She was seen by many as a kind-hearted woman. She took care of her father who was at nearly 75% Infection and cared for those that came to get the experimental treatments responsibly. So maybe she had one other amiable trait, but she annoyed Eric greatly. Even though she said she did it for the good of everyone, she still experimented on the twins... without their consent. Who would consent to such a devious sounding thing? Not Eric. She had a strong ideal though: that everyone was equal. That was a dream not to be seen in their lifetime....

Eric and Klaus had been walked into the building by the guard: a man wearing a hefty T1 suit. Liza, a nickname she hated by the way, so Eric used it obsessively, looked obscenely excited by their arrival. It was off-putting for the pair.

"Liza, you have quite the shit-eating grin there." He mused aloud, only for her to pout and turn her nose up.

"You can't rattle me today Eric, because I have something special!"

She almost giggled as she clutched her data pad to her chest. She wore a doctor's coat over her loose, blue pants and black top, which he could probably guess was sleeveless. Ladies always were *too hot* which really was their own fault for having a higher core temperature.

"Liza," Klaus copied the nickname. "Was that a First Gen Turbo Suit?"

She smiled brightly as she led the pair through the dimly lit halls and into a main area of the laboratory. She was too excited. They didn't like it...

"Yes Klaus," She was always calmer with Klaus. No idea why. "It's what I have to show you two!"

When they entered the room Eric quickly noticed her assistant, Casey, sitting at one of the consoles. The elder twin offered his most devious smirk to her. Coldest reaction yet: she sneered at Eric and turned her back. It seems even Casey is holding her tongue, which was suspicious.

Casey was Liz's assistant. She had a strong temper, but given her infection level the twins felt a bit sorry for her. Casey had white-silver hair and pink eyes, often making her stand out more than she wished. She lost the majority of her internal organs, and her ovaries were gone, as well as a majority of her intestines, leaving her more cyborg than Amaroxian. With her ankles also twisted in atrophy, she could not walk so was confined to a wheelchair. It was an extreme case of a low-level infection.

"This is a highly auspicious day!" Liza was a bit too excited. Eric felt that bad feeling return from the other day. "Thanks to all our research, the Daughters have given you two a reward for working toward a better tomorrow for the Colony and Districts!"

The scientist ran over to a large platform. Klaus and Eric looked up. Their jaws would drop most simultaneously. Standing atop the platform, attached to several wires that led into the computers, were two Turbo Suits, quite different from the ones they had been testing with for the past month. They seemed to match one another, save for a few key differences in helmet shape and hand accessories.

They had a jade sheen to them, like raw gemstone. The plating that bordered the edges of the jade metal were silver, likely Silver-Steel. Even the joints appeared to be made of more flexible looking, silver parts. Long tail-like forms hung from the two machines, but one appeared to have these flat protrusions that came out the back while the other was bulkier in shape.

Eric felt a sharp jab at his side. He was not sure when Liz had slid up next to him, but she jabbed him expectantly.

"Well, speechless aren't you?" She had that grin again.

He really hated that grin. "Are you stupid?!" He couldn't help but shout in anger. The technicians were used to the man's temper around Elizabeth. She had a serious screw loose in that head of hers. She always came up with these outrageous ideas that put Klaus and Eric on her cutting board.

Casey was snickering at his irritation.

"How can you not be excited?!" Liza almost sounded – hurt.

"Do I look stupid?!" Eric glared at Klaus who he knew was about to make a face.

The older twin did not need him adding sass in this sort of situation. Eric needed backup, not a turncoat! "Why would I be happy about something so stupid?! People have died using these things!"

Eric asserted his anger with great force. Normally women were not used to men disagreeing with them, but Liz has clearly grown used to Eric's habits and has learned to simply ignore his abrasiveness, to their regret. She now seemed to ignore his legitimate reservations on such a dangerous situation.

CHAPTER ELEVEN

Being The Difficult Ones

"Eric, those were prototype suits, these are ones I helped develop!" She said this, beaming with pride.

Eric smiled and nodded. "Oh well, if that's the case, that's *far worse*." He would assert his discontent here and now!

She, again, looked shocked by his words. Not only should she understand his hatred for her, but she should clearly understand that there is a limit to how reckless a person can be!

"Do you remember the last time you helped *fix* anything that is a machine?!" Eric wanted her to think carefully.

Liz was a scientist, so normally they had to be very good with Computer Science and Organic Science. Eric began to question the sanctity of the educational facilities beholden to the high-class when he first saw Liz trying to use a new computer, of which promptly became a paperweight after her attempt to simply open a program.

"Oh come on," She waved her hand dismissively. "When have I ever caused that sort of trouble?" She utterly denied it!

Of course! A woman would never admit to her mistakes, that would prove her incompetence!

"What about the time you tried to fabricate a machine that would give injections automatically?!" Eric brought up. "I nearly died!"

He did, the machine had fired various sized needles at his body, nearly skewering him. Eric was only thankful for his agility in the matter.

Klaus nodded. "I almost drowned."

"Thank you brother! Backing me up beautifully as usual!" He thought, pained by the situation.

That was right, he had almost forgotten. Klaus was trapped in a healing vat that Liz had adjusted to implement the twins' medication more thoroughly through their bodies. The technicians couldn't get Klaus out, but Eric was thankful for his brute strength as he managed to punch through the pressured glass.

"That was a program error." She refused again, blatantly!

"A program *you* wrote!" Eric asserted.

He was growing tired of her. Liz exhausted the man. This was why he did not need sedatives when she worked. After a while his body just gave out.

"Don't worry idiot twins." Casey finally decided to chime in. "I double checked the systems, so there should be no problem."

That was good. Casey was likely partnered up with Liz to meet up with this critical disadvantage in skill.

"Listen, she worked really hard. It's thanks to Liza that the systems have improved so much."

Eric didn't know why, but he could not force a remark. Casey seemed oddly supportive. Normally she was very negative about these sorts of situations.

Liz giggled and nodded. "These are the suits provided to us by the grace of the Daughters!"

Liz had a fondness for the Daughters the brothers would never understand, no it was more the case that Eric had lost his care for creatures that abandoned her children, be they Azi or Grul.

Liz supported her own efforts quite easily: "They were made using your specs! They are codenamed Cipher Dragonfly and Cipher Dragon!" She seemed so proud, but Eric furrowed his brows.

"What do you mean *our specs*?" Of course the older twin was suspicious, this was Liz. "Liza...." She pursed her lips at his call. She was hiding something. "Damn it Liza, what did you do?!"

She shrugged and hopped back, away from Eric. She was energetic. This was a terrible omen.

"Well, we were running out of Grant money..." She mumbled.

"Liza..."

"And it was getting harder to convince them how useful you two were, I mean you can be pretty uncooperative!"

"Liza!"

"I agreed to let you be the test subjects for the new Turbo Suit System my father helped the Military redevelop!"

Eric threw my arms in the air and sunk down to the

ground, crouching as he felt his head start to spin.

"I knew it. I can't trust Yhazi to really consider their actions."

He knew it was not a kind word. A Yhazi was an Azi who felt the need to keep the man at her teat at all times. It was basically saying she was the sort to keep things so close to her, she could not see the problems it caused on the outside.

That was when Eric felt the kick to his head.

"Eric!" Klaus called.

"*I can hear your worry brother, but damn she kicks hard!*" Eric fell flat on his back and groaned.

Eric heard as Casey wheeled up to his side. "Serves you right."

"Shut up." He groaned as Eric was helped up by Klaus.

Casey shook her head "There's no fighting it. It's already been decided. It's because you two are twins."

"What does that have to do with anything?" Eric wondered.

Grul Twins were looked down upon as inferior. Liz walked up to Eric, her pout from his earlier comment not yet dissipated.

"Because," Liz began. "It is because you are still able to use your suits with such a high synchronization, even though your Geroiid are now considered dead."

"Yeah, so?" He scoffed. "Besides it's only a fluke, nothing

we can help. We worked side by side for years." That was just normal for twins to be able to work together.

Maybe people that were without close siblings couldn't understand? Eric knew Casey and Liz were the only children to their parents. But the twins didn't know any siblings either so they had no standing comparison.

"Stupid twins," Casey sighed in exasperation, pressing her hand to her forehead, trying to relieve the migraine likely growing due to Eric's antics. "It's not something that should be possible, at all. Look,"

She seems to have pulled up an image on the computer screen with a button she had on her chair.

"According to all of the data we collected, the old Turbo Suits had failed because they used too much mental power to drive, but those who have lost their Geroiid's use seem to not suffer the mental exhaustion that come with it, but neither can they fully control the various functions of the Suits."

Liz nodded. "The Geroiid were both necessary and unnecessary because the billions of neurotransmitters could not move the machine's functions without a strong, processing Geroiid, but overusing the Georiid caused terrible side effects, including death!"

Don't say that so cheerfully....

"Wait, so Liza is saying because we can, and cannot use our Geroiid...?" Eric wondered.

"Liza proposes that because of your unique circumstance you can operate Dragon and Dragonfly, which are reputedly the most difficult to run because of the extra function of Flight on the Dragonfly and Power on the Dragon." Casey seemed convinced, but Eric was troubled.

Klaus seems to have picked up on it as well. "What about the Turbo Suit we saw coming in?" Eric was curious about it too.

"That was the Hammer Unit." Liz answered without skipping a beat. "It was a newly developed suit from the Military, but it still uses the old System. They have a different theory on why they would malfunction. I don't feel it's a safe route, but since the pilot is a prisoner..."

Right, prisoners were just animals to the scientists. They were disposable garbage that didn't need anyone's concern.

Casey seemed annoyed as well. "They're using an alternate system that digs not only into the Geroiid, but the nerves of the muscles and entire body's peripheral nervous system. It's dangerous because if the body is not getting enough nutrients or is exhausted, the user can burn out."

Another way to say that the pilot of the unit was as good as dead if he wasn't fed by the rich and kept fat.

"So?" Eric felt it was not their place. "So why should Klaus and I help?"

"Because," Liz put on a serious expression that was unsettling on her. "You either agree to this or we'll have no choice but to send you to the Marco Facility."

Those words shot pure horror through the twins' hearts. Klaus froze, and Eric could admit he was shaken as well. The Marco Facility was where Infected Prisoners were sent, cut apart and had their head, and sometimes still living, tissue experimented on. It was not a choice anyone made.

"But..." Liz said that and the pair felt a bit angry for some reason.

Maybe they were being unreasonable, but they were sure she was going to say something even more outrageous.

"Our laboratory is small and this grant barely puts us on the board..." Liz always complained about money. "If we succeed we get a bigger grant!" Liza always got overly excited about projects and the twins were, unfortunately, always trapped in the middle of them.

Liz was strangely driven toward equality. She was a scientist that did not follow the norm. She felt hypotheses were better tested with both genders. She was fond of her father and even paid to have him taken care of. It was touching, but she was still way off the morality coil with her openness to experimenting on the still-living!

"You don't seem excited..."

She looked to Eric with her bright, silver-colored eyes. It was as if Eric had already told her no and she fought to silently beg the man to show energy... He could not help but smile. In pain.

She was always proud of her work...

"I'd rather be dragged through pondscum." Eric was eloquent.

It was true and the truth always hurt. He could tell by the way her face twisted up into a pout.

"Are you stupid?!" Eric would utterly refute her attempts! "What sound-minded person would be excited about being poked at by a mad scientist!?"

Klaus nodded to concur with his sibling.

"Thank you for the back up Klaus."

"Eric!" The way Liza called his name irritated the man.

She called him as if we were... friends. They were anything but. Eric hated her, he did. He had no choice but to stand here and listen to her. He had no choice but to watch his brother and him play the role of a pair of lab animals.

Eric *was* irritated.

"No!" His voice raised. "I was planning to escape today, but I ended up being dragged into this stupidity!"

Eric lost his temper. He would admit he was overreacting, but it was a doubled response for Klaus' voice. He heard Casey snort.

"Idiot twins." Her witty banter was unrivaled... "How far did you think you'd get?"

Casey would continue to offer her insight as she rolled her chair up to the twins. Klaus has since slunk behind Eric. He was afraid of Casey for some reason. She was loud, but not really scary, at least that was what Eric felt.

CHAPTER TWELVE

The Dragonfly

"No clothes, no money. You think you'd get out of the Districts and into the Colonies?" Sometimes Casey's common sense annoyed Eric as much as Liz's voice.

Traveling on foot in Amaroxia was difficult. Though not impossible it took preparation. Maps were easily accessible through public terminals so planning your route was easy enough, but the borders were rigorously guarded. Identification was required whenever anyone wished to cross into a new city. The Chambers had a lot of traffic due to resources coming in and out of the farms as well as the Military and Science bases. It was a matter of security, though it was also not.

Those of the North were notorious for their mistrust of outsiders. Their border checks were solely for the assurance that non-Native or even escaped prisoners didn't make their way back. Though clothing was not a major factor in how you were viewed at a border it did determine if you survived the colder stretches of passages that had weaker generators which were unable to produce enough heat to keep some of the Runways thawed. It sometimes got so cold that some tunnels would completely freeze over.

"That won't stop us...." Eric began to shake with anger, but soon felt a pair of warm hands wrap over his own.

Eric's assertion was weak, flimsy. He knew the difficulties

of traveling across sectors. He's done it in the past, but he was still considered a citizen. He didn't want to admit it, but Casey was right. Without supplies their chances of making it half way through a tunnel was next to nil. It was aggravating and put into perspective just how helpless they were. They were trapped.

He looked down to Liza, as she stared up at Eric, her eyes practically sparkling with excitement.

"Don't worry. With this you'll be free..." She was very insistent about that word, and there was something seducing about it...

Free.

Eric had been seated across the way from the consoles, on a metal stool. The doctor's assistants had been hooking up wires and nerve sensors into his skin, pinning a few beneath his flesh in a few key locations: under his wrists, shoulder blades, and, finally, his pectoral muscles. His muscles twitched under their light touches. They were oddly delicate when handling this and it made Eric feel self conscious. Eric's skin showed clear scarring from where his flesh was continuously cut open and healed to allow the placing of the instruments. Because Casey was the primary assistant Eric being seated was for her comfort as it made it easier for the chair bound woman to reach his sensors to check their signal strength with a reader.

Klaus sat at the far end of the room on a bench, his bare feet pressing against the cold, steel ground. He sat with his hands on his knees, red-hued toes wiggling against the metal. Though often scolded for it, the younger twin refused

R.A. REX DRACO

to put on socks to fend off the icy chill that came with being further underground. The younger twin sneezed. A sharp glare was thrown in his direction Casey. She had a temper towards reluctant sibling. The quieter twin stiffened, hair bristling like a cat caught eating the canary. Klaus was, understandably, terrified of her.

Elizabeth walked toward Erick. "You'll help herald in big changes! Do you have any idea what that means?!" She clasped her hands together and stared down the criminal from the top of her glasses.

Eric looked up, sneering at the way her pupils contracted to near slits in the light of the red examination lamp Casey flashed over his body. "...no. Can we move on? We don't have time for this. Indentured servants or not, Klaus and I haven't had dinner." A smack against his chest caused him to jump. "Ow! Can you not?"

Casey smiled before her expression flattened. She pressed her palms over her chair's controls and shifted her torso so she could see Elizabeth. "I hate to admit it, Liz, but if we don't get chuckles here into the containment chamber we might hit a rolling blackout. It's getting to be that hour."

Elizabeth crossed her arms over her chest and pouted. "...you're right." She seemed to slump a bit before standing tall.

The woman pushed back her glasses and made her way over to a wall of computers, muttering. Glowing tubes of various colored liquid, bubbling and boiling, lay embedded in and between the maze of twisted, metal tubes and touch screen panels. A soft hum was the only indication that the machine ran on some actual power, rather than lying dormant, boiling beneath its own heat. As Elizabeth approached the machine: her glasses reflected the display as she began to rapidly type commands into the system via the mechanical keyboard. The loud clacking of the keys were soon drowned out by the hum of the generators, kicking the systems out of hibernation. This caused the building to rumble, groan under the change in pressure. The three of them watched as the manic grin drew itself onto her features as she woke her computer up.

Klaus laid his hand on Eric's shoulder. The older sibling swallowed. "She's, uh, a bit enthusiastic today..." Eric worried.

Casey rolled up beside them, the silence of her approach causing Klaus to jump behind his brother. "She found a way to time the reboot." The assistant grinned.

Eric rubbed his hand against the back of his neck. His fingers traced along the metal ring that had been fused to his skin. The ring was necessary for second generation models. It directly interacted with the brain with the support of artificial intelligence to allow perfect control of the exoskeleton with a nearly non-existence delay. Closer to the base of his neck sat a thick mass, a scar where the last reboot had nearly taken his life. The machines here weren't perfect. If he remembered much of the lab had originally been a pop-up facility so much of their equipment had been meant for temporary use. As long s they maintained their station here it caused much of what they had here to degrade as requests to the Capital for new consoles had been stalled for weeks already.

Normally computers had a safety in place for reboots so if a person was still hooked up to it the surge would be rerouted. Of course around anything Liza touches he expected things to go wrong in every which way. Unfortunately for him this was not the case for old machines falling apart at the seams. He turned his eye to the larger, unlit chamber. Silent, the fluid-filled capsule looked able to fit a man, but unlike the other parts of the computer, it was the only portion still in the lull of its mechanical hibernation.

As soon as his green eyes were upon it the fluid in the chamber lit up with a green hue. Inside of it sat an 8th model Destroyer Runner, type 1 Flyer. It was known as the DR8-FI-TS2, codenamed Dragonfly. With wings it was the only aerial second generation. Bubbles rushed through the chamber and soon the liquid began its draining process. The thin grooves along the chest of the exoskeleton lit up with soft greens and the visor screen glowing a deep cyan.

The sight always caused Eric's heart to jump. Though the machine wasn't alive he couldn't help but feel the deep gaze it put out. According to Liz the machine had a special AI programming written by a genius, but she altered it to suit her purposes with the two suits being set up for the brothers. This unsettled him plenty, but what bothered him more was the uncanny, yet familiar gaze that fell on his person when in the suit's presence. He felt something hit the back of his knees, causing him to lose balance and focus. Luckily for the distracted experiment Klaus was within reach and had thrown his arms forward to catch Eric. The prisoner glared back and down, only to spy Casey. She had rolled forward, which forced Klaus to move, and had jammed her knees into the back of Eric's.

"Move it or lose it, we have barely half an hour to reboot his systems. You don't want *Burn* to happen, do you?"

The main doors in front of the room slid open. "A **Burn**?" A light, feminine voice called.

Eric rolled his eyes and walked toward the chamber that held the second generation suit, followed in quick pace by his brother. Second generation suits were more sleek than the bulky first gens. Elizabeth and Casey turned to face the door as Klaus helped Eric equip his thermal suit. The black suit was lined with sensitive transmitters that read the small, electrical jolts generated by twitching muscles. It helped the exoskeleton accurately compensate for strengths and weaknesses found in the Amaroxian body, especially one riddled with disease. Standing at the door was Doctor Bell, head analytical chemist of the floor above.

CHAPTER THIRTEEN

The Ol' Hamster Wheel

Analytical chemists came hand in hand with facilities like Hurvor that focused on genetics and human experimentation. There were few places that openly practiced live testing. With with animal experimentation having become a long, forsaken practice, steeped in archaic sciences, there were new methods created to completely replace the need for putting another living creature at risk. Well into their past Amaroxians used vitrocell-kits. These kits replicated the division and biological response of living cells and the kits could be easily produced using native stem cells. Unfortunately come the War of the Sun so came a drop in the supply of vitrocell-kits. Prices skyrocketed as supplies plummeted. The price of transportation became too costly, as the kits needed to be specially handled.

It was not as if their supply was lacking as they were cheap and easy to make. It had what made them a landmark product in turning away from living test subjects. Alas, after the outbreak of the Mugenes virus what kits did remain held up in hospitals and other medical facilities were eventually used up in the frantic first two years in the rush to solve this problem.

Quarantine, isolation, vaccinations, respirators, hospitalizations, hysteria, violence, and eventually propaganda. Many were led to believe the disease has stabilized, but Amaroxians merely grew complacent. It was quickly spread that with the discovery of the Vox their lives would begin to return to normal. But the Vox wasn't a fix, just a bandage to a deeper wound yet to be closed.

Bell had thick, curly hair, red as the soil, skin a darker pale hue giving her a higher, natural resistance to red-light sickness. As a great niece to Hurvor, she had a lot to live up to. Being the head of analytical chemistry was an important position, at least among those who still searched for a cure.

Casey shook her head, motioning her hand to explain in more detail. "A burn is what occurs when a power surge happens while the suit and pilot are still attached to the home base." She began. "Because the shift is so sudden it creates a static charge in which a grounded machine could easily diffuse, but a person doesn't usually have time to ground. Some pilots in higher positions in the military have bypassed this problem by installing EMBPs."

Bell blinked, taken aback by the information. "Electromagnetic Bracelet Pulsers?" She sought to confirm, Casey nodding her head. "That's 7nexpect3d. I thought they were banned."

Casey sneered. "Not for the military. So long as it benefits the Daughters they're willing to turn a blind eye. It lets pilots not only diffuse the recoil from reboots but it can heighten their reaction time to the suit's prompts." She gave a dismissive shrug.

Eric slowed as he listened to the women talk. The other scientists in the room were insignificant, and frankly so were Liz and Cass, but... even them. The people who sought a cure... to them, he and his brother were just tools. A battery... Klaus felt his brother's hesitation. They both looked to the suit, Klaus sealing the back of his brother's thermal.

Turbo Suits were worn by humans.to compensate for their physical limitations. These portable super computers needed a constant supply of energy, in part due to the limitation of Cloud services to maintain a master file for the system. Without a recent save of their loadout it was a guarantee that months would be spent trying to regain or replicate the lost data, though more often than not it was not worth it. Without a continuous power source the energy cells in the suits shut down, turning them onto glorified paperweights. That meant even a small interruption of power between the machine and battery would force a reboot. Designed to do whatever it took to keep an up-to-date master file the machines were known to default to the living battery inside. Humans were a perfectly suitable source of power that gave enough time to store a backup.

Reboots would turn into Burns, this was when the pilot was jolted by the suit when it shifted its energy paths. Suits were connected to their pilots via cerebral mounted cables that were connected directly into the brain from the outer part of the skull, at its base. Surges often led to extreme burns around the base of the neck where they were attached. Sometimes it led to the battery's brain being melted... Eric had come close to a major Burn. He was unconscious for two days. It was perhaps the most agitated anyone had ever seen Klaus... It was the last, they hoped.

They had never seen metal bend so easily without a suited individual.

"Yes!" Elizabeth chirped excitedly. "I finally synchronized Eric to the Dragonfly. It was no easy task, let me tell you!" A suit only ever had one owner. Once that owner died, there was no replacing her or him. The user's neuromap is burned into the machine to allow for perfect control. "I knew they were wrong. Even if the parts were from an old suit, the control system is brand new, it was just a matter of adjusting power levels between the old tech, which is known for its lower usage of power, and the high efficiency of second gen." Her explanation was quickly getting away from her.

Bell pulled her hands out her coat pockets and held them up, laughing softly. Her cheeks pinched up as she chuckled. Unlike Liz's brown and tan Walker Suit, Bell's was yellow and tan, indicating her department in the second basement. She was a bit younger than Liz and Casey, but that didn't stop her from doing her part in it all.

After sealing Eric up his brother would meander off towards the workstation Elizabeth had been at. Klaus turned his gaze over his shoulders as he looked to the three women across the way. All about: the other scientists did their job. They continued to monitor and diagnose the interference created by the brother's active participation in their own experiment. After blinking a time or two Klaus turned right back around and continued to type on the terminal's console.

"Alright, alright." Bell defended herself against the rabid science girl. "But um, should your rats be in the experiment without you?" She pointed back to where Klaus had pulled out the keyboard by the chamber, Eric already having entered the suit with practiced ease.

Elizabeth whipped around. "Don't touch anything you hamsters--"

"Rats," Casey corrected.

"-- rats!" Elizabeth corrected herself. The belligerent pair ignored her, Klaus typing away on the console. Liz huffed and turned to face Bell, a bright smile on her face. "Don't worry, if the wrong sequence and password are entered they both get a nasty shock and the system will lock them out."

Liz wore a bright smile on her face as she ignored the stubborn man. "Also without the system passwords he can't start up the system to initiate the loadout sequence." She assured Bell, who gave her an incredulous look.

Casey sighed and leaned her elbow on her chair's armrest. "Did you change the password and exchange sequence from the last time you said that?" She questioned, determined not to let the woman's scatterbrained personality get to her.

"Ahhh…" Liz whined. "Yeeees?" She was hardly convincing herself at that point.

Bell and Casey stared at her, deadpan expressions on their faces. Elizabeth bowed her head and quickly pardoned herself before turning on her heel and making a mad dash for the console.

The experiment was simple: the brothers would have to work to synchronize with a pair of Second Generation Turbo Suits designed by Newberry's sector, specifically created to make use of the twins and their still functioning geroiid organs. But things were going as expected with the pair participating. Eric had entered the capsule that contained his suit, wearing his black, thermal jumper. He settled into the suit before it would seal around his body in a simple process, but it was the machine's startup that was complicated and Klaus made sure to interfere as best as he could.

Eric gasped as the cerebral cable vacuumed shut in the

space between the suit's plug opening and the small metal plate on his neck. There the line would remain attached to allow the computer to have access to the neuromap it was loaded with. This gave the user the power to move the machine with the thought of movement. Just like the brain worked with the muscles using electrical impulses, the suit would amplify these signals to trigger movement in the layers of nanowire and electrodes in the limbs of the exoskeleton. With the helmet attached it he pressed on the sides of the helmet which started a pressurization that would ensure the suit was skin tight.

Once the seals were sensed by the ring inside the helmet the vacuum kicked it and snapped the wire into place, locking the metal casing over the man's head. Tendrils of optic cables gathered and squirmed as they collectively drilled into Eric's cerebellum. By now the pain was a dull crackle in his brain, the sensations dulled further by light application of Vox serum that was pumped in small amounts through the cable. Due to the Vox's mild toxicity it was heavily diluted with micronutrients to ensure the medicine did more good than harm.

CHAPTER FOURTEEN

No Limits

The process was nearly done, all that was required was the passcode which would activate the final step of the program and finalize the loadout: data that would allow the machine's AI to function properly.

Loadouts were massive packets of data that the Suit's AI depended on to function. The first generation units used basic packs that typically consisted of conditional code that allowed a pilot to exceed limitations placed on the system's CPU for concern of overclocking. These instances were known to severely injure pilots, but those who could withstand even a few minutes of Overclock were invaluable. The risk was too high though so the second generation models were made with this in mind.

Bell looked over the data as she stood beside Casey. Fit was all too fascinating, but computer science wasn't her specialty so she would as the light eyed woman beside her. Despite how her eyes seemed no one in the building had more knowledge of the software than Ca a ey, other than Liz, after all Casey strove to surpass the Newberry woman.

"I didn't think I totally understand. How can AI think as fast as a person? I know it's come far, but it's been proven time and time again that a person problem solves more efficiently."

Casey reached up to her monitor and pulled down a window on the screen with her thumb and long finger. She continued to pull the window adorn before she used her index finger to drag the screen towards the left side of the monitor where Bell and her were. She flicked her wrist, opening the panel in a holographic screen that hovered between them.

"Despite that, " Casey spoke as she scrolled down the data to a simple graphic shoeing compatibility data. "Just look at how much better the pilot can do with the assistance." It was hard to deny the data.

Using the AI program specialized for the Suits insanely amped up speed, power, and reactivity. But as Casey scrolled, Bell would reach out her hand, signaling for her to stop. Blinking, the woman pointed to a stat block that looked out of place.

"W-what is that? Is that the upper limit?"

[Unit: Dragonfly]
[AI: Tiamat]
  [Systems: AR, HUD, Scan]

    * * * *

  [Suit Status]
  [Energy: ███████ 100%]

[Power: ███████████ 100%]
[Charge: ███████████ 100%]
[Heat Index: Normal]

<u>DMG</u> <u>RANGE</u> <u>Hit</u> <u>CRT</u>
100 5~10 +20 +15

[ACTIONS]
Flight Jump
Pulse Strafe
Pulse Shield
Cipher
[Inactive]
[Inactive]

"Why are these numbers so high?! Isn't this suit based off the Drake Model?!" Bell was beyond shocked.

Casey was about to answer her, but she would turn to look out towards the pods. Liz was losing control of the two again. "Liz!" Casey called, trying to get her to pick up the pace.

It was too late to stop the twins as they had initialized the main step which sealed the pilot into the suit, but Elizabeth couldn't get to Eric before he could enter the capsule, so Elizabeth turned her sights on the younger twin. She took a step to approach him, hands held out like a farmer trying to herd a rowdy flock.

"Klaus..." She sternly called. The young man glanced back over his shoulder, his brows furrowing at her stance. Feeling emboldened by her attempts Klaus would defiantly activate the sequence. "Klaus!" Liz shouted, jumping at him in an attempt to pull him away from the console, but Klaus was quite stubborn and stood his ground.

The dutiful younger brother reached his fingers into his sash before pulling out what appeared to be a microkeycard. The microcards were embedded with identity chips used to get into high security digital systems such as weapons systems which had limited access.

Elizabeth's jaw dropped at the sight. Lurching away from Klaus she began to pat herself down only to find the microkeycard clipped to her coat was missing.

"Klaus! You put that back, or so help me!" The woman sputtered at the shock of being pickpocketed! She knew Klaus was clever and quite strong, but she has never taken him for a dexterous sort.

Klaus, as belligerent as ever, slid the microcard into the slot integrated into the keyboard and entered the passcode, completing the sequence. If they had to stand here and be lab rats for a bunch of mad scientists then they could at least control this one aspect of their fate.

Eric had been working to synchronize with the Dragonfly's program for months and Klaus watched every step. They had become masters of their own suffering. Eric knew how to hook himself up to the machine while Klaus knew every passcode Elizabeth would use before she used it.

Bell and Casey watched the spectacle from Casey's workstation, rather impressed by the brothers' ingenuity. "I gotta say," Bell offered nonchalantly. "For a pair of lab rats, they're pretty clever. These are the ones that General Hochberg wanted? Pretty sure he wouldn't have stood for their insubordination." She chuckled.

Casey shrugged and leaned back against her chair. "It makes me wonder if he ever gets effective results with his work being so strict and by the book." Casey drawled as the other scientists quickly worked to compensate for the energy being diverted into the chamber. "She's pinned all her hopes on them. If she can figure out why they don't have the same level of infection as others their age -- she could save her dad." Casey pitied her coworker.

Bell looked to the chair-bound woman. "She doesn't believe that stupid story they tell everyone... They were on a farm in Agris their whole lives, orphans of the system. The Agris is in the Borvin Zone, all located in the Northern sphere." Bell reached up to her chin, rubbing at her jaw thoughtfully.

"But her dad, he was imprisoned in the Archon facility at the Capital, right?" Casey would affirm Bell's query with a nod.

Casey pressed her palm onto her chair's mechanisms, the machine pushing forward at its owner's command towards another console as one of the assistants struggled with the fluctuating power.

"Yeah, her father was imprisoned after the Conyard Incident and she's been working to clear his name, but so long as the military division maintains control over the Turbo Suit reform we'll just keep going in circles. The suits shouldn't be used for combat." She looked away. "I don't envy them. They're the apple of the Military and Scientific Division's eye. Both sides are fighting over them for the same reasons."

Bell frowned. "Your uncle means well." General Hochberg was Casey's uncle, the head of the Red Shield's Military division in the Provin Zone. He was in direct contest for their division's resources. "You know men only know how to bash sticks together. At least he still has a title, well after everything." The younger woman consoled Casey.

Casey winced at the stick comment. While she did believe there were things men couldn't do, she did not think they were invalids or only capable of fighting with one another.

"Sure..." It was difficult to decide who was right.

On one hand she was raised under the beliefs that men had ruined the world with their wars. A long held vendetta against the southern colonies created a rift between the groups, making trade negotiations difficult. A war had raged for resources between the two groups for years while they still had a surface to live on. Even now there was a distinct rivalry between the two territories that prevented their tunnels from ever directly connecting, leaving a stretch of badlands between the two states.

In the other case her brother had been a pilot during the Conyard Incident. He was smart, and was wholly against fighting or hyper development of Military growth in Red Shield, feeling it would just revert to days of olde where they were always fighting. He believed that they could maintain peace through negotiation and the Sisters. He died that day when his suit malfunctioned. But maybe it was best he didn't live to see the Council advocate the use of violence to control the growing unrest caused by the Mugenes.

Casey blamed the Newberry family, like everyone else, for years after. She believed them wholly responsible for the malfunctioning core. It had been Elizabeth's family that was in charge of the science Division and had written the program. Her father had been the first man in centuries to reach such honors. It had taken one night to destroy it all. She hated them and strove to her current position if only to usurp their prestige.

It wasn't until Casey was reassigned to Elizabeth's team had she come to learn the truth. And the most damning was that the Twins knew this too. As much as she refused to believe they were there during the Conyard Incident, and agreed with Bell -- there was something about their knowing it was the fault of the military that got her.

It was not just some wild accusation due to their headbutting with her uncle. After all he has come by to the lab more than once to express his interest in them, to which the pair vehemently expressed their hatred of the military.

Much in the way her brother had.

Men had few rights and even fewer positions of power in Amaroxia. Military roles, while typically male due to their reportedly more aggressive behaviors, were generally operated by female officers and government officials.

"That's all Eric and Klaus are to Hochberg, my uncle... The official stick bashers of the Sisterhood." Casey mocked dryly, causing Bell to laugh. "But Elizabeth sees something else in them. Something they had seen in my brother... "

CHAPTER FIFTEEN

All Over Again

Elizabeth slammed her fist on the console's frame. "Idiots!" Elizabeth was both horrified and amazed at Klaus' ingenuity and outright belligerence.

The chamber sealed shut. One could almost see the shit-eating grin on Eric's, now masked, face as the hiss of steam rose and swallowed any visible remnant of the glass tube. The process began soon enough and the pod would begin to allocate the suit's parts over the pilot. The thermal suit had small sensors that ran throughout the lining that allowed the unit to respond to even the most minute of movements.

Any twitch of a muscle, firing off of a nerve: the machine could read it the instant the pilot moved, but with that in mind it was only capable of such thanks to the AI that Liz had reprogrammed. Unfortunately Eric didn't have much confidence in her skills. He's ended up injured or left unconscious numerous times as a result of her tinkering.

As the automated system snapped the individual parts in place: the water served as a buffer to the heat produced by the process. Each part was sealed in place with heat, of which was taken off with the specialized pod, but the process was a long one. Even if a pilot wanted to, they could not simply remove their suit in the field nor could criminals steal them at their leisure. It was a lengthy process that has been optimized over the years, but the second gens were special.

When the gauntlet was affixed over his hand and forearm: Eric would blink his dark green eyes, turning his hand to face palm up. The ends of the fingers were uniquely tipped and the digits too thick for fine tasks. This suit was definitely a fighting unit. His gloved hands pressed against the glass as the liquid around him bubbled when the heat dissipated into the fluid. The metal digits reached out and scraped lightly against the glass surface. As the ends made contact with the crystalline surface they caught the light of the overhead blue light, which scanned over his form, finalizing the seal.

The process was far from done though and hardly painless. After each part was set into place they would send a jolt across the artificial synapses embedded within the black, thermal suit in order to wake the artificial skin and connect to the nerves of the body within. He tried to hold still as he felt the ends of his nerves crackle, but his arms trembled nevertheless as he tried to fight back the pain of the boot. The suit's systems were waking up from a week-long hibernation. Eric was a foreign plug-in until the suit was able to complete its scan of him.

Heart rate, Electromagnetism, Neuromap-- each was systematically checked by sending small pulses of electricity through his body.

Elizabeth smacked Klaus' hand away from the keyboard before shooing him off to the side. He hopped off, skipping a step or two as Casey wheeled up nearly taking him out. Bell followed, intrigued by the whole process. The woman had never seen a Reboot before, having simply heard the rumors and seeing the neurological scans during.

A reboot was quite a painful process for the pilot. When strapped into the Suit its system must load up and sync to the user. During such the body has to accept the interference of the machine so it had access to its biological sample to become one unit.

Casey scrolled through a tablet she had pulled onto her lap. "While I am surprised the idiots didn't kill each other, we do have another problem." The seated woman declared as she held up her tablet, which had data screens laid across the monitor. "His vitals are all good, but we have twenty-five minutes before a rolling outage, maybe. Given the idiot duo pushed the system before things warmed up, maybe less. The reboot takes approximately-ish, twenty minutes." Casey warned.

Bell turned to take the tablet and look over the data. The Capital posted times for blackouts which were practiced in order to maintain the set allowance of energy use across the colonies. Each colony had a designated amount of power per day depending on their needs and would be fed forced blackouts in order to maintain that. Amaroxia had limited energy and every hertz had to be used accordingly.

Bell handed the tablet back to Casey and crossed her arms over her chest, brows furrowing at the information. "That is quite a lot of vaugities for such a precise field such as neuroscience." Bell worried.

Elizabeth waved her hand dismissively as she worked on the console, recording Eric's progress. Klaus inched his hand near the console, only for it to be smacked away again. "You know that's crazy talk Bell! Science is nothing but vague theories." Elizabeth declared. "It's our duty to test them!" Bell and Casey flinched at her attempt to cover up her concern.

Casey sighed. "And what is the difference between you and a mad scientist again?" The grouchy assistant questioned.

Elizabeth paused in her typing and looked up. "Pain." A serious tone entered her voice that caught the attention of the others. "I don't want them to be in pain..." She would whisper so softly that the computer hum would drown out her gentle declaration.

"IDIOT." Eric yelled from his communication system in the suit, which roared out from the computer. "I was **Burned** last time!" He reminded them.

The shout was unexpected, many in the room flinching as Elizabeth placed her hand over the speaker to muffle the noise. She snapped a sharp look towards the glass container.

"Because you two did this last time!" Elizabeth accused back.

"You're a slow ass!" Eric bit back, jabbing his finger toward her general direction. "Maybe if you lost a few pounds in that fat head of yours you'd get around quicker! Egotist!" He barked.

Liz threw her arms in the air. "You try carrying the burden of a prodigy and tell me how you have to slog around all day with everyone's expectations!" She assailed back before returning to her manic typing. "I will electrocute you!" Liz threatened under breath.

Casey rubbed her eyes. "Liza, you're not helping previous concerns of you being a mad scientist..." She warned.

There was a moment of silence as eyes fell onto Liz due to her response. After a sharp glare was turned in their direction from their lead, they would turn back to their work. All around the other scientists worked to gather data, but they held various roles. Some managed the systems, but others were in charge of ensuring the medicine that was being added to the suit was diluted at the proper ratio. There was a handful that took care of less technical aspects that involved filing away and storing the information gathered into safeboxes.

Fires were not uncommon and after losing some important data in the past, after an incident in the Capital, it became second nature for them to keep backups of their backups. While the experiment was underway everyone had a role to play and this was just another day to them. But before they could proceed with the task any further a pop was heard as one of the generators in storage suddenly burned out. The lights in the room flickered as they began to lose power.

It was worse than a blackout.

"What the--?" Bell began. "Please tell me that was just the light sockets popping... "

Everyone in the room began to panic. Consoles were furiously worked upon to keep power diverted to the chamber. Eric began to scream in agony as the suit went into self preservation mode and started to drain him of his power. Klaus looked up to the tube, mouth falling agape as he sought to call out to his kin. But he could not find his voice. It was happening again...

Casey wheeled up to her console. "Shit, if we lose power during a Reboot something much, much worse than a Burn can occur." She began to search for the cause of the generator's overload, her eyes rapidly jumping between her tablet's scans and her console's calculations. "Something's not adding up. Why is there a rolling black out at this time?" She was sure. There shouldn't be one for another twenty minutes, and again in an hour.

Bell was taken aback "What'll happen?" Bell asked, starting to become concerned. The two weren't just there for them to experiment on and toss aside if they died. "Liz?!" She called with more urgency when she received naught but a racket of clacking keys from the room.

Elizabeth had just froze. Her heart jumped in her chest as she tried to speak. "I... he--" Her usually eloquent manner was stunted by the unsettling state of affairs.

She stared down at her screen, hands at either side of the monitor. None of it added it, in fact most of the numbers looked to be nonsensical code thrown in with her program. Her glasses were filled with the reflection of calculations running over and over. At the end of each calculation a red screen blinked with an error signal. Every attempt to get the generator back online had failed and with the winding hum of the power fading Elizabeth could only prepare for the worst.

One by one the lights above them shut down as the cold snap returned to the bioluminescent plants, forcing them into a deep sleep, diminishing their natural luminosity. The computers shut down one by one, save for the ones still on the remaining generators. None of them were connected to, nor could be rerouted, to the Suits containment chamber.

Elizabeth slowly raised her gaze and looked up. "...the suit is designed for self-preservation. It will drain any and all energy it can to stay online -- even their pilot..."

CHAPTER SIXTEEN

Conflict Of Interest

The darkness came suddenly.

For a moment everything would have seemed to have stopped. Beneath the grim stillness, though, there was a faint thrumming that would remind its owner that they were still alive, for now. Through the unsettling quiet he would focus on it, realizing what it was that made such an obtrusive sound, one that would dare break the silence. Eric's heart began to race; he pushed his thoughts to remain calm, lest choke in the fluid that was currently filling the tube and aiding his breathing. If he inhaled too sharply it would cause his lungs to become filled too quickly, unable to pull enough air from the solution before expelling it. Doing so would irritate the sensitive lining of the lungs. The last thing Eric had heard before his head started to fill with that familiar haze was the muffled voice of his brother before a wretched and inconceivable pain shot through his body.

The feeling was like jagged needles digging through every vein and blood vessel, snaking through the intricate channels beneath his skin. His muscles clamped down and every nerve-ending boiled with a violent heat that made his skin feel as if it were boiling, the touch of the thermal suit more apparent as the tiny sparks of electricity rolled through his bones like lightning over generators. His mind was starting to lose its grip on reality. He was starting to hear whispers, voices familiar from his past and ones he had yet to know in his future. The pain-induced hallucinations began in fervor as white sparks popped behind his eyelids, stirring the blanket of darkness that he began to drown beneath with every passing moment. The agony that pierced his entire body was like nothing he could think to put to words.

Perhaps this was what the end of their lives would feel like. A slow, inescapable death as your body turned on you and you turned to stone.

Regret surfaced as he lost consciousness, his body heavy, yet able to sit weightless in the fluid filled chamber. Maybe it was foolish for him to try and escape their fate, uselessly clawing through a system designed to keep them down. He was a fool to have brought his brother out into a world where suffering was all but guaranteed by the parts they were born in and the family they were born to. Locked to a caste, trapped in a gender worth little more than what it was needed for procreation.

Inside the facility they could at least be quietly forgotten amongst the rabble of fading memories and have a warm meal, a dry place to stay. In a moment between the lines of life and death: Eric had an envious thought which did to invade in the light of his regret. Had he been born somewhere else, in a different body, at a different time: he would have been able to do something with his life. How he envied his mother because she was already dead...

How was it that the man they met earlier that day, who had escorted them here, handle that old first generation suit when he couldn't even command his. Even behind his shut eyelids he could see the soft, pulsing cyan light of his visor. The last thing he saw on his system's screen before it all went dark was rejection.

[User incompatible.]

Flashing, laughing at him. A curse spat in his eyes.

But on the other hand did they really want to stay there in prison? Perhaps the twins should have been more eager to head to the labs than stay with that malformed, monstrous murderer who sold them like animals to slaughter. They wanted to go home, even if there was nothing left to return to. They wanted to be free, no matter the cost, but he now sees it was too high a price. And yet, that was a cruel irony, because they were never as free as when they were trapped in these metal straight jackets. They ran tests: running, jumping, and feats in an attempt to exceed the capability of the exoskeleton, of themselves. They pushed their limits.

The pair were intent on returning to their cells to plot their escape, even if that meant going to the Void. The Void was a place no one could navigate, could see. Their senses became empty and their eyes useless. There were many that said it was a paradise, but others said it was a quiet place you never came back from: torn to pieces by monsters. It wasn't an escape so much as it was running away. At least here they could make a change. As much as he annoyed Liz and Casey they weren't like the Military Division, though he was loath to admit it. They wanted to make everyone better again because living like this wasn't living. On the edge of your years until you became a decoration in some garden park.

The military had long since given up and just fought to live, like starving animals surviving on scraps.

The Void was that place beneath the soil: the hottest and darkest place in Amaroxia. Beneath the red soils the ground was said to boil and resonate with the spires of Roxaedian: the red center. It was said to be a place only the sinful went. It was the one place that your gender didn't matter. Men and women that were unable to serve the land were sent there for the rest of eternity.

Those who could no longer do good in the world, who could no longer rise to the challenges sent to them by the disease, were condemned to this eternal wandering in the silent abyss of the molten core. There, not even the healthiest Geroiid could divine its location.

At least that's what the church dictated.

The Sisters did well with their propaganda. They made the Mugenes seem like a test from the Heavens; it was retribution from their sins against the Sun. Many had come to believe that those able to surpass the suffering and pass on, survive, they would see the surface again.

A surface where the Sun does not curse the land with its light rather, bless it. Cults had sprang up throughout the capital and even as far out as the southern hemisphere, where no Amaroxians could survive as mortals.

These cults dictated the only way to be spared from the disease was to embrace it. The pain was a sign you were alive and the crippling erosion of flesh was reason to fight against the heathens that sought comfort in the darkness. Over generations Amaroxians grew accustomed to the pitch black of the underground. Light had become a poison that burned flesh and killed life. Cultists bathed in IR rich lights, flesh seared as a sign of their devotion. They wore robes to shield themselves from the green and blue light that fueled an Amaroxian's comfort in the darkness.

Eric thought back to a time where he had felt very much

the same. He had wondered what it would have been like had he been weaker and accepted his death. Would he even be here? But as he faced that monster the military created, an abomination that blindly served the Sister's will, he began to feel he understood what it was Elizabeth wanted.

She was a mad doctor, to be sure, but it wasn't that the woman had lost her grip on reality. Her ideas were simply beyond anything others could see or understand as they were now. The way she spoke to them as if they were annoying little brothers, family, it wasn't the usual relationship between a man and woman that was expected of you.

He remembered when he was first introduced to her on his farm. She had come from Sofu, a city located on the other side of the hemisphere. She had heard that they were still alive, generally healthy, when normally those their age were already starting to face the tertiary stages of the disease. It was baffling that someone from Sofu, of all places, would even know about their Farm.

Farmlands were just small pieces of the Colonies outside the cities, no different from the last. They were places food and organic resources came from. Theirs was just outside the capital. They were nobodies, but they were still considered citizens at the time. Just like everyone else their records were in public files. Their health history, their birth records and even their lineage was open for all to see.

It was just how it always had been. There were no secrets in Amaroxia, no privacy. From the moment you are born everything you were and everything you did was recorded and scrutinized. She had called the twins special, amazing. Words they had only ever heard on the mocking tongues of Saiers, those native to cities, when they came through with their harvest to city hall for their tokens. Teiers like them, farm workers, were just an expendable workforce.

His thoughts soon became dark.

Visions of that metal monster continued to haunt his passing into the other world... It was there whenever he slept, whenever he tried to dream.

CHAPTER SEVENTEEN

Forgotten Relic

Prior to their arrival to the Hurvor Laboratory the twins had faced an ominous sign of things to come. Had they recognized it they perhaps would have taken that chance to run.

Thinking back I should have noticed the way he spoke.

Like usual where Eric and Klaus had to head to the lab at the behest of Elizabeth. It would have been like any other time they were expected to go, but now they would hold permanent resident as decorations for the facility. They had been approached by Honchberg that morning. It wasn't unusual for him to pick them up, but it was strange that he came straight to the fields to collect them. Usually he waited by the detention center's entrance. He'd always seem too arrogant to come and directly collect the pair. Too proud to step foot in the infested halls, but that day proved they were wrong about it.

They were also greeted by a new face, one they would remember for years to come, at least the few years they had left to live. When the ATV pulled into the yard they had been put to work in, guards and prisoners alike stopped to gawk at the vision of the first generation suit. It was known as the Hammer Unit and it was said to be piloted by a former prisoner that had been a prisoner of the Marco Facility.

The Marco Facility was a nightmare. The name alone could strike a deep, debilitating fear into the hearts of even citizens, who were normally ignorant of the more unscrupulous principles of the world. After all they lived a life believing their leaders delegated for peace and put their prosperity before selfish gain. There were some who disagreed, but those voices were quickly silenced and turned into enemies of the state, examples who were sent directly to the facility in question.

The Marco Facility was named after Karin Marco who had invented the Amplifier. It was a simple tool originally designed to disable early exo-suit models during the earliest stages of the war. It was a simple matter seeing as the earliest suits were simple metal frames that sat over the body like a skeletal brace. But soon suits were given thicker and thicker armor to make up for the weakness and the Amplifier became obsolete. But Karin Marco modified the Amplifier for use in interrogations. Her facility became an important detention center for rebel gangs and violent criminals. It became a place known to have the ability to rehabilitate anyone to enter its doors, but the cost was one's mind. Anyone who was rehabilitated was said to become a mindless servant to their chain of command.

The current commander of the Marco Facility was a woman named Mai Aaron, general of the Cyan GHOSTs (Garrison Headquarters of Observation & Surveillance Tactical Security). She was said to be a dangerous soldier who commanded the respect of the Daughters and had enough grant money to do as they pleased because they brought results.

General Honchberg's arrival was not a private affair. Inmates still inside hung from the windows, curiosity fueling their otherwise dull and ordinary day. Whispers carried across the barren pit, scaling against the Twins' backs like jagged stone. Or perhaps it was the sheer terror. The military was, naturally, feared as the weapons of the Sisters. Tools that were blind as they were fierce. The soldiers were the monsters who came in during the night and razed a sector for the transgression of one. It wasn't uncommon for entire areas to be gone come the morning and the soldiers of the Marco Facility could be thanked for that, but it wasn't as if other parts of the military weren't dangerous, like Honchberg's Red SHIELDs.

There was no other life they knew. Entire groups would disappear overnight if ever a whisper of mutiny crossed the moles that lived among the citizens. If they suspected a Roxoid was being sheltered in a colony or farm, power would be shut down in that cell, crippling everyone. Amaroxia was dependent on their power plants and energy for their livelihoods. The plants ran on unstable geothermal energy.

Their survival.

It gave them access to farming equipment such as spore exteriorizing evolvement devices, otherwise known as SEED vats, and a means to stay protected against the cave ins cause by geothermal shifts which most colonies were protected against with SHIELDs, sonic helio ionized emitting light domes, which were put in place after Geothermal plants began generating non-stop energy to provide power to the capital's defenses after the first outbreaks of Mugenes.

The domes separated. They controlled. Some even believed they were a sign for worse times to come.

The doors of the vehicle slid open at either side... a metal claw wrapped around the edges. Boots of black-steel hit the trodden ground... Over 200lbs of metal wrapped the frame of a person. Steel pauldrons covered the shoulders, arms guarded by ebony, thermal regulating cloth. Tempered metal weighed the chest down: figure hunched forward, counterbalanced by the metal dorsal fin.

Brass colored spikes protruded from the shoulders, the visorless helmet covered in electronic modules, from front to back over the ears to assist in hearing. Visual sensors compensate for the heat produced by the armor's most basic functions. A hiss of hot steam escaped the metal... the person?

A whirring noise crackled from the back wires that hung loose...a T1 model. There had been stories of suits becoming unusable when their users were welded -- trapped inside of the exosuit.

The dangers of Gen one suits were well known by all suit users.

The machine stood to the side as a figure jumped from the vehicle. The crunching of packed dirt beneath the heavy step caused a measure of red silt to billow into the air, the slamming of the door causing the vehicle to shake. The pair has never seen a first Generation this close before. The heat that emanated from the armor had been suffocating. Rivulets of steam rose from spaces between the joint plates with any excess getting released, forcibly pumped from valves on the neck. It was, overall, an awesome sight.

It was what Eric would recall as he struggled between his consciousness.

The technicians hurriedly worked as sirens rang through the facility which warned of the impending blackout. Bell would lend a hand, stationing herself at a console to help backup the system files. The most troubling aspect of the blackouts was when unprotected systems would lose months worth of data. Due to the limited resources provided to the scientific community: digital data was rarely backed up.

Cloud services were prioritized for the military. What was worse was there were little to no resources to store, what the government felt were, unnecessary volumes of data on the Nodes. Nodes were data grids connected to Pylons that transmitted the data into the government's servers.

Casey had rolled up behind Liz's computer only for her eyes to widen. "LIZ!!" But it was too late.

The deep, reverberating hum that had been a familiar song in the background would quickly reshape into a burning scream needling in the back of the mind. One by one the systems would shut down. Starting at the largest draw of power: the pods would be the first to cease function. Following that the fans would go, then the consoles, finally, the lights. The murmuring voices of the scientists fell into equal reticence. Elizabeth would release a shuddering exhale as fingers dug into the metal of the console.

She had been frantically entering commands in order to prevent the system from powering down so that the emergency protocols wouldn't initiate while Eric was still hooked up to his suit.

The light of the pod faded as the systems completely shut down.

Klaus stood beside Casey, eyes unblinking as he watched his brother's body float in the fluid. Casey sat up in her chair, pink eyes focusing on the younger brother. She couldn't discern his expression. Though dark, there were a few emergency lights that buzzed underfoot, threaded out via wires throughout the laboratory's floor.

What could she say or do? Despite their position in society, despite the twins' lot in life these two were not city born men. They were from the plantations out in the barren zones. They were a different breed. They were more aggressive and thought for themselves in ways city born men would never align themselves to.

In short Klaus was violent, he was dangerous and was not remiss to express his anger physically. They all knew that there was only one person in this room that Klaus would kill for, who he would protect. The younger twin slammed his clenched hand onto Casey's console causing the station to shake. The chair bound woman flinched and sat back as she stared into his deep, green eyes feeling a shudder run through her chest when he focused on her. Why did they seem to glow in such an unnatural way?

"Dr. Newberry!" One of the technicians called as they pushed to stand, their focus on the pod.

CHAPTER EIGHTEEN

The Skittering Rats

All eyes would fall upon the capsule as bubbles fought against the swirling fluid inside. Harsh bursts of powerful flow occasionally hit against the glass surface with enough force to cause the heart of those watching, lurch. As if fighting to escape the bubbles began to collect at the top of tube. Several moments would come to pass before all seemed to become still inside the confines of the pod. The suit was as still as death, staring down into the room a lifeless sentry: cold, unmoving. Suddenly the visor of the helmet took on a deep, red glow before fading into a soft cyan hue. The suit began to shift within the fluids, stirring them once more, seemingly fighting against its binding cords that attached to vital points of its shell.

The wires and tubes that were attached to the suits major points of contact: the scapular thoracic joint between the shoulders, the sacrum on the lower back, the two brachii triceps on the back of the upper arms and the hamstring region on the back of the upper thighs. They were important due to the fact that they ran along the major muscular roads that followed the Meridian's Flow, a path of nerves used by physicians, the military, and surgeons used to heighten the connectivity between various kinds of data processors, connectors, electronic brains and the nervous system. This allowed the currents from the wires to run faster through the individual to communicate with the machine. In the case for the Military Pilots it was the communication between their pilots and the suits that have become known as Turbo Suits, a unique line of suits among the hierarchy of Amaroxian

Exosuits.

"Casey!" Elizabeth turned back to look to her assistant. "We have to get him out or else--!" It wasn't as if she wanted him to die, but why were they in such a rush to do something that could get them killed?!

She couldn't get him out so long as the connectors were still attached t o the suit. The tubes are what allowed the computers to measure the machine's data, the pilot's vitals, and every calculation required to keep the systems from crashing. Elizabeth hurried over to the monitor beside the pod's controls. Leaning forward she would push her glasses back against her brows, but a thick layer of fog would cloud the glass. The woman would haphazardly brush her thumb over the glass of her lens, risking leaving behind thumb prints as sweat began to pour from her pores. She attempted to clear the steam that blocked her vision between her frantic typing as robust waves of heat flowed from the malfunctioning machine.

As Elizabeth hurried through the logs racing across the screen she would find herself unable to make any sense of it. All across the screens were indecipherable lines of numbers and letters, a formless code that was a garbled mess of corrupted data that looked to have become a ghost image on the screens of the now powered down machines.

The metal sheaths over the fingers flexed, the ends pointed into curved tips like a beast's claws. A soft whirring sound began to rumble from the confines of the fluid-filled prison, the entire structure vibrating. It grew louder, now a grinding noise as if metal gears were scraping against one another. The sound was unsteady and even began to stutter.

The sound grew layered as dull beeping noises began to wash over a rapid thumping. Bit by bit the sounds sped up until they hit a pitch and the reverberations would meld together creating a deafening scream of metal before the suit pulled back its arm, ripping its connections from the casing causing a dark, almost black ooze, to bleed from the detached lines. Slamming its claws into the glass with enough force to crack it, the machine's other bound limbs would continue to break from their bondage with a monstrous force.

The scientists gasped out and flew into a hysteric panic as the suspension fluids began to spray from what they had thought was a minor breach of the cabling, but upon closer inspection the Suit had even managed to rip panels from the pod's inner surfaces.

"How is it still moving?!" Elizabeth rushed to the capsule. "H-he should be dead!" Though it was the least desirable case, what else could Liz think now that the Suit's power had been rerouted to its driver?

Klaus had not moved. For several moments he stared up at the capsule, watching as the Dragonfly tore through its chains. He was unmoving, all the while watching their efforts come to life. The General was telling the truth. That was all it took.

Thinking back to when they were picked up by the General and his soldier they had asked the pair a simple question.

"If they give you the power to change your destiny, why don't you? It looks like you'll just die on the cutting block at this rate. Do you know what it means to be free?" The philosophical question was a ruse.

The man was military. They cared about only one thing: more power. So long as Elizabeth's group was testing the T2 suits the longer the Military would have to wait to get them. If they handed them over though, as their pilots, they could not be thrown away. A Suit, more often than not, never chose another Pilot.

Klaus raised his brows, Liz's doubt raising his hackles. "Oh?" Klaus looked up from the monitor, his focus now Elizabeth. "I thought you had faith in my brother, but I guess he was right about you." Elizabeth took a step back, her head turning to the younger twin as he stepped out from around Casey's console, in his fingers another microkeycard.

Casey moved to push her chair's buttons, only to find they didn't work. Looking down she would see that, while standing beside her, Klaus had tampered with it. There looked to be damage from the laser soldering pens they used to repair computers. The chair bound woman snarled, turning her gaze to the miscreant as he held up the pen, taken from one of the technicians, with a smug grin on his face.

"Klaus, what are you doing?!" Elizabeth moved to rush after him only for the man to jump back.

Despite how the pair looked they grew up out in the plantations. They were more physically fit than a bunch of scientists who sat around consoles all day.

"You shouldn't worry about me." Kalus stood in front of his brother's capsule as the exoskeleton continued to smash its claws at the glass. "We promised to escape together."

Klaus turned on his heel and rushed toward the secondary

capsule which held the suit he had been training with in an attempt to synchronize with it. The glass on Eric's capsule finally shattered and a wave of the suspension fluid rushed out towards the group, forcing them to pull up their arms in order to brace themselves.

Casey slammed her fist onto her console as Bell moved up behind her to help move her seat. "What are you going to do, you idiot?! Nothing's powered up!"

The Dragonfly unit jumped from the pod, glass crunching underfoot as it moved to stand between his brother and the meek lab-rats. These cowering scientists were the real rats. They were a pestilence that wasted resources fighting a disease, fighting a war that could not be cured, won!

Bell shook her head. "H-how is he moving?! I thought the system hadn't been loaded, he was going to Burn!" She panicked at the sight, unable to act against the monstrosity. "Why is it making noises like that?!"

Casey quickly pulled her tablet from the side of her seat. "It's corrupted." Bell shook her head, unable to understand as she wasn't experienced in computer language. "The voice generation is controlled by a computer. The helmets are layered with pressurizing materials that prevent the drivers from being crushed when they go deep into the planet's mantle! So their voices can't carry from the helmets easily." As was expected of Military missions. "It's running τ-synthetic speech generation, but if there is a portion of the system unloaded it fails to trigger the generation process. That's what you're hearing. Give me a moment I can--" Casey was sure she could complete the generation manually so long as she could hear the paced pitch and tones it was expressing.

In that moment the power came back on. Everyone was shocked because that wasn't normal.

"W-what?!" Liz pushed to stand as she had tumbled to the ground when she lunged at Klaus. "Blackouts last twenty minutes, at least!" It had only been five.

A shadow rose over Liz. Elizabeth would nearly take a step back, her head slowly lifting until the Dragonfly unit was in her line of sight.

"Liz, run!" Bell and Casey shouted as they looked over the generated text. It read as followed:

"LET'S SEE HOW YOU LIKE BEING TREATED LIKE RATS. SCATTER. SCATTER. SCATTER. SCATTER!"

CHAPTER NINETEEN

Dragons Breaking Free

In a storm of glass and debris Dragonfly's prison would be shattered. The crystalline rain would tumble down in a shimmering display of destruction. The heavy, metal boot would slam down against the lip of what was once the door, metal twisted and bent up as the heavy suit weighed down the thinner panel. Its armored hands reached out to grip the edges of the ruined egress before it ascended from the raised platform like a celestial being descending from the heavens, but for all those present it was more like a demon raising from the bowels of the abyss as fires began to break out when the machine sparks reacted with the chemicals spilling from the torn and frayed tubes that had once supported the metallic beast.

Its glowing visor dimmed, the sounds of whining internal components slowing to a complete stop as Dragonfly ceased its movement. As suddenly as the chaos began everything seemed to come to a halt, silence now hanging over the once clamoring and panicked voices. The dull sounds of typing could be heard in the background as technicians scrambled to get everything back in working order. Automated systems began to put out the fires, sealing the flow of actinic fluid.

"Ma'am!" One of the technicians called out to the leading figures from a distance.

The voice carried from a room towards the back of the facility. The laboratories found around Amaroxia had the tendency to follow a similar floor plan. This allowed workers to move between buildings and sectors with less time spent attempting to reacclimate to their new environment.

Looking around, at first, it was difficult to pinpoint the

voice among the swirling swarm of warbling murmurs and screeching electronics. Eventually one could spot a head of cropped, blue hair which was brushed aside, leaving much of the rest of their head a short, buzzed cut, peeking out from a door frame. The room itself had a soft, red glow as the emergency lights had switched on, providing a small amount of sight, though looking at the young man it did not seem to matter either way for him.

Over his eyes appeared to be installed an artificial means for the man to see. It was not the same as bionic eyes which were available to most people that lived within the Capitals, but he seemed to be wearing specialized military brand that assisted in scanning, reading, and compiling data. It was something useful for data scientists, which he was. His companions struggled to keep up with the overwhelming amount of data coming in from the computers.

"What happened?!" Casey called out, Bell leaning back to look over the rows of consoles.

"Ma'am, it looks like the mainframe computer is shutting down as well." That put them in a difficult position.

Without it they would be unable to redirect the information they were sending into the AI's program. They could do it manually, but it did not allow them to install large enough packets to slow down the Ai's automated processes that told it to preserve itself at the cost of everything and everyone else around it.

"Is it the Parameters?" Bell would ask.

The young man would nod. "Yes, should I start downloading the data clusters and start uploading them into the qubits?"

"Do it." Casey called. "Fast!" they were losing momentum.

The longer they spent trying to argue with the AI the less time they had to actually maintain their stores of data. If they lost it it would be impossible to reverse engineer the suit to rebuild the old program. It was written with old technology and was yet to be converted into modern qubits. The current neural networks were also incompatible with the Quantum qubit that the AI's program was on. It was, by compare, an incomplete picture of the total process.

Liz sighed out, placing a hand on her chest as she felt her body relax, the burst of adrenaline waning as a headache began to coil in the back of her skull. A strong grip came to rest upon her shoulder. The woman smirked and reached up to touch the hand, only for the warmth she was expecting to be replaced with a frigidity familiar to one who had spent her life around these machines.

Looking up: the scientist was confronted with the menacing visage of the Dragonfly's visor. From a distance the polarized eye shield had a uniformed appearance, but up close one could see the individual cells that made up its optic system which fed directly into the Pilot's brain. Each tiny, geometric 'eye' was made up of numerous quantum fiber optic cables so finely bound together that the Suit systems can manage 10k megapixels of imaging data creating vivid views of a 3D space.

Distorted rumbling rattled from the Dragonfly, sounding akin to the vibrating tymbal membranes of Burmite Cicadas. The sound was loud and struck deep against the chest. Liz flinched and squeezed her eyes closed, the cloying grasp of the Dragonfly tightening before it lifted her off the ground. The sound would repeat once more. The woman blinked her eyes, slowly turning her eyes to peer at the grotesque helmet.

The Dragonfly's helm was uncanny. It had a humanoid shape, but the mouthguard protruded slightly. It could open up in a butterfly motion, like parting automatic doors. She knew beneath that covering was the suit's rebreather and the Suit's unique Haptic Mandibles where, when extended, it can scan vibrations in the air to accurately process a 3D map of its environment with sound.

"Liz!" Casey would shout, unable to move because her seat's functions had been destroyed by Klaus before he entered the pod. "Bell, please!"

The doctor would nod before hurrying towards the pod. The capsule that housed the Suits were designed with Kill Switches that completely shut the machine out of its powersource and home console to prevent it from sending and receiving data. The woman rushed past the Dragonfly. The Dragonfly's chromium wings suddenly spread: four thin apparatuses attached to the back and layered with honeycomb shaped anti-gravity nodules that allowed its balanced flight with the propulsion system that was installed on its back.

"-----" Once again the sound rumbled from the Dragonfly's voice modulator, Liz's eyes widening when she finally parsed the sound.

"Wait, Bell no--aah!" Elizabeth shouted as her body was suddenly hurled into the doctor, both women sent to the ground as Bell had reached the switch. "Bell! Are you okay?!"

"The Switch!" Casey shouted.

Liz looked up, pushing herself off the ground, but as she reached for the button the Dragonfly's fist came down over the console, smashing it to pieces. The machine's visor would light up and begin to slowly pulse.

"NO!" Elizabeth nearly screeched as she jumped up to grab the Suit's arm. "Casey, he's activating the system!"

"What?!" The chair bound woman leaned forward to look at her monitors.

She was right! The Dragonfly was sending a digital signal right into their systems, activating the Dragon's startup process. As all hands attempted to stop the process they would find themselves locked out of their systems and alarms going off as the facility was compromised.

"What now?!" Casey looked up, the red lights of the lab flashing slowly.

One of the technicians looked up from the security cameras. "We have a problem!" She pulled up the visual on everyone's monitor.

There the team would see the General making his way onto the property with a full battalion of footsoldiers in C-Suits, basic exoskeletons that gave an edge to bodies crippled by the disease. Charger Suits, C-Suits, were proto Turbo Suits, and serve as a basis for all Suits to come after.

Liz pulled Bell to her feet as they looked to the screens. "That asshole!" Liz fumed.

Once again the Dragonfly would make its call.

"You're an asshole too!" Liz spat.

Bell would look at Liz in question. "What happened?!"

Liz shook her head. "He's using base DTMF to communicate, I don't think the Sensory Speech program fully loaded before it was disconnected. He's saying: 'We should scatter like rats, before we're caught in his trap'."

"His trap?" Bell questioned. "Casey's Uncle?"

The Dragonfly moved towards the Dragon's capsule and would slam its hands into the front hatch before squeezing a bend in the metal to give himself a good grip before ripping the portal from its frame. The now useless sheet of metal was thrown across the lab, causing a number of the workers to shout and run from the incoming wreckage. With that the Dragon was now freed from its hold, the twin machines working together to free the Dragon from its wiring.

Once the suits stood side by side it was easy to see that they had been especially designed for the twins. The machines matched in almost all parts, but the Dragonfly had Chromium wings and the Dragon Chromium, hydraulic flexors that made its arms' strength immeasurable. The machines stood shoulder to shoulder, their forms distorted by the rippling heat from their destroyed pods and intense presence due to the amount of constructive interference the machines radiated off of one another. Alone the machines could work well, but when together their digital waves worked to strengthen their processing power making them a destructive force.

CHAPTER TWENTY

A Mutiny Burns

The two machines would stand shoulder to shoulder, their visors backlight brightening. The Dragonfly's visor was a deep green whilst the Dragon's was a shimmering blue, which made it difficult for the average Amaroxian to look it in the eye. The bright light was painful to their vision and only served the Dragon model as a close quarter combatant. It made it difficult for the Amaroxian's naked eye, or the scanners installed in their systems, to easily pick up its movements.

The Dragonfly raised its claw threateningly, the curling mechanical tones rumbling from its helmet. "------!"

The Dragon nodded. "**We aren't going to let you keep us here anymore. We're going to be free.**" The Dragon's voice modulator seemed to be functioning and would translate their brother's words. "**We'll never let you cage us again!**"

The two machines would break their ranks. The Dragonfly would charge to the left and the Dragon to the right. The power behind their movement was so forceful that the air between them cracked, nearby screens shattering under the snapping of the air. Together the two machines would tear into the facility, decimating the surrounding terminals: tearing apart the consoles and making sure that every piece of shelved hardware was shattered, splintered, and shredded while monitors were mangled.

"Bell, get Casey out of here!" Liz called.

Bell was taken aback by Liz's urgent call. "W-what about you?" She moved to hurry to Casey's side, the chair bound woman's chair was non functional in its basic use.

"I'll slow them down!" Liz turned to run to the back of the

laboratory where the security room was.

Fires began to break out across the facility which needed to be brought under control. With the help of some of her technicians: Liz worked on getting the fire doors shut, the metal doors sliding down between the designated fire egresses across the multi-level underground laboratory.

Bell would hurry through fleeing technicians and those who continued to fight against the destruction by uploading what data they could into their servers and downloading what was left to their tablets.

She pushed Casey along whose chair, though no longer mobile, could still access their systems. The light haired woman would connect to the nearest terminal and start sending out an emergency call to the Capital.

Outside of the facility, the C-Suit units began to surround the ground level of the laboratory. The Hammer Unit stood by the General, Hochberg smirking as he stood with his arms crossed over his chest. The man's face was disfigured by disease progression: scars pinching back skin on the left region of his face, paralyzing movement in the muscles where skin was already beginning to calcify.

The military made sure to recruit the most desperate and those easy to manipulate. In this day and age of Amaroxia's era: there were few who would willingly join the military and become tools of war. Being raised in a society that viewed men as little more than violent animals, yet made it mandatory for citizens to participate in military training for a year: continued to perpetuate the stand.

It didn't help that many of the men that maintained their ranks after the mandatory year-long training were often poor citizens that would have been forced to return to Plantations and Mines. Those that stayed ended up being branded as warmongers and could do nothing to change the minds of others when they were allowed to retire near the end of their life.

People were afraid of war, afraid of those who had learned to kill. With their lifespans cut nearly in half it was impossible to convince people these soldiers fought for them, served them, and it forced many to return to the bases and use what was left of their life repairing the grounds by building barricades, repairing walkways and sometimes becoming material for the stone walls that separated sectors.

At least that was the rumor circulated by those who were sent to Military Camps to work to their final days and never seen again. After all when one's body turned to stone at their death there was nothing left to bury. Graves that held the remnants of people who have passed from the disease were known as Gorgon Gardens and what remained of their people, these haunting sentries, it was a cold reminder that they were slowly being carved out by thee virus. Despite this clear evidence of death: there were no Gorgon Gardens found near bases.

Steam would express from the Hammer's plates, the spaces between the thickly armored unit's chassis was the only means for it to breathe out excess heat generated by the Suit's basic functions.

"Sir," the Unit spoke with a heavily modulated voice, the synthesized sound twisted by the pressure of the helmet's seal. "Those red-foot..."

Hochberg snorted. "They'll do it. The one thing you can trust about Reds is that they are obsessed with the idea of freedom. When you live in a society you can't have irresponsible notions like freedom getting in the way of progress, but so long as they think this will unchain them from that inescapable fate they won't stay quiet."

All he had to do was plant the idea.

"Eric!!" The name echoed across the burning workshop.

The Dragonfly came to a stop as its foot came crashing down onto yet another pitiable instrument. Its claws flexed, the gears no longer whining with strain. Its head would turn, the glowing visor dimming as a visible scope focused in the center of the mask before it fell onto Elizabeth.

Her heart jumped, feeling she could almost see him glaring at her from the confines of the helmet. She shook her head, regaining her courage.

"You asshole! If you side with that miser and give him the units he'll just kill more people! We're trying to save lives!!" Her voice broke as she shouted.

Panicked debates would fade unto whispers. The Dragonfly would turn itself completely to face the company of biochemists and observe them for a moment. The primarily female collective did have a few male dotting their ranks, but all seemed to share the same look of disgust at the actions taken by the prisoners.

Like he had rights. He has broken laws and now that he paid his dues to society he wanted to throw a tantrum! That's what their looks said.

They didn't understand.

The Dragon slammed one of the computer towers to the ground before stepping over it and walking to their sibling's side. The Dragon placed their hand on Dragonfly's shoulder.

"Don't confuse us." Dragon accused. **"We didn't deserve this."**

The Dragonfly's visor dimmed before the two would turn and make their way to the hallway leading to the building's exit.

Outside: the Hammer Unit was becoming impatient. "Let me go in!" They moved forward, only for the General to hold out his arm to stop him.

The Hammer looked to the General. The man appeared to curl the right side of his mouth into a smirk. Before they could ask, Hammer raised their head to follow the General's line of sight. Hammer's optical scanners gave off a copper glow before they returned to their dull light.

"Those bastards." Hammer was pleasantly surprised.

Out from the main doors the Dragonfly and Dragon unit emerged. These were the Second generation Units. TS2: known for having a more stable power supply and AI assisted neural loaders. These two were the Cipher Twins, their units were customized for their unique Geroiid frequency.

The Geroiid organ allowed Amaroxians telepathic neural waves and served as a light sensing organ as well. But to see a pair of suits specifically designed around high functioning Geroiid...

"Boys!" The General held out his arms, motioning to the ATV as the Hammer turned to climb aboard, back into his seat. "Shall we go? Leave my niece to stew for a bit?"

The Twins nodded their heads and moved to approach the vehicle, but Dragonfly came to a stop, looking back to the Hurvor facility. There was a sense of regret. He wanted to stay and continue making a difference, but he was seduced by the idea of their freedom. He wanted to become a master of his fate.

Despite the misunderstandings, despite the judgment others held: the military did not diminish a man's ability to exist. Be it fighting, building, cooking, cleaning -- joining allowed them the chance to expand their lives beyond the Capital domes and square borders that surrounded Plantins; hell soon they would be free from the crumbling walls of that hellish detention center.

Not to stand on ceremony Klaus would look to his brother

and call out to him.

"**Eric...**" The Dragon reached out, touching the ends of the suit's fingers to the Dragonfly's chest. "**They'll be fine.**" They hadn't created enough havoc that the place would up and explode.

Eric was reflecting on his actions. His heart hesitated, his body conflicting. He wanted to persevere, but what was it he could do besides throw up his middle finger and force Liza to choke on his farewell?

He knew that well, but he couldn't help but feel troubled. "------" Dragonfly responded.

Dragon nodded, understanding. "**I pity them too.**"

The Dragon Unit would jump onto the back of the ATV, followed in close step by the Dragonfly who hung off the back of the vehicle.

CHAPTER TWENTY-ONE

Shaking, Stirring, Soils

Three of the four C-Units that arrived with the General would pack up. One team was to remain behind and assist in evacuating any scientists that survived and arrest them, placing them in the detention center so they could be questioned. The Dragonfly and Dragon Units broke all known protocols for producing Turbo Suits. The TS series was meant to act like an insect's exoskeleton and support the body creating an immense increase of strength. The team refused to divulge their programming methods now that the units were complete, which had angered the General.

The roars of burning fires crackled through the air, as a thick choking smog started to spill from the facility. The sounds of shattering glass fired off in repeating tumbles as the thick roles of smoke poured from the facility.

Inside the technicians rushed to put out risky fires and save what data they could. "Doctor!" A familiar voice called out.

Liz, Casey, and Bell turned their heads to the sound of the voice. The young blue-haired worker hurried over to the women, holding what looked to be a microcard in hand. As he held it out Liz's eyes widened as she recognized it. Holding out her hand as the young man set the memory card down she would blink.

"You finished converting it?" She nearly cried.

The team had been working to convert the AI into a format that can be used on the computers in the capitals.

"Of course ma'am. Should I deliver it?" He asked as they looked around.

"I --" Liz hesitated before Casey moved to push her shoulder. "Eek!" She startled, reaching up to catch her glasses as they nearly fell from her face.

"Don't hesitate, isn't this what you wanted? We have to leave anyway. There isn't gunna be anything left, look!" Casey motioned her head, Liz following the movement towards the pods. The fires have already begun to melt the more delicate components on the pods.

"N-no," Liz shook her head. "You're right!" She looked to the blue-haired technician. "Can you do it?"

The young man smiled, moving to tuck the chip in a case before looking behind him as two other assistants approached: one with silver hair and another with green.

"You can count on us doctor Newberry!" The green haired woman assured.

The silver-haired man shook his head. "Letting Honchberg win after all this would be a kick in the face!"

"Guys..." Liz was touched. She was glad this team was assembled for this task.

They originally came from different labs across the sectors with one coming from the capital.

"Alright, we'll finish putting out the fires! You three get to it--!" Liz's orders were cut short by the feeling of the ground shaking underfoot. "What was that?!"

Hochberg had seen the system's promise. After all, it was originally written by Janis Rolanberry, Elizabeth's father. He had seen it back then when no one believed he could write a system that synchronized with the Geroiid organ, bypassing the brain which most TS units at the time were directly linked to. It saddened Hochberg, that his friend had become a scapegoat for the military. His brilliant system would rewrite history and who held the reigns of power.

Like snarling beasts: the light frames vehicles sped through the Runways, towards the wider tunnels. The strained creak of the ATV's suspension systems made audio of just how hard they pushed, the engines even started to pop when they were pushed beyond their limits.

The cavalcade of vehicles burned through the badlands, making their way to the Borvin Tunnels. The whole of the Amaroxian society was buried underground after the War of the Sun, when the galaxy's brightest star rained Ifreeti down from the heavens to destroy man for their hubris. It had been foolish of them to think they could keep burning toxins into the skies and suffer no consequences. Now they lived like moles: thousands of kilometers underground between the crust and spinel, within the mantle. Amaroxia's surface had originally been made up of nickel, iron, basalt and other mineral stones that produced a natural red-hue. Even deep beneath the surface the red stone that made up the planet bore deep into its center where the people had come to settle. Beyond that it was mostly unknown, but many believed the spinel lower mantle of Amaroxia was all that supported the spherical planet as its center was an empty Abyss.

They had time to make it back to base, but their urgency was because of the horrors one could find deep in the Abyss. The ceilings of stone would crumble, crack: debris was unsettled by the speeding jeeps. Were they unable to keep their current pace the sound alone could cause the dry passages a final resting place.

Amaroxians burrows consist of a complex system of tunnels. Deep tunnels to runways often open up into chambers where cities are built. Plantations are built across narrower Farming Runways which lead directly to production lines, separating them from the normal tunnels traversed by foot and vehicle into main thoroughfares. The Runways connect the larger Tunnels and sometimes open up into wide

Turnarounds that make easy work of reroute traffic between the Highways situated between Chambers. City Chambers are always built at a lower incline to the Tunnels via slanting connectors to prevent cave ins.

But the supports were in constant flux, always in need of repairs, but with the dwindling population it was difficult, if not impossible, to maintain the infrastructure of Amaroxia's Tunnels. Even as one rode through the unsettling groans of the weakening foundation would one day be the end of the civilization, but for now they survived dangling on a thread of luck and time.

But it wasn't always easy to ignore the dangers of living underground. An underground habitat needed to have conditions to be just right. If the soils were too soft quicksand quickly became a hazard across the walkways, but an even greater danger came in the shape of wildlife. Amaroxxiana were not the only lifeforms here underground. Ravenous predators and dangerous disease spreading creatures roamed in the open tunnels carved out for their convenience.

A deep, resonating, rolling boom soon echoed through the Runways. The convoy of soldiers and their purloined goods were mere kilometers from the threshold into the Tunnels, which were more stable as they surrounded the Capital city. They would be safe, but the rumblings grew closer and closer still until the solid ground beneath the wheels of their trucks quickly began to crack and separate: fissures began to extend out like roots, interconnecting and soon becoming much larger crevices that were soon impeding the vehicles, one becoming lodged in a trench as the dry soils broke open. At the speed in which they were driving the vehicle carrying the C-Units in question would flip and slam into the nearby wall of the passage, further destabilizing the transport,

The Hammer Unit would look back as the Dragon and Dragonfly pilots stood. Dragon was in the back seat of the ATV, and would suddenly stand to observe the situation. But no sooner had it become riotous, it would quiet down. It wasn't until Dragonfly's alert that any would know something was wrong.

Dragonfly had been unable to fully download its system's data packet before it was disrupted, but it was still able to scan the field. The Dragonfly was equipped with a full-scan sonar that was able to create a full, detailed image of the scan field. Its current range was upwards of x from where they stood.

"-----!" The beeps were clear, at least to the military personnel.

"Sir!" The Hammer called out. "Below!"

They could feel the sudden seismic activity pick back up. "Like hell!" Honchberg grabbed the wheel of the jeep and made a sharp turn as the ground itself seemed open up before it would erupt out like a lahar: mud, stone, and other pyroclastic debris.

The action forced a loud screech of metal rubbing on metal to snap across the air like a spark of lightning ripping through a powerplant. When the General jerked the wheel of the jeep the vehicle responded with an equally outrageous response and would sharply turn with enough strength that the military truck would begin to lean, threatening to roll.

"Hammer!" The General shouted as he strained against the wheel, which fought to turn back to its default position.

The pilot moved to stand. Hammer made sure to grab onto the sides of the bars that served as the vehicle's frame. For him it worked as a brace as he would lean with the jeep before jerking back and pulling the whole of their weight against in tandem, pulling left as the jeep rolled right.

Quickly realizing his action the Dragon shifted his weight and hurried over the back of the vehicle. He wrapped his hands around the bumper and hung his body low on the back as he rolled his weight on the same side as Hammer, helping him level the jeep again. The long, mechanical tail that served as not only a tool for balancing but an extrasensory tool would slam with a frightening force into the ground.

The hit was so powerful that the dry bedrock beneath the mechanical limb shattered, shifting as if it were sand. The bounded coil of metal and optic fibers would bore several centimeters into the ground creating considerable friction. The tail was more like the hydraulic arm or manipulator of an excavator. It functioned similarly, but was more flexible and could be controlled by the pilot no different than their arm.

With the pair's action they were able to rebalance, allowing the General to increase their speed and barely escaping the Driger's deadly actions. The ground all around split and debris rained from above.

CHAPTER TWENTY-TWO

Into The Abyss

To any Amaroxian there was no deeper dread than the darkness rumored to be found in the Abyss.

For Amaroxians the Abyss served as their physical manifestation of hell. It was, in all its mythos, a threatening existence that threatened to devour the Amaroxian's desire to succeed. Their inability to challenge its presence is what, more often than not, prevented their progress into zones they had dubbed: Abyssia.

There in the Abyss was a nothingness that was said to reside at the center of their world. It had no light and no feeling: no means for them to know up from down where they were thrust into an endless wave that ebbed and flowed around meaningless destruction. What was worse was that they were taught if they died, prevented from being collected by their kin: they were marked to be consumed by the Nauo: a reaper that had pink, wrinkled skin, a long tail that curled at its end, and vestigial wings from which glowing lichen grew. Its face was sunken, almost emaciated and their eyes had a deep green glow within pools of black.

Despite Hammer and Dragon's efforts the vehicle had fallen short of its target so as soon as the wheels hit the ground so did the Driger's body. It had not gone far enough to evade the seismic strike caused by its body's slam. The vehicle was thrown several meters into the air, its passengers escaping as the soils tore across, taking out the remaining jeeps.

"**Look out!**" The Dragon's pilot pushed to stand to his feet, grabbing onto the exposed frame of the jeep before he moved to climb back through towards the front.

Despite the vehicle being violently rattled by the Driger's slammed: the Dragon's pilot had no problem moving through the chaos. He held out his left hand toward the General, the suit's forearm covered in a metal gauntlet similar to the Dragonfly's. Unlike other suits the twin unit's gauntlets were larger and seemingly less dexterous, but their defining property was the fact they had more fine-tuned motor skills with more advanced proprioception for pilots.

The units hit the ground and soon looked into the face of death itself, demise screaming with an inhuman noise that ripped through the soul. A Driger, monstrous demon that altered one's sense of reality. Their sizes were incalculable and could measure anywhere from a meter in length to seventy or more and a weight that exceeded the load bearing force of the ground for as soon as its serpentine-esque body settled: the land itself was unable to support it and tore apart under its size along.

"----?!" The loud, tonal beeping that sang from the Dragonfly could not be understood by the others.

Dragon understood him though. "How does it move so fast?!"

Dragon was able to grab the General before he fell from the vehicle's side. His other hand reached out to grab the wheel and kept the axel from twisting suddenly, lest they lose control again.

"Muscles!" Hammer called. "Its entire body is nothing but a bundle of muscles!" The Hammer has seen Drigers launch themselves clear out of their exit burrows, dragging more than half its body from the ground.

Its body, from nose to tail, was a tube of grey, wrinkled flesh with patches of scaled carapace fitted along its side in sporadic patterns. At its sides were small, impractical limbs that flailed around, serving more as sensors to allow it to orient itself once it was on the mantle surface. Drigers lived deep underground near the spinel layer where it fed off the composite magnesium/aluminum mineral crystals. But there were times when Driger broke through the layers into the mantle where it hunted Amaroxian vehicles and other machines which were composed with the same composite mineral.

THRRRREEEEEEEEEEEIIII

The shriek was gut twisting. A sound mixed with the guttural braying of a Hellhound and the taunting cackles of a Gnoll. The sound shook one to the core, because the sound carried through the air devastating the already weakened Runways and Tunnels.

"What was that?" Dragon raised his head as the sound seemed to shake the very foundations of the passage they pushed through.

The General settled back in his seat, pushing Dragon's hand off. "It's calling for backup."

The twins looked to the General. They never heard of such a thing. Why were they calling more?!

Hammer moved to stand against the jeep's frame, his back against the higher bar as he looked back to the mayhem. "It may seem strange but they are pack animals, but with as many vehicles as we have they will not be able to drag them down into their nests alone." Hammer raised and looked to Dragon who had settled between the general and him. "They eat metal." it made sense, but Driger were normally so far below they were rarely a threat, let alone those of that size!

"----!" The Dragonfly would beep, but the sounds could not carry over the feral wails of hunger from the Driger before it turned its predatory focus on Honchberg's vehicle.

With a murderous intent the subterranean creature would

throw its upper body towards the van, jaws unhinging as flat, blackened teeth crunched down on the transport like it was willfully fighting back. The power half of its body seemed to remain in the ground as it anchored itself. Lifting its upper half along with the vehicle in its jaws it would clench down and begin to flail from side to side, slamming the twisted metal against the ground, sending all bodies scattering.

The Dragon rolled to its feet before holding out its hand where, at the underside of their forearm ran a fuel hose that pumped out volatile, combustible propellant towards the crimson tips of its claws that were superheated. When the claws were ignited they would light the fuel that could send out a stream of devastation, but the downside was clear: it had a large area of effect and could take out the rest of its team.

Those that were able, took cover. The Hammer unit hurried to the General's side, helping the man to his feet.

"Retreat!" Honchberg shouted as he motioned down the Tunnel.

Dragon's scanners attempted to find a safe point to strike the beast at, but the system would indicate with numerous, red crosses that there was no viable point of contact.

"Boy!" Honchberg shouted towards the Dragon Unit.

Clenching its fists the unit ran back as the remaining C-Units, Hammer and the General retreated toward the Tunnel's edge. The Dragon unit slid to a stop as his system's warning beacon went off, alerting him of the distance the Dragon unit had fallen back. Over the visor it could see the marker for their brother's unit indicating they were three meters away and nearly at the halfway point of their acceptable range limit for their synchronization: at five meters.

The debris above no longer fell in small, crumbling chunks but now rained sizable pieces capable of striking a man dead. Out in the field of destruction as the Driger flailed with its so-called prey: was the Dragonfly unit. They seemed to be staring off, hands having come over the sides of their head.

At some point after the Driger's cry, the sound created a disruption in his system caused by the beast's transverse sound waves, interfering with his suit's. The nanites in the suit's system began to go haywire as they had not been fully activated during its startup process.

[RED System update has failed.]

[Missing data packs identified:]

["sofp": 4, {vox.tsxe}
["sofp": 2, {axon.tsxe}
["sofp": 0, {nodus.tsxe}

[user:nanite replacing data packs]

[Resetting RED system]

[Prepare to eject user.]

"**ERIC!**" The Dragon unit reached out toward their twin. When the Dragonfly unit didn't move: they shifted their weight to hurry after them, only for a weight on their shoulder to subdue them "**What--?!**"

Looking back the Dragon unit was grabbed by the Hammer. "[Stupid kid! You'll be crushed!]

It wasn't until Hammer pulled them back that a heavy stone came crashing down, sinking into the ground right in front of them. Bit by bit the Runway would start to cave in.

The Dragonfly unit could only watch as the forms of the squad disappeared to cover the threshold. They could only drop to their knee as the suit powered down, leaving the pilot with no strength of his own. Slowly the visor would darken, vision going black as all light was pulled from his eyes.

"*Klaus...*" Was all Eric could think as the ground around him shattered: his body sinking into the soils.

With one last pull the Dragon unit was thrown across the gates as the stones collapsed with a resounding crash, finalizing the barrier of red rock that now separated the units from the Runway. It was not until the alert sounded down the Tunnel that the Dragon unit fell to their knees. The passage took a deep, burgundy hue as the lights began to flash, warning of the dangers.

Over their visor the Dragon unit helplessly read their system notifications scroll by.

[...scanning for {DR8-FI-TS2}]
[...scanning for {DR8-FI-TS2}]
[...scanning for {DR8-FI-TS2}]
[{DR8-FI-TS2} signal lost...]
[{DR8-FI-TS2} signal lost...]
[{DR8-FI-TS2} signal lost...]

--

--

--

[...system reconnecting.]

[user:nanite restored.]

[Missing packs restored from last saved point.]

WHIRRR WHIRRR WHIRRR

[Initializing...]

And the visor would switch on, the fallen twin taking in the view of the deep, purple monitor before he would notice a new command prompt.

[Deactivate RED system restrictions? ▪ Y/N]

Eric would blink and shift his eye to command the cursor.

[Y]. . . [Confirmed.]

CHAPTER TWENTY-THREE

Waking Up Tiamat

After selecting the command the visor shut off. Suddenly being thrust into darkness once more left the feeling of deja vu burning in the back of one's mind. Though Eric's heart began to race the young prisoner had to remain calm, lest choke in the fluid that was currently aiding his breathing. The helmets were all filled with the same liquid found in the suspension tanks: Jule Vapor.

Though the vapor was seen as dangerous it was necessary for the pilots to be able to work under the intense pressures of the various underground environments. It would vary from the Asthenosphere in the lower mantle which was over 500km from the planet's surface to the boundary of the core mantle over 2500km down. The lower one traveled the hotter it became. Less and less airflow existed leaving less breathable air available and, the most problematic situation: magnetism. Without being able to feel the planet's magnetism an Amaroxian was without a sense of direction and could, potentially, fall into the Abyss as not even instruments were as accurate the farther down one went.

Once Suit and Pilot were synchronized they would depend on the liquid, which was saturated with pure oxygen, until the fluid was fully drained.

The last thing Eric heard was the muffled voice of his brother calling out to him before the pain shot through his body. His mind was starting to lose its grip on reality as the hallucinations began. He suspected the nanites had started to eat through his brain tissue. He heard that if they were not connected to a consistent source of power they would drain the user.

The pain that pierced his nerve endings was like nothing he could imagine. Perhaps this was what the end of an infection felt like. Death. Regret surfaced as he lost consciousness. Maybe it was foolish for him to try and escape, to bring his brother out into a world where suffering was guaranteed. Inside the prisons they could at least be quietly forgotten. In a moment between the lines of life and death: Eric would have a thought.

How could that man that brought them here handle that suit when he couldn't even handle his own?

His ears would pick up the familiar sounds of his suit starting back up. His body felt like it was crushed under hundreds of kilos, which if his suit had shut down as he fell through the cave in, it was not surprising. The units weighed over 90kg. Little by little he would start to feel his body, the numbness that had spread all over beginning to fade as the AI's nanite system pumped him full of doses of $C14H19NO2 \cdot ClH$ in order to wake him.

When he opened his eyes there was nothing but darkness, but soon he would hear the familiar tone of the Dragonfly's AI.

-
-
-

[System booting.]
[{DR8-FI-TS2} RED Protocol]
[Callsign: Dragonfly.]
[AIS: Tiamat]

Sitting up Erick, once again, finds himself assimilated as the pilot to the Dragonfly. The system dialogue scrolled across his visor with unfamiliar prompts.

["sofp": 2:{vox.tsxe}]
["sofp": 4:{axon.tsxe}]
["sofp": 0:{nodus.tsxe}]

[Packs Installed]

Pushing to stand, the Dragonfly would move his eye across the field of vision. With the axon.tsxe installed he now had full use of the helmet's ommatidia photoreceptors, the microglass cells that dotted every centimeter of the visor. The darkness that filled his current location was removed thanks to the backlight on the axons that allowed the Amaroxian pilot to use all of their ultraviolet vision.

Unlike most Tunnels or Runways there were no lights wired through this particular passageway, but it was clearly dug out by Amaroxian hands, or at least machines, by the symmetry of the paths. There was clear evidence that the Driger from earlier had passed through here frequently before it eventually surfaced. There were burrow marks along the walls which were made by their mouthparts as they dug through their environments.

Blinking Dragonfly would allow his eye to drift, controlling the basic functions of his system. Before he was unable to even access his terminal because the tracker hadn't been properly calibrated, but now he was able to pull up a multitude of windows, none of which seemed to help.

[Location: Unknown.]

[DRK8-TS2 unit out of range.]

[Comm Tower: out of range]

[Wayfinder: N/A]

"...why is the wayfinder not working?" Dragonfly would take a step forward and soon realize why.

[Posible demagnetization or nearby ferromagnetic source.]

The Dragonfly would hold out their hand, the folded Chromium wings raising off his back slightly allowing the wings to become exposed to the UV pack on the suit's thoracic joints. This made the wings emit a soft, red fluorescent light that greatly lit up an area. To an Amaroxian's eyes red light could be downright blinding, but thanks to the cyan film over suit goggles.

The soft glow from his wing pack would help provide him with light and give him a moment to gather his brings and orient himself to the passage. He needed to calm his panic, unable to help the overwhelming sensation as survival instinct kicked in when plunged into a pitch dark void.

He needn't feel around in vain and possibly collapse down an unknown pit. Looking around he found that, after being knocked to his ass, he had fallen several meters down. His suit's wings were functional, but without access to his Wayfinder he would be unable to activate his system's Flight Mode.

Shifting his wings with a simple sh9ft of his shoulder muscles: the suit precisely controlled the mechanisms that allowed the plates of Chromium to move. In doing so he adjusted the focus of the glowing wings. Scanning his immediate surroundings he found himself in a massive, collapsed chamber.

The difference between a chamber and a simple open cavern was the unnatural arcs carved to create load bearing structures. They are sturdy enough to prevent the ceiling from crashing in and can withstand the small quotes created by the pressure of steam generated in the still active geothermal vents, which are very few and between on certain regions of the planet.

"Dammit." Dragon reached up to rub at the back of his head, fingers brushing over the CN cable connected to the back of their skull. "Maybe I should follow its trail..."

Turning to face down the chamber he could see the clear path the Driger had been burrowing. Typically they stayed lower in the planet's layers, but this one seemed close to the mantle."

One could tell by looking as the dig marks seemed to tread higher along each layer of the stone's strata. It should be easy enough to find a way as long as he follows the ascending marks. Without the Wayfinder he wasn't sure if they ran east or west of the Tunnel. His Suit had shut down before he was able to process how close they were to the next Tunnel.

"What was that Driger though?" He had never seen it before.

[Bio-Analysis...]
[...]
[...]

[- Perovskite Driger -]
[Clade: Allokephale]
[Order: Rodere]
[Diet: Gasthrolith]

[Perovskite Drigers are found in the Magnesiowustite Layer, 2000km below current layer.]

He shook his head, looking up. "So we're still in the Pyroxene Layer?"

[Affirmative.]

That was good. They were still in the main layer of the mantle where Amaroxians were settled, meaning they weren't close to the Void, the Magnesiowustite Layer.

"But if that's the case why was a Pero up here?" They were Void dwelling Driger. At first he thought it was just a Garnet Driger, which are normally found roaming just beneath their Pyro Layer.

Amaroxia was made up of four Layers of mineral composites before reaching the solid core: The Crust, made up of scoria and hematite, or was. After the War no one was sure what remained aboveground. Then there was the Pyro, known as the Pyroxene Layer, made up of ferromagnesian minerals. Some areas of Amaroxia are so dense with Ferromagnesian that it can be impossible to triangulate using Wayfinders. Next was the Spinel layer, a mineral rich layer that the Military complex mines for their use in semi and superconductors and as insulators from magnetic fields. Beneath that is the Void, or the Magnesiowustite Layer. Ferropericlase: an anisotropic layer of the planet that cannot be measured as it constantly changes. As far as Amaroxian tools can tread there is naught but darkness within that layer.

Just another hell.

"Biosonar. Find a passage." Maybe something was hidden he couldn't see in the debris.

At his behest the suit released a wave of sound. Watching his visor he would see that a passage was hidden out of site behind a larger boulder. It looked to be about the size of a Runway, which were carved out in designated heights and widths, so it could be recognized at a glance. If he followed that he could make his way to a connecting Tunnel. If he was lucky.

But his luck for the past few days has seemed to belong to the devil.

Folding his wings back the Dragonfly would start off towards the Runway in hopes of reaching a Tunnel that was at least recognizable.

CHAPTER TWENTY-FOUR

The Menu Screen

Despite the glow of his wings, the edges of the path played with the shadows, ensuring that the edge of his vision was shrouded in a consuming darkness. Amorphous forms of inky specters shifted as the light danced off the debris that had fallen from the passages above. It induced a primal fear. The cloying anxiety pulled the man back into his baser instincts: returning him to a time when his ancestors were small, scampering prey shrouded in a seemingly everlasting darkness as they were constantly hunted by larger predators, toyed with by evolution.

Even now his body struggled to evolve, to change. He still felt stiff, movements rigid as he found his new, metal flesh difficult to accept. Was this what he was from now on? There was no way he could get out of the suit without a station. Even if he attempted to break out of the metal suit it would be futile because the unit would not free him so easily, not without taking his life. The nanite AIs depended on a constant source of power or they would die and the microscopic machines were programmed to survive, regardless of the cost.

It was why suits were never piloted by decorated military officers, not anymore. Not since the Conyard Incident.

[Warning.]

Eric felt his heart jump, eye drifting to the side at the warning signal that popped up in his field of view. Rocks, ash, sand but there was nothing there. Was it a false alert? The RED System was supposed to be perfected.

The RED System. It was a restructured program that replaced the Synaptic Hardware Integrated Encephalon

Loadout Driver System, the SHIELD Systems. The Systems are what allowed the pilots to ride their suits. The amount of mental strain a suit put on a person was monstrous. The brainwave technology used pushed the suit to respond to the mind's external commands, but it came at a cost. The old SHIELD System had a 58% mortality rate, where the RED System reduced that to 15%. The Military refused to believe that this was a result of the program change, but rather it had to do with the quality of the pilot. The younger the pilots they used the lesser probability that they would lose a rider.

Turbo Suits were originally designed for the surface, but when society returned to the Underworld they had to be reimagined to better accommodate their needs. Necessity was truly the mother of invention because it was not until the Mugenes outbreak that people thought to change. With the sickness crippling the body and destroying the environment: the suits were changed to better support their dying race.

"It's suffocating down here." He wasn't a Saier. He wasn't born in the cities. He wasn't used to this choking sensation of traveling these twisting mazes of Tunnels and Runways. He was from the Farmlands. There they lived in wide open spaces, unbound by the dome that stifled the fresh air in the Capital. "Maybe we were better off staying." Alone the doubt began to consume Dragonfly.

His twin, his brother. He was his confidence. He was his courage. It was too dark to truly see, even with the glow of his wings lighting his way. Fear began to gnaw at the back of his mind. The soft rattle of shifting soils. The silhouettes that seemed to follow him. Whenever he looked back, nothing was moving, but the more he thought the more he realized that the Driger wasn't gone.

The beasts were massive, but the Pero Driger that had attacked him could reach the edge of the universe with just the end of its nose, its length was immeasurable when compared to ordinary Driger. That was why they couldn't run. The majority of its body was still hidden underground and tore at their solid footing whenever it moved. He heard the AI's voice again.

[Warning.]

Dragonfly whorled around, but there was nothing there.

TREEEEEEEIIII!

The sound rumbled in a subsonic wave, Dragonfly able to feel the frequency against his boots. Feeling the fear seize his heart the unit took off running.

The [Warning] flash on his FoV began to glow a dim yellow from its orange hue, the shift in color indicating the degree of threat, its proximity. In the corner of his peripheral Dragonfly could see something. It was like an eye watching him from the shadows. He wasn't sure how long he ran, or how far he went: all he could remember was when he dropped to his knees, pushing into an unmarked Runway, trying to put distance between himself and the Pero Driger.

The glow from his wings dimmed until it was dark. He heard a soft whirr in his helmet before the visor lit up. Light, at least enough to see one foot in front of the other. The passage was narrow, forcing Dragonfly to use his hands and shoulders to feel his way through the tight path. Reaching out his hands: the tips of his metal claws dug against the stone. It crumbled beneath his touch easily, showing how little water was in the soils. It told Dragonfly that he was still in the badlands. Nothing could grow here and it was as if all the water was sucked out from the formerly moist, clay ground.

Dragonfly soon came to a deadend. "Shit!" He raised his fist and slammed it against the obstacle. "Huh?" When the side of his hand dug into the wall it made a dull sound. "Tiamat." He would call to the AI.

[Scanning.]

The wall was made of sedimentary stone. It was dry, loose, but more importantly with a quick Bioscan he could hear the short bounce from the sound wave. Since his other scanners were down due to the ferromagnetic interference he was only able to use his soundbased scans, but it was all he needed.

He could see the scanner working in the corner of his visor, the image always in his peripheral. What interested him was the window to the upper left that read [BIOMETRICs]. He moved his eye to select the window, but was startled by a tone sounding, alerting of the scan's completion.

[Scanned structure is only 30cm thick.]

30cm. That was nothing. He flexed his hand, the metal gauntlet starting to feel more comfortable over his skin. Pulling back his fist the unit would slam his weight down onto the wall as he threw his fist into the thin barricade. With a loud burst Dragonfly was able to blow the wall out into what appeared to be a larger Tunnel, but unlike the one he had been in this one seemed maintained, as the previous one looks to have been abandoned decades ago.

[Wayfinder accessible]

The pilot perked up. "Oh?" Glancing back towards the narrow adit he passed through to arrive at the Tunnel, "I'd rather not go back if it's possibly a Driger..."

He came to a stop, gaze drifting towards the ceiling. He had fallen far, far enough that he could no longer see the ceiling. It was just utter darkness as the unnatural lights could not reach so high. He reached up to rub at his chin, but was startled. He looked down to his palm. The metal that covered his limb was starting to feel like his own skin, more than it had at the beginning. The digits were thick, the dense metal protecting him from the heat and pressure typically found in their subterranean society.

Shaking his head he would reach the suit's metal gauntlet towards the side of his head. At either side of the helmet were silver, metal discs that served as galvanic cells that produced small amounts of electrical energy to bolster the systems that ran through the helmet. The tips of the metal claws tapped against the sensor, activating it. After a few scrolls through the system options he would find the [Suit] menu which held the vital menus for the Suit and Pilot.

■[Status]
[Wayfinder]
[Bioscanner]
[Tiamat tsxe]
[ᵏ/eeẑ]

"What the...?" Dragonfly's eyes drift over the last option, but as he attempted to select the menu he was given a prompt by the System AI.

[Access Denied. Pilot lacks sufficient clearance.]

"Then why is it on my menu?" He shook his head. "Nevermind." Tapping the [Wayfinder] option he would start by getting a scan of the area. It was distinct from the previous Runway as it had clear markers of a well traveled road.

[Location pinged. Data files added: Nyxia Tunnels, Sector S2]

"Nyxia? But that's near the Equator." The pilot was in shock. The Porvin Zone was located in the Northern Sphere. The Equator was on the South's border.

The Nyxia tunnels were dug out during the pre-Sister eras. If one could believe there was a time where the Sisters had no power within the Council. The tunnels would lead down towards the Southern Hemisphere. There had been talks about opening trade with the Southern spheres, but as the Sisters gained influence many began to rethink their actions, worried that the two spheres had grown so far apart in their cultures it would only encourage conflict. Desiring to maintain peace the Southern Spheres and Northern Spheres agreed on a non-interference pact. The only route that they would share was the route that traveled from Erinyes to Aglaophotis, a pair of Military bases outside of their respective Capitals that had once been a single manufacturing plant for Helio panels.

Where had he fallen?

CHAPTER TWENTY-FIVE

This Isn't Paradise

It had begun with a mine.

Amaroxians had once lived on the surface of their planet. It was a beautiful world with a crimson red landscape, with vast plains and rolling hills. They had six seasons and moderate weather. The inhabitants had become masters of their land and were able to live sustainable lifestyles in harmony with the world's balance, but one day there was a never before discovered mineral ore that had been mined up from a certain quarry. This stone had become revolutionary to Amaroxian society, but at the time of its discovery: it was considered a rare commodity.

It could only be found in the lowest strata of the planet's surface and digging any deeper than what was allowed by the government's regulations was against the law as it put at risk the delicate balance of their environment. There were many laws in Amaroxia dictating strict control over the use of power, recycling, and other acts of business that best preserved their growing power as a race. With the universe moving and many alien races visiting worlds in an exodus of freedom: they needed to be ready.

Eomite. It was seen as the first organic ore within their galaxy. It was a mineral that could be grown, renewed, and used in various areas of industry that replaced the more wasteful use of space for farms and mines. Eomite could be used for everything from fuel to fodder for beasts! It had a composite that provided ample nutrients required for most carbon lifeforms to survive, including a dense supply of nitrogen that encouraged rapid growth.

All these benefits yet, at the beginning no one was aware how versatile it was. At first they had seen it as a possible building material. It was durable and became strong when heated to a certain temperature, but was also malleable. These vital attributes would not be discovered until it was too late.

Because of Eomite's scarcity those able to find the ore above ground created a market of supply and demand. Those who could supply the ore were able to demand prices. Much of the time the ore was collected by the government for experiments and attempts to cultivate it as Eomite required specific conditions to grow aboveground. Eventually these actions created a criminal element that caused many groups to start fighting over any available supply. According to their history a tragic event in the past triggered the start of the War of the Sun. The event in question is dependent on if you are from the Southern Hemisphere or Northern.

As it went: A small company was delivering cargo between towns. This group was shipping some Eomite from a local quarry to the nearest research facility as it had been bought up by the Laboratory. Whether the workers were from the South, or from the North, changes: but the group was attacked and brutally murdered by a rival company who resold the stolen ore to the labs for double the price. This created a rift between the two companies that had once encouraged growth with their rivalry, but when that line was crossed there was no going back, and conflicts only became worse.

Within a year of the conflict the kinetic properties of Eomite were discovered. When properly exposed to Ultraviolet light it would release energy that could be harnessed as electricity, a power source. Charger Suits were exoskeletons designed for use in the Military, but often used by the Industrial sector for heavy labor, especially government contracted jobs. These suits were available throughout Amaroxia, but were expensive to maintain.

With the shift in the economy C-Suits became the ideal riot gear for criminals who could afford to purchase decommissioned sets scheduled for incineration. They would modify these suits with deadly arrays and weld additional sheets of metal to serve as protection against projectiles. The original C-Suits were simple prosthetic-like structures that wrapped around the body so had no protection. Eventually the Military took notice and developed the first Turbo Suit, named for the turbine engine that was designed to amplify the use of Eomite as a source of kinetic energy.

Lines were drawn. It became a war of us versus them and, in time, the incredible leap in technological advancement came to a grinding halt. The creation of Eomite Turbinechargers that allowed incredible outputs of clean energy. Helios Light emitters created static barriers using electromagnetic compressors which protected from space debris. There were also advancements in bioengineering allowing Amaroxians to restore domesticated species once extinct. In the blink of an eye everything returned to a stagnant rerun that looped over a static filled background as the noise of a news anchor, who had the job to announce the end of the world, weeping while trembling.

But soon hellfire rained upon the land at the war's progression. The surface became uninhabitable. The War had not been with nature, but with one's neighbor. The side that had started the conflict differs on where you are born in Amaroxia because, even today, and the ones that ended it were the gods.

Those seeking to avoid the growing conflict between the Southern and Northern Hemispheres had broken apart, these groups still present today in Amaroxia as the North believed in Military prowess and advancement through the power of man's ingenuity, working with nature to ensure they could fight the land were it to ever turn on them again. The Southern spheres focused on growth through Science and artificial intelligence was as much a part of their life with machines as it was with nature.

"Not that it matters..." He would say to himself, feeling his face contort in annoyance.

His kind seemed to constantly be in conflict one way or another. And though history spoke of such things being of male influence there were some who had suggested an alternative history that involved female leaders. Of course such topics were viewed as propaganda, slanderous. There was no archaeological, historical, or cultural proof of this surrounding the Amaroxian society. Eric couldn't care either way. To them he was no longer a citizen and hardly a person.

"Tsk. Does that mean I'm just Dragonfly now?" It was a strange feeling to think of oneself as a machine, but he was feeling that there was less and less of a difference between where his body ended and the machine began.

[Warning]

The suit's system would alert the pilot of movement picked up on its scanners.

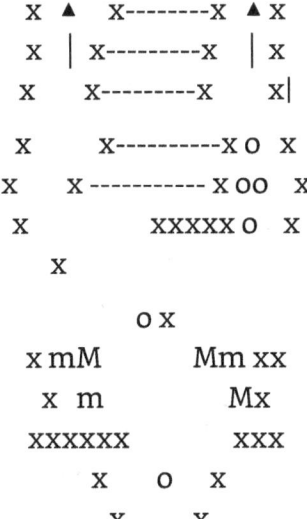

x | x
Xx ▼ xx

"This warning is way too late to be useful. This is saying the nearest lifeform is nine kilometers away!?" Dragonfly would complain, confused by the received information. "Shit, is it another Driger? Or a colony of Driger?" There were other markers on the map, but the Bioscanner was a vague estimation compared to the more accurate 3D scanner, but that was taxing on the system and required time to collect.

The suit would have to release Electromagnetic Detection Devices, or EDDs, that would zip around in the air and scan an area that had already been pinged by the System, but it had the added burden of needing the ping to not already be in data files and there needs to be a present electromagnetic field which, in Amaroxia, are lacking in the Void and can be interfered with at Crosspoints.

[Negative.]

The system called just as Eric hurried out the narrow corner and towards a stone pillar, these pillars part of the numerous arches that kept the passages stable.

"Then what, or who?" He would ask, expecting a clear answer.

[Humanoid Targets: 3 Roxiod, 2 Pharyst.]

This was a problematic revelation. Peering around the pillar the Dragonfly would be able to see as the five targets crossed over the horizon and into view. It was likely one of the many gangs that were known to wander the abandoned tunnels that littered the Pre-Sister Era construction projects.

Roxoid were what they called any native or non-native Amaroxian that had more than 50% of their body augmented with machine parts, which staved off the degeneration from the virus. Pharyst were non-native races that came to inhabit Amaroxia before ports were closed centuries ago and eventually became part of the population. One would find more Pharyst on the Southern Sphere, the Northern Sphere having strong feelings of exclusion given the Worm's Spine, the sky elevator, was at the center of the Agartha Capital...

"By the looks of it they're all Reds too..." From a glance the Dragonfly pilot was able to notice they were wearing old, discarded C-Suits that they painted over with red dye, which helped absorb the UV waves put out by most Amaroxian scanners.

"The ceiling collapsed around here boss!" One of the men shouted.

CHAPTER TWENTY-SIX

Gangs Of The Abyss

At first the Dragonfly pilot thought to confront the group, but upon seeing their modified exoskeletons he thought better of it. Though the T2 models were reportedly a major upgrade from the first generation he was outnumbered 5 to 1. It was clear these individuals weren't just going to lay down their arms and talk either.

[Warning, external scanning in progress.]

The system would warn the Dragonfly of the enemy scanners going off and searching for him, but there wasn't anything he could do, no where he could hide in this open chamber.

"Boss! There's a scab creeping!" One of the goons called.

The TS pilot raised their head and shifted their weight onto their left leg.

[Warning! Incoming assault!]

A loud whirring noise whistled across the cavern before the support stone he was hiding behind became nothing but rubble when heavy machine fire made contact with the stony sanctuary. The solid stone support had crumbled to gravel, its collapse kicking up a fine mist of debris and sand that filled the immediate area. Thanks to the system warning the Dragonfly was able to roll out of the way in the nick of time.

He used the dust cloud to conceal his movements, the enemy suits drawing closer with impressive speed. His visor let off a dim glow, easily spotting amidst the murky fog of ash. He pushed to stand, the suit's joints no longer netting off its distinct grind from his earlier movements. The pilot's axon focused as the mapping over his vision showed an incoming bogey. Dragonfly dove out the way before another shot lobed in his direction. This blast of energy curved at the last moment and slammed into a nearby boulder, having mistaken it for an enemy.

Aside from the percussive rounds they appeared to also have homing rounds, which could become problematic for the pilot were they armed with several loadouts. The wall of stone that had acted like a barrier between the main path and the side routes typically widened for vehicles as opposed to foot traffic, was not rubble and the five suits would approach the wreckage of stone in search of their target.

"There!"

He could hear as their shouts drew nearer, the heavy steps of their modified integuments a noisy clatter amidst the quieter movements of his suit. Weight seemed to make a difference between the suits and their mobility. The Dragonfly was made for flight so it was considerably less burdensome on the pilot if they wanted to move with quieter steps. Such was not the case for the augmented scrap suits and they were excessively sluggish when completed to the second gen, but they had more material making them sturdier than the Dragonfly, meaning taking a direct hit from their weapon fire wasn't an option.

"I need a way out. Tiamat."

[Calculating.]

The pilot spied the progress bar in the corner of his visual range. Three minutes. He was crouched down behind another obstacle, hoping he could ride out the timer, but the enemy suits were drawing nearer. With every second he stayed still, the wider the target on his back became.

"Shit." He wasn't sure if he was speaking out loud or talking to himself.

161

It was hard to tell as whenever he would speak there seemed to be a muffled echo that started to swim between his ears. It could have been because the fluid in the helm gave that feeling whenever he moved. But that seemed to trouble him. Was the helmet properly filled?

"Not important. Where was it?" His mind had a habit of drifting when he was feeling stressed.

This was definitely a stressful situation. He tried to be aware of his surroundings now that there was danger, but he hasn't gotten used to the readings across the visor. There was a lot of information. It wasn't due to a lack of literacy. Despite growing up on the Plantations he held a high reading comprehension. It was what Klaus and he would do on their off time. It was more an issue of recognition of the layout.

He laid his hands flat against the rock wall behind him, the palms of his gauntlets serving as directional sensors. His minimap pinged with the suits. Every step they made, every sound, drew a three dimensional map that allowed him to plan his movements. A suit was drawing up near his left side. His Chromium wings locked when he shifted his shoulders, the minute muscular twitch acting upon the billions of nerve sensors that made the suit act like a second skin.

When the muzzle of the enemy suit's gun peeked out at his peripheral: Dragonfly slammed his hand beneath the nozzle: pushing it up and forcing the unit to misfire. The blast ruptured the ceiling above, creating a rain of rock and dust. The gang would shout out as shots were fired in the Dragonfly's general direction, his attack pulling him from his place of hiding.

The leader of the gang stood furthest from the chaos, his refurbished suit a higher quality when compared to his gang. It was clear at first glance this man was the leading figure. Shifting his weight the leader turned his head as the scope over his eye scanned the foreign pilot. The scope attempted to overlay the shape of the Dragonfly to other suits in the database that were left over within their repurposed scraps.

An [ERROR] notice would flash on his screen. That was inconceivable! The database had every known Suit in the library, even decommissioned ones. It was what made it easy for groups like theirs to find junkers that have been tossed aside by the complex!

"What?" The leader huffed. "His suit isn't in the system! It's unmarked!" It had no recognizable frame nor had it a serial number that it could scan. It was neither marked as a Military Construct Unit, MCU, or a Scientific Construct Unit: SCU.

Two of the enemy units would attempt to pincher Dragonfly while one made their way through the outermost part of the chamber in order to sweep around in an attempt to ambush their target. The fourth looked to the leader who started to laugh.

"Boss?" He was a little concerned by his boss' unhinged laughter. "You okay?"

The gang's boss would lean back, mouth parting in a twisted smirk. "Is this guy an idiot!?" He looked at the mook. "Oy, this is some unmarked suit. Maybe it's one of them prototypes they test in secret. Whichever it is close in on him and rip the suit off his body!"

"But boss," He would step forward, his firearm at hand. "Don't the higher models have a pilot lock system?"

The exosuits that began to have individual names such as the Turbo Suit and Dynamis Suit Units had a failsafe system which prevented them from acquiring a new pilot. It was a result of a certain incident in which a Military Construct Suit was stolen from a dead pilot. The criminal in question rampaged across a sector located across the Erinyes Passage that killed members of the bases the North and South

Spheres traded between. After that suits were given a unique identification system that turned suits into junk if their pilots died.

But this left any MCU or SCU Suits at risk so most have been disarmed and it's become harder for gangs to find ones with weapons, but that didn't mean they weren't learning to refit them.

The boss would smirk, raising his hand, the metal bones of his exoskeleton groaning under his flexing motion.

"Don't worry about that. Primark can take care of that. Just rip his body off those bones!"

The goon nodded, turning to call out to the crew. "You heard him boys! Flay him!"

"""Raaaaaaah!""" They called in unison, blood pumping at the prospect of getting a new piece of equipment!

"Shit..." Dragonfly was annoyed. It seems the group got riled up by their boss. What did they mean that they would peel him out of his suit?! It was his! "Bastards, that damages the suit and--" Puts him at risk.

He's already partially fused with the Dragonfly.

[Scan complete.]

The system lit his visor up with data. According to the map there was a maintenance passage where generator shafts were buried as they crossed between Chambers to maintain the planet's power grid. They were not contained within the main passageways in the case of accidents. The maintenance passages were typically more stable on account of their importance.

The Dragonfly couldn't just go. He needed to divert their attention before he went for the tunnel.

"Where did he go?!" He could hear one of the men shouting.

The sound of their weapons loading could be heard echoing across the chamber. "Spread out!"

The pilot peered around his hiding spot. "I have to engage them, at least for a short time. I can't have them following me."

[Targets locked.]

The system marked the five targets, the leader being the furthest out so not a viable mark. "Right..." He'd have to be quick about it.

CHAPTER TWENTY-SEVEN

Within The Shadows

The Dragonfly pilot was far from keen on the thought of having to face five opponents on his own. He wasn't a hero and far from a trained military officer. He was a former farmer with a short temper and shorter range of attack. The Dragonfly had only one ranged ability and it was currently [Offline] due to having no ammunition. The problem of being separated from the one military officer willing to arm you.

"Found you!" Goon A called as he jumped at the pilot, swinging down a metal staff.

Kicking from his crouched position: the Dragonfly took off running. A dull rumble escaped his Chromium's booster, but because his wings were locked they did not activate. The metal staff slammed into the stone he had been hiding behind, tearing a gash into the surface.

This goon was a Pharyst, a non-native Amaroxian. They were known as Arglions. A tall race of semi-aquatic amphibians that primarily inhabitated the Southern Sphere. On average they stood at 228cm to 243cm. Their bodies were covered in a thin, breathable carapace with fin-like crests atop their heads, along their dorsals, and on their chests. They were originally inhabitants of the Deltotum Galaxy, but had been systematically purged from their home planet.

A few tribes would arrive on Amaroxia before the sealing of the Worm's Spine and eventually settle among the population of the South Sphere, but what a Arglion was doing in the North was beyond Dragonfly because, as far as he knew, they had been barred due to the illegal trading of illegal cross-bred creatures sold as domestic pets.

They were fast moving, even on land, so posed a significant problem in the patched together junker exo he wore.

Before the pilot was able to settle the other fellow, whom the Dragonfly pilot marked as Goon B, was a Roxoid and was the Arglion's backup. When the Arglion missed, Goon B rushed in with a slashing unit attached to the arm of his refitted C-Suit. Dragonfly was able to jump back, only to be forced by Goon C, another Roxoid, who had a ranged aperture attached to the shoulder of his suit.

Roxoid were Amaroxians or Pharsyt that were sufficiently augmented. While uncommon in the North as it was frowned upon, it did happen among higher ups who could afford the price tags of replacement parts. It was much a more accessible service in the South, but without restrictions this often led individuals getting upwards of 75% of their bodies altered. Goon B seemed to have much of his limbs replaced save for his left arm and Goon C had nearly half of his upper body augmented with machine parts visible on their sparsely dressed forms.

Goon C fired his blaster in the Dragonfly's direction. He remembered the goon had percussive rounds so he made a mad dash for open grounds, which was a good call because the blast turned what remained of the hiding spot into a small, smoking crater.

Good D was the problem. A Roxoid he had the homing rounds. He was parked in an open space so he could target the Dragonfly. The Suit anchored itself into the dry soil and would take aim. It was then Dragonfly heard the warning in the system.

[Warning! Focused targeting detected.]

Over his visor he would see the system light up a narrow passage. It was the one mentioned earlier. So he had to make a run for it or be blasted. Could he dodge it?

"What are my chances!?" He looked back over his shoulders, the tail-like appendage hanging behind his suit acting as a counter balance.

[...5% chance to dodge. Ill-advised.]
[Alternative actions:]

[Flight Jump - 75% chance increase]
[Pulse Strafe - 35% chance increase, route alter]
[Pulse Shield - 75% chance increase, unknown collateral]

Pulse? He knew all he had to do was unlock his wings to make a quick jump, but what was the pulse option? "Pulse?" He would ask aloud, maintaining his current speed as he could hear Goon D charging his blast.

The system would bring up a screen of information.

[Pulse - The Chromium Anti-Grav Pack can be staggered: fast charged and released, to create a pulse that can be used to act like mag bursts.]

Showing a diagram of the small dome his wings were attached to, it seemed that it was not only capable of assisting in flight but creating bursts of energy?

"What's the burst's range?" He asked.

[...4 meter radius.]

[Radius can be increased with an upgrade to pack size.]

It seemed he had his answer. Fine, they wanted to take his suit?! "You bastards can pry my cold, dead corpse from it!"

The boss was a Pharyst, a member of the Kirin tribes. They were seen as animals to the Northern Sphere, but the reptilian hominids were dangerously intelligent. Many in the North bargained it was because of augmentation, a taboo brain transplant from an Amaroxian who was at the final stages of the Mugenes infection, but there has never been proof one way or another.

"Idiot!" The boss bellowed! "Don't hit him directly! We want the suit in one piece!" The boss had no idea that the Dragonfly could take a direct hit from the blaster.

The goon would nod and fire, aiming for a spot to the right of where the Dragonfly would be coming up to.

The time between Dragonfly receiving data from the system and the Roxoid charging his blaster was all but half a minute and when the droning hum of the blaster loosed the Dragonfly acted!

The device that housed the Chromium wings charged up, but quickly stopped before he released a burst from the pack. His wings unlocked and spread to balance his frame before he released a Pulse Shield that covered his back in a sudden eruption of energy. When the homing blast landed beside him and set off a powerful explosion that released more dust and debris into the air the gang could only watch and wait. That strike should have had enough force to send the suit crashing to the ground as there was enough force to upend a truck.

Dragonfly was able to use the blast to thrust forward, wings and tail balancing up before he dove into the narrow opening. He grunted, body stuck between the walls. He squirmed a bit, using the suit's mobility and hurriedly pulled himself through.

When the cloud of dust settled the gang were stunned to see he was gone and naught was left but another crater.

"What the hell?!" The boss erupted with fury. There was no sign of him, but he couldn't have gotten far. "Find him!" He wanted that suit! With it he could finally take down that cocky Zeta!

His men would nod and split off in three ways. Tunnels circled around so there was only a matter of time before they would be able to find a path that connected to the Suit's route.

The sound was deafening.

The whistling projectiles was one thing, but the force in which they hit the wall behind the Dragonfly was another. The explosions rattled his entire body, right down to his teeth. He had rushed forward and would not stop, lest risk getting caught in the crossfire. Adrenaline rushed through his body and his legs didn't stop until he slammed into another wall which brought him to an abrupt halt. He had brought up his arms to protect his body and managed to do just that.

When his vision focused and the dust kicked up from his sudden breaking, settled, he was able to see the damage he had done.

His gauntlets had burrowed several centimeters into the stone from the force of his stopping power. Shifting his weight he pulled his hands out, the stone crumbling around him. Dragonfly turned his palm up, metal covered fingers rubbing together to crush the stones that remained. The simple motion easily turned the rocks into dust, which he would brush down against the front of his chest.

"That was surprising. How much power did I use?"

[98% of Pilot's charge remains.]

"W-what?!" His eyes darted around the screen before landing on the previously forgotten [BIOMETRICs] option.

Unlike the previous Status screen it hadn't any information of the suit's condition. He knew that suits needed to be charged and if he wandered around too far from a base he would be unable to recharge the suit and would find himself stranded. If the suit couldn't move he couldn't move and there was no way for him to exit the suit without a proper Station to remove the sealed parts.

His eyes would land on the option, the visor shifting in color slightly to indicate the screen shift. The cyan glow dimmed to a softer cerulean.

[Loading...]

[Unit: Dragonfly]
[AI: Tiamat]
[Systems: AR, HUD, Scan]

* * * *

[Suit Status]
[Energy: ▆▆▆▆▆▆▆ 100%]
[Power: ▆▆▆▆▆ 100%]
[Charge: ▆▆▆▆▆ 98%]
[Heat Index: Normal]

<u>DMG</u> <u>RANGE</u> <u>Hit</u> <u>CRT</u>
100 5~10 +20 +15

[ACTIONS]
Flight Jump
Pulse Strafe
Pulse Shield
Cipher
[Inactive]
[Inactive]

"What?" The pilot felt himself step back reactively. "What kind of numbers are these?!" They were far from the norm.

On average suits had a 20 damage cap to prevent

171

overheating and even if the limitors were unlocked through overclocking 40 was the ceiling of what the machine could put out. The numbers were based on the pressure a suit could put out. The numbers were in kN, or Kilonewtons meaning that a suit that could put out 40kN was converting over 4,000kg in force.

100 was just excessive!

"How much damage difference is that to the Charger suits?!"

A tone would ring from the System.

[The power between the pilot's Dragonfly and a Charger Unit is a 6000 point difference.]

The Dragonfly would count. "That's 10,000 units of force!" He would have turned the Chargers into scrap metal had he faced them directly!

Not to mention the suit's charge was still quite high given his actions. He was turned into a toy for a Driger, fell an untold distance down into a tunnel and had evaded a small gang of probably raiders. They liked stealing exosuits from lone military scout groups or digging around Military Recycling Plants to steal decommissioned suits.

"How long could I hold charge if I avoided combat?"

hypothetically, because he was sure he wouldn't be able to avoid all combat.

The familiar tone of the System rang between his ears, alerting him of it waking from its idle mode.

[If going through the average day by day tasks of an Amaroxian the Pilot's power would last five years.]

That was nonsense. Five years sitting in a metal suit of skin, if he was living a normal life? Utter bullshit. Was Liza expecting him to spend his entire life as her plaything?!

CHAPTER TWENTY-EIGHT

Abandoned Halls

Amaroxians spent countless generations building their underground world. Originally these passages were first dug out for research. The more work that was done underground it did not take the society long to learn they could harvest the vital resources one could not find on surface mines. Below the planet's crust they discovered new mineral elements that had yet to be observed in nature. So far there had been numerous elements already known by various sources of knowledge across the universe, but within Amaroxia's galaxy there had been well over 300 since the last iteration of the table.

The two most important ones discovered on the planet were Eomite and Unbotainium. So far there have been no other places in the galaxy where one could obtain Eomite. This had become the economic backbone of the planet in its heyday, but all too soon it became meaningless. A surplus of resources bred green and greed turned to war when there wasn't enough to possess.

When Unobtainium was discovered it had first become a joke among metalworkers. The metal had properties similar to old stories of a fire colored metal that was able to create weapons able to absorb or temper souls. While weapons and the like made of the metal didn't have the capacity to do such things it was still a unique metal that, if they could get enough, would allow them to colonize new planets or even create something akin to antimatter and create massive pools of energy that were nigh inexhaustible.

But beyond its disreputable mythological properties Unobtanium, or Scarletite, it had the capacity to create parts for quantum computers that far exceeded the traditional components in terms of power and longevity. The alloy had a unique red color that was capable of conducting high indexes of heat without degrading or losing shape, it conducted with greater force than gold, and wasn't capable of rusting. Unfortunately it became too valuable as a resource and with the increasing difficulty in finding it: it became expensive. There was a bit of irony as not only was the metal named after the legendary mineral it shared traits with, but it also quickly became a rarity that was strictly guarded by government agencies.

In the end the war had begun over a scrap of metal, but escalated over a life.

"Doctor Newberry!" A voice called out to the mad mistress.

The blonde-haired scientist was making her way out of the Hurvor Laboratory, arms full with a crate that she would deposit by the ever growing pile of what the members of the team were able to rescue. The fires weren't terrible. Many of the facilities were built to prevent the spread of fire as well as their growth. Most materials were designed to prevent fire as much as possible but, unfortunately, there was no such thing as a machine being fireproof.

The woman would sigh, reaching up to wipe sweat from her brow. "Aahh..."

She looked over towards the voice calling out to her, smiling widely, glasses catching the glow of their lantern.

"Oh, it's you! Long time no see." Liz giggled, her lips curling back in a mad grin. "Did you find what I was looking for, Junker, my precious gem~?"

Junker was a curious figure. Garbed in tattered tan and grey rags that reached down to their feet, there was little one could see of their body save for the heavy, steel-toed boots on their feet and the augmented gauntlets over their hands. Even their face appeared to be covered by a curious mask that helped them breathe.

By their name alone Junker was a Diver: someone who dove through landfills and other places such as abandoned sectors as well as old gang dwellings for parts, information, and anything else that could be of value. Dives like Junker were holy relics to people like Elizabeth who were quite rich, but not powerful enough to get the information she needed legally.

On their back they carried a heavy duffel backpack stacked to a ridiculous height with spare parts and other odds and ends. A blush would seemingly appear over their mask.

"I bet you say that to all the Divers!" They would reach their arm back behind them, shuffling through a few items before pulling into view what looked to be a small lockbox.

As Junker and Elizabeth spoke Casey and Bell would make their way out of the building. Casey carried out a crate on her lap as her chair's buttons repaired again, allowing her to move around again. Bell followed along with an arm full of datapads.

"Oh no." Casey came to a sudden stop, sulking a bit in her seat.

"Eh?" Bell chirped as she followed Casey's gaze.

"Junker..." Casey hissed with disgust and annoyance. "Another headache we don't need."

Meanwhile Dragonfly's pilot hurried through the passage. As he walked around, parts of his map that were missing seemed to fill out. This was an old Pre-Sister passage that was built before the first Sister was born. The Sisters were a special group of individuals who would eventually grow and create the Daughters: a powerful Council that eventually took over the old Theocracy of Amaroxia.

Though there seemed to be some data in the old Systems that allowed him some knowledge of his surroundings.

Despite having a generous portion of the map available to him: the tunnels were difficult to navigate. It was a labyrinth built to confuse and disperse enemy invaders. Before the Daughters were in charge it wasn't uncommon for raids to frequent smaller sectors.

It was said most of the raids were due to gangs from the Souther Sphere looking to steal from the North's wealth of knowledge and what internal fights that had occurred were due to their displacing citizens and forcing them to act desperately. Back then they lacked the government's support were they not part of the Helios cities, which were protected by the dome apparatus that can only be found in Capitals these days.

"I didn't think these sectors were still accessible. Is there any information on this place, Tiamat?"

~Tink~

[Around the end of the Separatist Era numerous sectors connected via Nyxia, Amaroxia, and Vradixia were victims of frequent raiding from a group known as the Eryth Confederacy. This tunnel had been collapsed by the Cyr Legion after the creation of the Daughters Council.]

Dragonfly came to a stop, his head turning up as the name struck him as familiar. "The Cyr Legion? Why is that familiar?"

[The Cyr Legion were the unified armies of the Cyan GHOSTs, the Red SHIELDs, and the Yellow CROSS before they separated after the Conyard Incident ten years ago.]

"That's right..." He would come to a stop by what appeared to be an old road sign. "When I was younger they were still being called the Cyr Legion by the older folk." Reaching out his hand came to rest on the metal post where archaic Roxaedian, the original script written by Amaroxians before it became New Matrix. "Can you translate this Tiamat?"

~Tink~

[You are now entering Ikelos.]

Dragonfly's hand slid from the sign as his head turned up to the horizon where he came face to face with the ruins of a Pre-Sister Sector. Ikelos, the Capital of Dreams.

An underground corkscrew built jutting down into the planet's belly. Supporting arches, parapets, and other foundational columns: the City of Dreams was the first city built at the end of the Exodus: when the last colony of Amaroxians settled into their assigned homes. With the aboveground no more and space limited people had to be carefully assigned their living spaces. Ikelos, being the last settlement built to that vein: had become a dream for its residents because unlike other cities they were not assigned a specific capital. Whereas some were focused on important industries like food production or mining, Ikelos had been simply assigned a recreational city and could focus on what they pleased so long as it encouraged others to visit and recirculate money into the closed economy.

Since the start of their journey underground the society had many ways of constructing stable underground tunnels that far outlasted ancient monuments and were flexible enough to withstand the natural shift of the soil due to seisms. The ground beneath their feet were patchwork roads of mismatched stones flattened into the surface to create an absorbent, flexible road that stretched from the end of one wall to another.

The tunnels themselves were labyrinths of interconnecting subways with rails built along the wider sections of the underpass. The footpaths were walled off from the rail lines with reinforced walls. These split paths were simply called platforms and it was the expectation that they were shared with smaller vehicles that had fairly decent maneuverability. In more modern capitals it wasn't strange to witness the perfect ebb and flow of man and machine along the platforms.

Originally carved out as mines: the first underground settlements were made for miners and quarrymen. These mining communities had shops, municipalities, and other of the creature commforts one found above ground. As the wars increased these towns were forced into eminent domain for building bases that were unreachable by enemy forces.

Soon places were needed for doctors, scientists, and other essential workers. Deeper tunnels were dug and larger communities built. Ikelos serves as a remnant of this history as its construction followed the model from the Sun War eras. First the main shaft was dug out with supporting ventilation shafts along the way. Fans were built to take in old air that allowed it to be safely recycled. Once well ventilated electricity was run through the planned space before chambers were dug out. Inside these chambers platforms were built every ten meters, the one below supporting the one above until solid ground was reached and built on top of flexible concrete.

All of this was built in a circular design, winding down to the center where a reservoir for water was built which pumped fresh water throughout the system.

But this was not the way they build the Chambers anymore so seeing one still intact was like stepping into the past.

CHAPTER TWENTY-NINE

The Forgotten City

As far as Dragonfly could observe there appeared to be endless walkways swirling up into blinding heights. On each circular platform were buildings which were equivalent to four city blocks on one platform. They were huge and even if he were to walk from the center edge to the outer edge nearer the walls it would take at least ten minutes. The web wall structure with the self-supporting parapets bound by the stone walls made the structure nigh indestructible, unlike the more modern "islands" they currently built.

If not for the hollow sound of wind one would be unable to tell that it was abandoned as it showed next to no sign of aging, despite the dust and overgrown foliage.

Down in the connecting catacombs the gang had fanned out to search for the Dragonfly. They made sure to keep in contact via their headsets. The gang called themselves the Red Rebellion. They differentiated themselves from other groups with the red dash marks brushed across the backs of their machines. These were rubbed on using paint made from redsand, which eventually ate into the metal and became a permanent part of the structure. Gangs across Amaroxia served themselves and were said to be beneath the living for they subsisted on the suffering of others. It was not seen as a crime to kill members of gangs because of their reputations and disruption of the already collapsing economy.

Amaroxia was a closed economy. It was advantageous because the raw materials vital to their day to day lives made it cheap and easy to produce goods. Citizens were wholly self-sufficient and had no issue investing in new businesses or the government spending in the forms of grants and growth.

Unfortunately because of having lost contact with outsiders there were many goods that were on their way to extinction because Amaroxians were unable to produce them and have grown dependent on them, such as Goraynium. The toxic mineral had become the cornerstone of their society's energy production, but seeing as it had been the cause of Mugenes its use stopped.

With no cure on the horizon there were some places that still used the ore as a means for cheap energy. This became the norm for newly built sectors. New sectors had to buy power generators from the Capital which cost a great deal, leaving a sector with a debt they had to pay back within a number of years or the generators were taken back. As these new sectors were independently built by a group of citizens with the help of Planners and Miners: they had no backing from the government to build cities, which differed from sectors. Sectors were built by independent groups and cities were built by the government. Power plants sometimes could not be built in their sectors due to the costs, especially after the completion of terraforming a purchased area.

One could not simply build anywhere and had to purchase pre-designated plots of land from the Capital. Anyone could buy these plots so long as they had the money to do so. But if one was unable to get the plot to turn a profit after five years the government would take back the land and make use of it or demolish it.

Gangs like the Reds would disrupt these growing cities and sectors which often got damaged in their raids. Instead of putting money to build their area these locations were forced to spend on repairing damaged property.

"Boss!" TThe Red leader raised his head hearing the call in his ear. "The Erebin passage collapsed."

"Shit," He responded. "Make sure to update the maps. I'll

send a message back to the commander after we rip that little shit's spine out of the suit!" Koper was the boss to this gang and as a Kirin he had a bit of a superiority complex and was peeved that Dragonfly had gotten away so easily.

Kirin were immune to Mugenes and it put them at the front of the illegal energy plants that still used the Goraynium ore as a source. The problem was it sometimes forced them into dangerous, underpaid labour that caused them to resent Amaroxians. Kirin tended to be the highest number of Pharyst that populated North gangs.

Two of the Roxoid members found their way down a still-lit passage. Their suits were fitted with close range raiments after spending their ammunition trying to take down the insect. He was quick, but they didn't seem to have any ranged abilities if their interaction was anything to speak from.

Rab and Bar were cousins, both born in the South Sphere. When they were done with their primary education they emigrated to the North Sphere in search for work as Junkers. Unfortunately for them they ended up at the pointy end of a debt after gambling for a Feed Ring. Feed Rings were handy for Miners and Junkers alike and, as the name suggested, the ring provided food in the way of microorganisms for Pigdog sniffers. These creatures were used as scent animals and could be taught to identify, locate, and even alert for certain scents making it an invaluable animal to domesticate.

Feed rings made it easy to fed the creature as it served as a small, active biome that encouraged the production and growth of these microorganisms which supported the symbiotic animal survive the long periods Junkers and Miners were on the move for. Feed rings were expensive though and sometimes took those in these professions years of generational wealth to afford.

The bet had been a trap to pull them into the gang so now they are paying off their debt for the rest of their foreseeable futures.

"Rab," The augmented male called to his kin, motioning his head toward the west end of the tunnel. There appeared to be a break in the parapet that separated the rails from the walkway. "Check over there, Ima look this way." he motioned his arm, body caged in the exoskeleton that was more like an exoskeleton than it was a suit.

Rab nodded and made his way over to the hole in the wall. He dropped down from the platform, as the rail was at a lower level to prevent accidents from occuring when excess water would drag along the sides of the subway cars from the sluices.

Bar made his way toward the eastern end of the space. The easternmost wall had a ramp that led up to the second ring of walkway. There was a break in on the incline, but jumping over with the suit was an easy task. Upon reaching the next level of the spiral: bar would make his way to the edge of the walkway.

Looking down he would spot his cousin walking along the rail. Even though he was only up on the second ring from the ground it was high up, at least ten meters up. Unfortunately from this height it wasn't a terribly clear view. The numerous fungal roots that stretched along the platforms, almost like roped bridges, impeded his vision.

There was a suspicious silence. Even though he could clearly see Rab moving down below, at least between the webbing of roots, he couldn't hear him. Did the roots distort the sound? Places like this were natural amplifiers of sound, so it was bizarre he felt more like he was at the bottom of a pit rattheer than the top of a bottle.

Rab's suit pressed forward. Though heavily augmented that didn't mean his stamina was inexhaustible. Running around underground passages like these could wear the body down, despite any evolutionary advantages one had as an Amaroxian. Amaroxians could withstand the pressures of the deepground passages due to their denser bones and slower metabolisms. The suits made it easier for them to go longer, but charging them was expensive. Larger gangs like the Reds had ways of hacking directly into the main power grid, but other gangs had no choice but to raid cities and sectors to keep their suits charged. It sometimes forced citizens to fight back which ended up creating more of a problem and loads of property damage from the skirmishes.

Power was a precious resource in more ways than one, after all.

Rab tapped the corner of his head piece and over his visor he could see the blurry visual of his suit's power indicator.

[Charge: ██▬▬▬▬▬ 45%]

"That's probably three more hours of power." Rab nodded. "Good." Without his firearms he would be able to use a lot less charge."

~Dwop~

"Huh?" There was a blip on Rab's radar, but no sooner had it been picked up did it go out. "Piece of shit -- Ima have to ask the brain to fix it when we get back." Looking around there didn't appear to be anything beyond the old railcar that sat gathering dust and growing fungus.

The speedy vehicles were how citizens used to get around the tunnels, but as power became scarce many sectors and cities became unable to power their railcars and they fell out of favor for less power hungry modes of transportation like jeeps and skycars, which were like railcars but depended on magnets and could only be built is specific locations with decent altitude.

While Rab scoured the old line the Dragonfly had managed to run around to the opposite side of the deserted car. He sat crouched beside one of the open doors. As Rab passed by his line of sight he would duck down.

"How strong is his gear?" He would watch the system keep the enemy suit in its scanner's range.

The pilot was able to see its outline past the thinner walls of metal that the discarded railcar was made of. It didn't seem his radar was strong enough to see him. His opponent's footsteps were excessive: the metal of Rab's boot hitting the metal of the rail, occasionally clapping down when the magnetic track pulled him firm to the surface.

~Tink~

[It is estimated that one hit from the Pulser will destroy the fragile frame.]

Fragile!? Those frames were made of Silver Steel! There was no way they could split like stale bread. But from what he was reading from the system's scan of the repurposed Charger Suit it was hard to argue.

[Unit: RR Charger Unit 24]

[AI: None]

[Systems: Radar, IC]

* * * *

[Suit Status]

[Energy: ▮_____ 10%]

[Power: ▮▮_____ 20%]

[Charge: ▮▮▮_____ 45%]

[Heat Index: High]

DMG RANGE Hit CRT

5 1~2 +0 +1

He was surprised he could pry so much information from

the unit, but if the AI could determine its Charge, finding its Power and Energy wasn't far beyond imagination as they used similar outputs. But what horrified him was the difference in overall ability. The enemy's 5 damage compared to his 100. Perhaps this was why the system insisted his opponent was fragile.

Looking down to the palm of his gauntlet a blue energy radiated from it. It was the outflow from the Grav unit on his back. Reversing the outflow of the Chromium's radiation he could push it through the forearm of his suit. It could focus the vibration and energy there rather than at his wings which assisted in flight. The push force could knock down an anchored object with ease, which was why to take flight a pilot needed to take a running jump much like a Raybird.

~Tink~

[Enemy unit reaching acceptable distance.]

Right. If he didn't act quickly he could lose the element of surprise and he would hit his radar's range again. See the weakness of a C-Unit's radar is if their target was too close it would disrupt the readings giving a false-positive to a ping. So long as he maintained about a meter within range it couldn't read him.

Dragonfly would quickly round the back of the railcar, his steps silent. The energy that allowed his Grav pack to create anti-gravity force could be applied to the Dragonfly's gauntlets and boots as they had specialized magnets that connected to the Grav sub-system. This was the reason why only Second

Generation suits could use flight: their oversized boots and gauntlets allowed for the space to carry the excess weight with the AI assisting in the management of the extra calculations.

Lowering his center of gravity by crouching: Dragonfly would make sure to 'walk' along the rail, which opposed his boot's polarity and caused him to 'hover' ever slightly. Not a sound was made as he crept towards Rab.

CHAPTER THIRTY

Broken Toys

Rab continued his search. Though he no longer had the advantage of a long ranged weapon neither did his opponent. It put them on even ground. On his head he wore a metal visor which was attached to the neck brace of the exoskeleton. He had raised it off his head as the radar wouldn't net him much profit in such a crowded area.

The Tunnel itself was a fair size: over six meters wide and several kilometers long with a ceiling height of thirty meters. The railcar was four meters wide and four and a half meters tall. Since it was only two cars, the engine and a passenger car, it was currently only seven meters in length.

That alone would take no time to search, but the excessive clutter scattered around left behind numerous hiding spots. Heavy slabs of concrete that had fallen from the Tunnel's ceiling and platform littered the degrading cement paths. Heavy splits in the stone ground created deep gouges that made moving around difficult. The webs of fungal roots created a tangling foot trap that could stall the older models. Not only did the roots have strong tensile strength, as evident in the hanging blocks of stone they kept suspended above, but they were difficult to remove when inside a C-Suit model.

Rab hadn't seen any critters roaming around, so he was thankful for that. Abandoned sectors like this often fell victim to am'lo and other troublesome fauna. The mushrooms and lichen colonies weren't too troublesome so long as you avoided the fungal roots and slippery lichen patched.

What was most frightful were the Suneater flowers. These plants have developed to survive underground with their human counterparts but in the stead of remaining domesticated many of the plants had gotten out of their housing either through theft or lost when on shipment routes: it had learned to survive on what meat it could below ground.

Without intervention a Suneater plant can grow hundreds of meters. They have long leaves that stretch out like tentacles. Each limb-like leaf is covered in red, feeler-like tendrils that excrete a glue-like sap that can capture prey. Once stuck in the mucilage the leaf curls up, trapping prey and carrying it to its 'mouth'.

What made avoiding the plants difficult is that they grew in dark places and have been known to grow in crumbling ruins where prey all but fell into its trap. There were other dangerous plant life underground, but many were due to poisons or dangerous obstacles in the environment that exosuits had difficulty with.

A soft glow emanated from Rab's C-Suit. On the front of the chest bar was a headlight that glowed a soft blue. The color was easy for Amaroxians to see in and it made certain colors pop out for them. In fact, if an Amaroxian's eye was caught in blue light it gave off a sharp glow due to the tapetum lucidum, a tissue layer in the back of an Amaroxian's eye, that made seeing in the dark easier, as long as there was some light.

Rab reached out to a slab of concrete. Threaded through the block were titanium rods, sturdier than the ferro rods used in the temporary walls meant to stem the flow of traffic. This meant the block was originally part of the tunnel and not the platform. It made him nervous to think parts of the tunnel were possibly still collapsing.

The sound of crumbling stone caused Rab to jump. Turning around in a sharp turn, he held up his arms in a defensive action. His limbs were barely covered by the suit's metal frame, but it offered some protection were something to fall on him. He had to be ready for anything. The tunnel was unstable. He didn't know how old it was, but with its infrastructure ignored anything could happen.

Focusing his eyes he took note of the debris tumbling off the neglected railcar. Its rusting hull was slowly being reclaimed by the local mushroom colonies, the roots wrapping around the metal frame like a snake around its prey. Many areas looked as if the metal's been eaten away, either through erosion, or the rust breaking it down. His pale eyes traced along the car, traveling up to the roof of the rotting, metal box.

From behind Rab a dark shadow would cautiously weave between the curtain of roots that hung down from the roof of the railcar. With every step Rab too, the Dragonfly would march forward, disguising his movements by shadowing his opponent. Slowly parting the silky, white tendrils the Dragonfly would stalk towards his target. Rab came to a stop when he reached the nose of the car. He leaned his left hand against the twisted frame as he carefully peered around the corner. Dragonfly would reach out his hands.

-

-

"RAB!" His cousin would call from above, but it didn't look like Rab could hear him. "Damn, what's with this place's acoustics?"

Bar would pick up his pace, trying to hurry around the ring to get a better visual on his cousin that wasn't impeded by the roots. As he made his way around he would start to get around the dangling tangles. He slid to a stop as he saw the blue glow of the Dragonfly's components creeping up behind Rab. He would turn on his radar and sure enough: at Rab's coordinates there were two pings.

"RAB!!!"

-

-

-

"What?" Though he could not hear his cousin he would catch a flicker of movement above him.

As he raised his head, Dragonfly's claws came down around Rab's face and throat, dragging him to the ground with a deadly force. The sound of the exosuit hitting the ground struck with such a thunderous force that the sound shook the Tunnel with enough strength to dislodge debris and cause a shelf of dust to rain down over them. Bar stumbled as he tried not to be thrown with the force.

"No!" Bar panicked and scrambled to the edge of the platform. His eyes darted around, the radar unable to pick anything up. "Rab, come on man..." No movement.

The panicked Red would try to pick up his cousin's comm on his setting, but there was too much interference in the area. When the cloud settled Bar pushed up off his knees. The Dragonfly's glowing systems looked like the glare of a demon peering out from the Void. The lashing tail whipped around, clearing the remaining dust before the pilot looked back and over his shoulder towards Bar.

"You bastard!" Bar jumped to his feet and ran back towards the ramp, the Dragonfly's scanners focusing on him.

At his feet lay the mangled twist of Rab's body and the exosuit. The amount of damage done around the neck made it nigh impossible to discern whether it was man, or had been a machine. It took one action and the Red was turned into the very pigment that now stained the ground and side of the railcar. The Dragonfly unit stood with its arms at its side.

A warm, red liquid dripped from the cold metal, the digits occasionally twitching as the pilot's adrenaline reached its peak. It was the first time he's killed anyone. He didn't mean to

-- he was only going to pin him, ask him questions. The suit's power was excessive. What the hell did Liza plan to do with something like this?! This wasn't for curing anyone!

[Warning. Pilot's heart rate reaching redzone. Injecting with serum.]

The pilot could hear as a soft hiss of air popped through his suit. He felt the pinch of a needle piercing his skin before a burning sensation flowing in through the base of his neck. The pilot reached up, resting his hand against his neck. What was that?

[Heart rate at optimal level.]

"Did you just drug me? What was that? Why?"

[Affirmative. It was a dose of the Vox serum already running through your system, but it was undiluted. Pilot's heart rate was exceeding safety parameters. Any higher and it could interfere with the system's synchronization.]

"So I panic and you reject me?" Lovely.

He gasped out, removing his hand as he was smearing blood and grease over his suit. Staring at his palm he lamented his action, but it had been self defense and -- an action of unintentional overkill.

[One remaining enemy unit.]

The system would target Bar's unit just above them. Raising his head the Dragonfly would see as Bar rook off running. He would hesitate, but if he let them get the advantage he may end up scrap metal. He wasn't a combatant, professional or otherwise. With enough of them, even with this suit's power, he could be overwhelmed and subdued. The very thought terrified him.

As the serum rushed through his system he felt himself begin to relax, his mind thinking clearly.

"It's me or him." Extending his wings, Dragonfly would

dash off, using the Pulse to boost his movement speed.

-

-

-

A blip inside Bar's visor called his attention. He hit a spot where the comms system was working. "Boss! Boss! He killed Rab! He smashed him with his godsdamn hands like he was a bug!"

Koper sucked his tooth in annoyance and turned to look at the two remaining flunkies by his side. "We're calling for backup. We want that suit in one piece, and in our hands."

CHAPTER THIRTY-ONE

The Next Stage Down

It had been like breaking apart dried soil. When Eric had that unit in his hands, in the Dragonfly's hand, it was no different than sifting dirt between his fingers. As he ran he continued to try and convince himself that it was still he could protect himself. If the situation was flipped they wouldn't have hesitated to rip his corpse out of his suit. Even still... He'd never kill anyone before. Not even an animal. Living near the city all of their food was supplied by the city via rations. They were dried, calorie rich crackers that provided all the nutrients they would ever need. The taste wasn't bad, but after living on the stuff for your entire life eating just became a chore.

Eric was crouched on the ground, struggling to wipe his hands clean off the stain in the red soil. All it did was mix and become more pronounced. Now instead of the blood and grease drying between his fingers now the once silver colored hands were a murky burgundy that no longer reflected the dim, blue light of the glowing lichen. It was a poison, death. All around everything was dying. Even these old settlements had become nothing but ghosts, shadows of the dreams of a better tomorrow. These locations weren't always named like this. Ikelos. The prophecy. It had been here that they first started processing the ore.

There was a man who had said it was wrong. He tried to stop the government, but was accused of treason and thrown in jail. It wasn't until five years later that they started seeing the first effects of the ore's unique radiation. It disfigured, twisted, and eventually turned you to stone. What was worse was that it didn't just affect man. It mutated plants, poisoned the land, and began to kill domestic animals and wildlife. It didn't discriminate, unlike them.

It only took a few months after the first breakouts for the two main government factions on Amaroxia to completely collapse. First they began to embargo trade of certain resources until they were outlawing members of those factions from entering each other's borders without strict documentation. It had been a tense relationship since they settled underground. They dug deeper and traveled farther to get away from each other. That meant there were places where even hands wouldst go. After his encounter with the suit he ran deeper into the settlement. He didn't have a complete map of this area, the system drawing one up as he went. At least on this way he'd know where he had been. Following the tracks Eric made sure he put enough assistance between him and the remaining gang members.

When he was far enough from the remaining figure the system flashed a message over his visor.

[No enemy units in range.]

Eric's hurried steps slowed before he came to a complete stop. He's been on the move since escaping the laboratory, so he hadn't the time to really absorb everything that had happened. So far all he had been able to definitively deduce was that he's been separated from his brother and had fallen down at least two stages. Stages, simply put, were the territories. Since Amaroxians rarely dug out Tunnels horizontally from each other, reducing the risk of cave-ins, most tunnels were dug out in a vertical angle at different depths. Each base of land at said depth was called a Stage. So far, according to the incomplete map, he was about three Stages from his incomplete location, obviously excluding the travel spent through the tunnels themselves.

~dwop~

Eric turned this eye towards the data stream that began to

compile on the left of the visor.

[High pressure detected.]

[400 meters ahead.]

"What?" Eric looked up.

He had been following the passage for twenty minutes already, the mechanical tail-like appendage curled up, the tip of the extra limb extending numerous sensory filaments that writhed and twisted like the twisted tentacles of those man-eating plants.

[Scan complete. Active Geyser Field ahead.]

Geyser Fields are terrestrial phenomena found deep in Amaroxia. They were known for being highly active and dangerous, harbouring many fierce predators. There are creatures who have adapted to the intense heat, like the Giant Waterbear and wild Pigdogs. The dangers of being digested, gored, or burned were high, but if he wanted to put an obstacle between him and the remaining gang members the Geyser Fields were a top choice.

"I'll reach it in another fifteen, twenty minutes." He murmured, seemingly to himself. "Shit. Won't it be 3 in the morning in fifteen minutes?" He looked down to his wrist, turning his palm side up.

There on his wrist appeared the time on glowing, blue numbers, as well as the cardinal direction he was traveling. According to the systems tools Eric was traveling southwest, away from the capital which sat on the Northern pole.

Checking his system's remaining power again he would make sure he had enough energy left to make it to the next Stage.

[Loading...]

[Unit: Dragonfly]
[AI: Tiamat]
[Systems: AR, HUD, Scan]

* * * *

[Suit Status]
[Energy: ██████████ 99%]
[Power: ██████████ 99%]
[Charge: █████████ 97%]
[Heat Index: Normal]

"What the hell? I still can't believe this thing had barely drained. Maybe it's a glitch?" If it was some sort of error he needed to make sure he got through the Fields before his power went down. "Where's the nearest base?" At his query the system responds.

~dwop~

[The closet base with an accessible charge station is located two Stages down.]

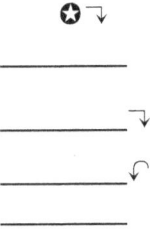

"Of course."

His disappointment aside, Eric would eventually arrive at the Geyser Fields. It took him almost twenty minutes, finding the slog on the uphill slope difficult. He was still growing used to the machine and found his body's movements sluggish, even staggered. It could be the fact he hasn't eaten in over ten hours, but with the medicine still pumping through his system he couldn't find his stomach craving a meal. The fields themselves ran on for over fifteen kilometers both ways, vents dotting the distance like sporadically sown crops. But these crops burned. Any one vent could erupt with a spout of water that could melt the skin off a person and have been known to frighten even the largest Drigers. These were some of the only areas in the underground that were safe from Driger nests. Be that as it may, the other dangers far outweigh the benefit of evading the subterranean wyrms.

The fields themselves were typically found in areas with heavy Geothermal activity. Many cities depended on Geothermal energy to function so it wasn't a surprise that one was so close to Ikelos subway where a number of generators could be installed and the boiled water subsequently pumped into homes for use. It was not uncommon for locals to use the hot rocks for cooking or even some brave few that sought to collect the mineral nodes from the fields as they were an important source of nutrients for those who could not afford the rations from the Capital as they were payment for selling resources to the government. It was a setup that Eric highly doubted existed when Ikelos was still a prosperous state, but it was something he remembered at the very least.

The man walked to the edge of the field. The steel boots sank slightly in the softer soils, which were still red as one's skin. He watched for several moments as massive arcs of the heated water burst from the vents with loud cracks and visible shaking of the ground. His visor scanned all that was in range, drawing part of this into his system's memory. It was best to have as much of the map saved in the case he ever had to come back through here to make his way back up. For now he needed to hide from that group and ensure his charge would hold out until he could either make it to the charging station or find his way to a tunnel that led back up at least one Stage which would put him close to the Enshu Stage.

"Alright, so far the suit hasn't started to heat up..." It would take much longer to cross the field, but Turbo Suits were famed for overheating and exploding. "I'll just need to hurry along. How much time do I have to cross before the system overheats?"

~bwop~

[01:30]

"So I have an hour, thirty out there? I'll have to keep a running pace." It would otherwise take three hours to travel the distance, even in the best of conditions, but he would need to actively pass and evade the superheated vents. "Here I go!"

[01:29]

[Unit: Dragonfly]

[AI: Tiamat]

[Systems: AR, HUD, Scan]

* * * *

[Suit Status]

[Energy: ███████████ 99%]

[Power: ███████████ 99%]

[Charge: ████████ 97%]

[Heat Index: Warm]

CHAPTER THIRTY-

Two
Heated Steps

[00:29]

[Unit: Dragonfly]

[AI: Tiamat]

[Systems: AR, HUD, Scan]

* * * *

[Suit Status]

[Energy: ▐████████ 99%]

[Power: ▐████████ 99%]

[Charge: ▐██████ 97%]

[Heat Index: Hot]

He was halfway through the field. He didn't know what was waiting for him at the end of his endeavor, but Eric didn't want to be pinned under anyone's thumb. Nor the government, not the gangs, and not even the so-called rebels. Everyone seemed to fight for their own selfish reason and so did he. In what short life he had left he just wanted to go home with his brother and see their mother. At least be with her when she succumbs to the disease, if she hadn't already. Life on the farms only seemed to exacerbate the degeneration.

The last time Elizabeth had checked him he was at Class B. He was halfway from a full-blown infection, but by comparison to others the twins' age their progress was relatively slow. It was what made them valuable, at least more so. They were perhaps the first twin males to survive to adulthood since the start of Mugenes. Everything went to shit when it arrived. It had been their greed and irresponsibility that set them on this course. Nothing in life was ever free, not even energy.

Flexing his hands, his body almost fully acclimated to the suit, he could feel the exoskeleton acting like a second set of bones that strengthened his body, though it made his movements tighter and he felt constricted. Perhaps it was just his mind. Having to wear a second skin of metal couldn't be something easily adjusted to, but the movement was. He began to pick up his pace as an alert rang at the side of his visor, warning him of the increasing heat index. Inside the suit he had yet to feel a temperature change, but he could see heat begin to radiate from the joints of his suit. Regardless of how strong the system appeared to be at first glance: it was still a prototype. The Dragon and Dragonfly Units shouldn't even exist, let alone using this AI.

He didn't know much about artificial intelligence. He knew it served a major role in industry, solving problems at speeds that people could not. Though they could not yet present what Amaroxians felt was true emotion, lacking the ability to procedurally adapt to interpersonal scenarios, they had been taught to mimic tone and practice socially acceptable conversations to a point where it was nigh indiscernible during a day to day basis. They had their uses, but they couldn't farm long hours with limited mobility and they failed at other interpersonal industries for their low adaptability. There just wasn't enough space to store near infinite possibilities in a scenario.

"How much farther?" He felt it was easier to breathe now that he had become more used to moving in the suit.

Instead of fighting the micro adjustments he moved into them. It made recoil less jarring. Regardless of what he did there was no helping the feeling left in his muscles when the machine suddenly sent signals to his muscles through the pulses of electricity.

~bwop~

[10 kilometers remain. At your current pace it is calculated you will arrive in 42 minutes.]

But looking at the timer displayed by the AI in his visor he had only 27 minutes remaining before his system overheated.

He could only move at his own speed. Not only was he still getting used to the suit he had to pause frequently since he wasn't struck by a spout. He only had seconds of warning from his locator that could feel the seismic vibrations and measure its distance from him. By the time calculations concluded he would be at risk of stepping right onto a vent as it erupted. To prevent this from happening he would hesitate when the scanner pinged the simple map he had of the assumed area. Unless there was considerable tectonic activity there shouldn't have been much change in the land since its last full scan. Without satellites they depended on more rudimentary methods for collecting Map and topographical data. This meant they could only update their map data every few months.

"Isn't there a way to move faster and not be blasted?" It was a rhetorical question so when the system's tone rang, indicating it was running the query, he was taken aback.

His questions phrasing seemed too vague for the computer to earnestly make use of, but it scoured the known database quickly and redraw the scaled map in his visor before overlaying a route. The star, which indicated his location, was somewhere near the south east quadrant of the field. A line drew through a proposed route that both reduced the time and used the frequency of the eruptions to charge the safest possible route. There was still a 15% chance he could be struck by a stray burst. The variable was inescapable seeing as vents often released at random, nowhere near the last.

Finally the route was complete and showed the pilot a way to run. If he made full use of the suit's ground speed he would be able to cut the time in half.

"But this looks like I'll be cutting right over vents." He didn't seem enthusiastic about the prospect of getting his ass toasted out there.

~bwop~

[Probability of minor injury at 15%.

Probability of burn injury at 5%.]

"What, why only five?"

[The Dragonfly was optimized for open field combat as well as traversing precarious terrain which would also include lava fields.]

That meant the suit was a lot sturdier than he has given it credit for. But no more hesitating. If he didn't take off now his chances of injury or even fully overheating were increased. It took a minute for him to collect the information and put his questions up. He had 26 minutes remaining on his timer....

[00:26...]

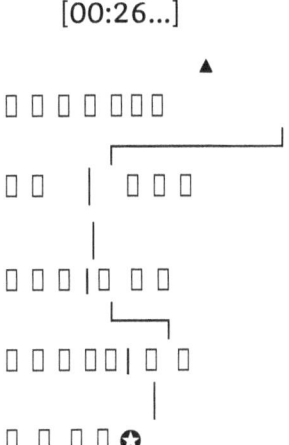

Eric took off down the path. It had only taken a thought and his body just let go. His main concern was burning to a crisp or being left with a heavily damaged suit and being trapped on this Stage with no way out. He had to get back to his brother because without him -- what could Klaus do? He was quiet and let others push him around. After being taken from their home he had to become the one to speak out because every one of them wanted to use and manipulate the pair for the pair they carried between their legs.

[00:24]

Faster. If he didn't move faster he was going to cook in his own suit.

~bwop~

[Warning. Heat Index reaching Critical. Start system cooldown?]

"No! No!" Eric had to make it.

He could see the end of the field. Even as the noisy geysers blasted off beside him one after another, clouding his sight with steam and spraying the boiling water on the metal shell.

[Heat Index at Critical. Forced system cooldown initiating in order to maintain the life of the pilot.]

At the bottom right of his visor he could see the rapid countdown for the restart. He pushed every ounce of his strength into his legs, but he wasn't strong, body weakening every day from the withering plague that was consuming the whole planet. Every day he got a little weaker and the goal he reached for was only that much further out of reach.

The Dragon reached out his hand towards the horizon, the boundary of the field within sight. Staggering forward his hand slammed against the ground. He fell to his knee and felt the ground rumbling like a beast's hungry stomach. A geyser beneath him began to turn over and start to erupt. At the last second he was able to roll out of the way of the vent. He would kick off the ground and take off running once again.

[Forced system cooldown starting. Going into offline mode.]

The suit became heavier as each system began to shut down, dragging Eric beneath his weight. He wasn't sure how long he had before everything was gone, but he continued to push himself. The kilometers counted down, but it wasn't enough. Darkness soon consumed his vision as the visor shut off, leaving him in the complete darkness within his helmet. There was no means for him to see outside without the helmet's camera, the visors merely serving as a direct portal between his eyes and the lens outside of the mask. Try as he might to drag himself forward he could no longer feel his body moving. Finally the suit hit the ground mere inches from an erupting vent, his fingertips reaching for the lip of the opening.

The Dragon lay motionless in the burning fields.

Eric could feel his consciousness leaving him as the suit forcibly injected him with something. He could no longer fight and, as with the machine: he shut down.

CHAPTER THIRTY-THREE

No More Stars

Several stages above Ikelos, General Honchberg had arrived with his entourage at the Red Shield Military Base. From the building's interior Klaus would watch as the men unloaded the gear and computer hardware they had managed to abscond from the Science facility with. What hadn't been caught and eaten by the fires was taken with the group so that they could download the data on their server connections without hindrance. Politically the military had more power than the science corp, though this wasn't how it used to be. Before the Conyard Incident the Science Corp's word was law, but they were now seen as fallible and prone to operating dangerously, disregarding protocol. To get the equipment back they knew Newberry's group would have to file a report with the main branch of the council in order to reclaim their work. If the military took their data it was assumed there was public risk attached. It would be determined whether or not any of the data had bearing on the safety of Amaroxia as a whole. Honchberg was well aware that Elizabeth's research was seen as dangerous. The AI programming she was using was not only experimental but was technically still illegal. That type of artificial intelligence was outlawed fifty years ago due to the risk it carried. It was seen that the Dragon Systems had a habit of taking over the native operating systems they were installed in and overwriting code.

Unlike the tower pillar structure Eric found himself in, Klaus had arrived at what was considered a modern marvel. The underground had limited space and was difficult to build in without premade supports that, in the past, took months to prepare. Now they are simply built into the stone to create a foundation which took half the time. The solid stones were used as a buffer against Driger and other dangers within the environment. Solid, silver steel metals were shaped into sheets and laid out within the carved spaces creating a natural, almost undetectable structure. The metal, thereafter, was painted black to hide it from scanning equipment. After the foundation was set into place the inner workings of the bases were constructed with similar layouts to expedite setup.

The entrance was typically found on the Western front. It was a metal arch that had massive bay doors which were blast proof. Inside was a small communications room. Windows that faced the outside could easily view incoming and outgoing vehicles that entered via the garage slope that rode down into the main base. These checkpoints served not only as a means of security, but they also ensured no vehicle could get near the base without being seen. Long and wide windows made visibility outside the base easy, but also gave extra security as blast shields could be lowered over the structures.

To get to the main point of the base one would have to ride a lift down. Once on the main floor the base opened up into a cross that led to the four major points of an Amaroxian base. To the north was the Armory, where weapons were stored and suits were repaired and charged. Next, heading east, the barracks. Here soldiers could find the mess hall, sleeping quarters and recreational areas. To the west was administration. Here soldiers could get mission briefings, find superior officers, and get pat. Finally, to the south, was the medical ward. Here injuries were treated with the best available technology, sometimes outclassing even the Capital's hospitals.

The General entered the base, a communications officer informing him of multiple situations that required his attention. The officer would hand Honchberg the tablet, of which the man looked over. The communications officer appeared to be wearing a second generation suit outfitted for long and short ranges communications. On his back he appeared to carry a rifle that was seemingly attached to the back of his suit.

As Klaus started the officer would look back, feeling the gaze. Honchberg paused when he realized the shift in the officer's attention.

"Leave it for now. I'll report to the Council as soon as we have their remaining hardware hooked up." He returned the tablet and stepped aside, the officer excusing himself. "Klaus, walk with me." The General made his way towards the lift.

Klaus had not left his Suit, though given the choice to when they arrived. His brother told him he shouldn't trust people like this and he felt the same. Ever since they arrived they looked at his suit, made comments. He had a bad feeling and something told him not to give them the chance. When he heard the General his eyes stayed on the view before him. He had been attempting to connect with the Dragonfly's comms the entire time they had left the Hurvor Laboratory.

[...scanning for {DR8-FI-TS2}]
[...DR8-FI-TS2 unit out of range.]
[Comm Tower: RS-S2-L1]

Over and over, nothing seemed to change no matter how many times he tried. Sighing would stare in the man's direction before finally following. He supposed he could give it a break for a moment. Reluctant he would turn to face the General and walk onto the lift. Klaus kept his head forward, but eyed the panel the man pressed. He seemed to use a combination of passcode and microkeycard. Keeping this in mind Klaus turned his head to focus on Honchberg.

"What do you want to talk about?"

"Your role." The older man chuckled. "You seem to be tense so I figured I'd explain the status quo and where you will be expected to while here."

There was a moment of quiet between the men, but seeing as Klaus had no objections Honchberg would continue.

"Now it will be an adjustment coming to the Military from a prison. Unlike the prison where they let you run wild there will be more structure here. You will be expected to pull your weight or you do not eat. You are not just given food because you dug a few holes. Here you will have a list of tasks and the number of tasks you complete by the day's end will determine your rations earned." While he talked Klaus seemed to turn his head away.

The man was only half listening to the General. He continued to scroll through his Suit's menu bars in hopes he could find a way to connect to his brother's suit. Without Eric he lost exactly half his power and combat ability, at least according to the data being brought up by his System. Honchberg let out a deep sigh and would raise his hand to pat Klaus' shoulder.

"Don't hold out too much hope. It is very difficult to survive in the Stages below even with a Suit. There are gangs and roving am'lo all over the place. You need to focus on surviving. Your suit is still properly charged, correct?" Klaus was silent a moment, but would nod. "Good. Follow me to the training room."

"I want to sleep." Klaus' words were unexpected.

"Ah..." Reaching up to rub his fingers on his chin he tried to adjust himself. The response was wholly unexpected. "Are you sure? If so let us get you out of your Suit.."

"No need." Klaus shook his head. "I need to rest. I'll do whatever you ask in the morning."

Honchberg sighed. He didn't want to push the man before he had him settled with them. "Very well. I will have my lieutenant get you in the morning. You met him already, the man in the Hammer Suit." The General tried to be friendly with the young man and even smiled, but to no avail.

"Alright." Klaus seemed resistant to any attempt the General was making to be approachable, but he was also not being pushed. "Where are the beds?"

Afterwards Honchberg would walk Klaus to the barracks. "If you need something to eat you can get something in the mess hall, though we only open it at certain hours. Since you've no credits to your name yet I will be sure to leave your name with the cook and they will get you a meal until you start earning." Seeing as Klaus was no longer willing to speak Honchberg left him to his business.

The room was lit by a single, blue lamp that hung overhead. It seemed to have no manual control, which he expected. The room itself was a box of black metal, matte with no sense of space to it. It had a single bed with simple sheets that were somewhat clean. There was a metal trunk that had an electronic lock which was unprogrammed. It would likely be for his belongings he would later receive. Maybe a uniform. Most groups had uniforms, even the prison did. At the end of the room, right across from the door, there was a window that had a view of the underground chambers that surrounded the base. Klaus walked over to the window and would attempt to open it, but the glass had no means for it. Sighing he would pull the trunk by the window and seat himself down. He stared up only to find the ceiling was naught but stone.

"There are no stars down here..."

CHAPTER THIRTY-FOUR

Five Days Remain

Klaus did not sleep comfortably that cycle, but how could he? A lifetime of having his brother at his side, and the day spent fearing the worst had come of their separation ensured that nightmarish thoughts plagued his mind through his attempts to sleep. It did not help being in, what he felt, was the enemy's territory. By his very nature Klaus was one to give others the benefit of the doubt, but the time spent with Eric at the prison had ensured some of his sibling's cynicism rubbed off on him. Instead of sleeping, not that he felt he could, even if he wanted. The suit was still a terribly strange environment for him, the man had spent his time familiarizing himself with the System.

Klaus' AI was called Yamata. Since he didn't have a flight suit Yamata's support primarily focused on his terrestrial combat functions. After a bit of weaving through the menus he also learned about the Nexus. It was a central hub of data that held the whole of Amaroxia's knowledge. Being from poorer roots Klaus had never been to any of the Hub Libraries available in the city that had direct access to the network of terminals within the capital. It was amazing to think that he could connect to it from such a distance.

Using his newfound link the young man spent the night reading files containing the public data concerning the Newberry family and their experiments. He was surprised to learn of the practicality of the Newberry's work around the Artificial Intelligence systems they called DRAGON, which stood for Data Routing Aggrandized Global Open Network. In short these were a connective system of multiple AI that worked something akin to a hivemind to collect, sort, and focus data to active users to make quick and accurate decisions from combat orders to mathematics calculations.

What made the DRAGON AI different from most others is that they were designed to prioritize the user where most AI tends to prioritize the resulting data. It was what made the current government wary of it. In the stead of taking the whole into account these systems took the individual's before the collective's. To the Sister's Council this looked dangerous because it made them feel as if a Suit wearer would choose to abandon the ideals of the collective to selfishly survive. In a world where survival was difficult stacked with the crippling struggle of an ongoing plague slowly reducing their numbers, all that mattered were the numbers. Klaus was beginning to understand the system in a way he had never thought he would.

The poor had little. The rich had much, yet neither had nothing. Those who could abide by society's rules were supported by the government. They were provided with food rations that seemed to be reduced the further out from the Capital you lived. They say it is because it is much harder to transport goods too far from the production line, given the danger of rebels and inability to find fairly healthy couriers that could make the trips. Clean water didn't exist. All the water in Amaroxia had been contaminated by the toxic seepage from Goraynium processing plants. Though it was not ideal, they were still provided for and always had a source of food and water regardless of their wealth. Nothing was for the criminal. Criminals were outside of the system and were forced to forage for food, to process their own water. They were not worth the charity of society. A true state of poverty was said to no longer exist. But it was all an illusion of equality and a facade of access to necessities. The welfare of the citizens was the government's means of survival because if the people were unsatisfied the Council was on their last leg. The Conyard Incident brought with it many questions, numerous doubts. Insofar as what Klaus would discover was that food was purposely withheld from the more distant Farming units because it was assumed that they kept a portion of what they grew for the state. There was a generalized assumption they all stole because, as per the law, it was said that a Farmer must relinquish their entire crop yield and in return they would be given enough food from the government to survive. From what he discovered, the government also had programs within the capital that provided the wealthy with increased supplies and credits for sending their children to Military Academies. So long as their support continued the cycle. The government would feed this privileged class who could afford to purchase space within the safe barrow of the capital through generational wealth. And the privileged will stand by the government so long as they are fat and fed. Growing up they were far from poor, but without a large family they would be unable to afford a place in the capital. Klaus remembered how they struggled, how some nights his mother went to bed hungry just to see them fed enough.

~bwop~

{User's biometrics reading abnormal. Proceeding to inject serum to prevent syncope.}

~bpst~

Klaus would arch his back, flinching when he felt the needle press into his lower back. "What--?" He was startled.

Closing the windows on his visor, by pinching the air in third-dimensional space, he would sigh and glance around the room. For a moment he had thought someone was coming in and triggered the AI. Outside he could hear the soldiers participating in their daily routines. A cadet was sent by to drop off his breakfast, but Klaus didn't trust food he didn't grow himself. Standing from the bed, where he had been lying to read over the information, he would walk over to the windowsill where the young man had placed the metal tray. He recognized the food. The pile of shiny, slightly gelatinous blobs was cultured meat spread. The substance was usually spread on boule, a hard baked bread with a soft interior. It fueled fat, protein, and carbohydrate reserves. Beside it were diced chunks of biopolymer edibles that were packed into cubes before cutting into portions for a high protein yield in a small portion. Last there was a pile of diced, water mixed synthetic fyto, a plant-based mixture. While edible it was all machine processed food that wasn't appetizing to him.

He turned his gaze toward the door. *"What are the chances I get out of here unnoticed?"* He thought.

Klaus had quickly become used to the system, his body adapting to the connections in and outside of his body, so he knew how to use mental commands for the AI.

~bwop~

{Chances for undetected departure is currently at 25%}

{Due to anticipation of User's reveal among the base-users chances of undetected departure have been severely reduced}

Canting his head Klaus would put his hand to the door. Well that makes sense. If he perhaps showed himself yesterday and settled to rest... but they would know what he looks like, no?

"Wouldn't that decrease my chances if they met me?"

~bwop~

{False. User's familiarity lowers the degree of alert base-users would process.}

Klaus thought for a few moments. He couldn't easily leave to find his brother nor could he convince them to look for him in Driger territory.

"If I join them, how long do you think it will take for me to be in a high enough position to do what I want?" But instead of an immediate answer there would be silence on the AI's end.

Turning his head slightly the visor glowed bright for a moment, as if the machine thought of something. The long tail-like tentacle was rolled up and over his shoulder, which kept it out of the way. Klaus was already capable of controlling the finer movements of his suit.

~bwop~

{*On the User's current experience it would take four years.*}

The man frowned within the helmet. "*That's a long time...*" Highly disappointing. Was he so incapable?

~bwop~

{If User can increase the efficiency of his current state, the time for mastery will significantly reduce.}

"*So if I get better I will progress faster?*" It was basic really. "*What if I became three times more skilled than I am now? Using that as a base, how long would it take?*"

The machine was quiet again, seemingly calculating. In the meantime Klaus reached for the automatic sliding door, which opened. Stepping out of the room he would look down the left and right hall. He could see on his visor where Honchberg was, his suit having saved his biometrics for quick identification. Before going to see the man he was hungry. His first goal was the mess hall to find something that was grown from the ground to eat. Starting on his way his eyes moved to glance up to the side as the calculations completed.

~bwop~

{If User is able to increase their current output by a multiple of three: User will be capable of seizing complete control of the base within five days.}

Klaus would grunt. "Five days it is."

CHAPTER THIRTY-FIVE

Day One

Klaus made his way through the base, heading towards the mess hall. He had hoped to fill his stomach with something other than the processed rations of the military. Despite the funds they claimed from the government, much of it was spent on maintaining their weapons, base upkeep, and the soldier's pay. Anything of their budget left went into uniforms and food. Klaus felt it was a waste not to focus on food. Without food a man couldn't work. He was always someone who thought strongly of such a value because of the lessons his mother left them with. It was difficult for her to care for them both, but as a result they became more self-sufficient then most grown men these days. If Klaus had to take a guess, from the passing interactions he's had since coming to this base, General Honchberg did not run the place like he thought he did. He was no fool. Though this base painted a scene of a place blessed with equality, only an idiot would think it true. Women have maintained the status quo for millennia already. It would not be changed so easily and with just a bunch of pretty words or wishful thinking. He knew how women thought. He was raised by one and taught of their less scrupulous behaviors. They were not wont to relinquish power that easily. It was part of the reason he felt he could take true control of this base in no time. He just needed to train and chip away at their illusion of unity.

Upon entering the cafeteria the Dragon-user was struck by the overwhelming chatter that filled the room with a heavy fog of flapping lips and wagging tongues as each conversation seemed to carry its own diverse range of noise which stood from anywhere to braying laughter and snorting contempt. He was thankful the helmet filtered much of it out, but being a combat suit made picking up noise with ease, but it also allowed him to filter much of it to allow him to focus on individual discussions so he could gather intel and turn it against them. Getting into the queue lined up by the counter, he would begin to sort and identify conversations by importance. Of course his entering the mess hall wasn't such a simple case as entering and blending in. He was the only person present that was fully suited where others were either in the required heat suits and the rest in the base's uniform. It was easy to determine who was in charge just by the segregation of members. There was a group of women who had a sitting space closer to the windows that overlooked other parts of the base. Their uniforms consisted of a mix of the expected regimentals and some wore the heat suits that he had beneath his exoskeleton which indicated they were pilots. They looked young, with the oldest looking eighteen or nineteen.

Making note of that he looked over to the other tables where the rest of the soldiers were left to sit among those of their ranks or on their own to hurriedly finish what could be their only meal of the day as they were often inundated with training and spent more time with duties than at mess. Approaching the main counter Klaus would place his mechanical hand on the surface, the mask's visor looking towards the server. They appeared to be a young soldier with the role, either as a punishment or a means of stretching tasks since most occupations on the base had to be filled by soldiers since outside help could not be counted on with the level of access required to see their more confidential information the bases had at hand, especially with suits in their control.

"What can I get you?" The soldier sounded tired, looking a bit degraded for having to do this kind of work.

Klaus tilted his head, eye turning to glance up at the corner of his visor he would notice the AI bringing up information on the soldier. He didn't know it could do that, but considering the soldier's information would likely be registered in the Capital's database, it was not a surprise either. He quickly read over the information.

Name Rank Status
Aaron Kebs Private Active

Call Number
OHL-2302RS

Base
Red Shield

The way the call numbers worked was that the first three letters designated the origin of the prison, laboratory, or city the soldier originated from. In Kebs case it was the Hurvor Laboratory. The next four numbers were their unique identifier and the last letters was the base they were stationed at, which they were currently at the Red Shield base. The identification sheet had a picture of the soldier and a marker indicating they were Capital soldiers as opposed to Mercenaries or being a soldier from the other territories. While not allies, the Northern and Southern Hemisphere shared a base on the Western Sector of the Underground so the specification of allegiance was a necessity.

"Hello Kebs, the General talked to me about you. He said if anyone could help me it was you." Klaus' words were empty praise, but the man who was often neglected by his superiors was attentive to the words of appreciation.

There was a moment of hesitation from Kebs, but he finally nodded. "If I can help. What do ya need?"

"Is there any fresh produce here or food that hasn't been shaped and squeezed out of the nozzle of a machine?" He would pause and point back to the kitchen. "I had asked a few before and it seems no one else knew the answer to my simple question."

Not wanting to disappoint Kebs shook his head. "Don't worry, I'll check!" Hurrying to the back of the kitchen the other line workers would give each the other a look of confusion at Keb's abandonment of post, but not wanting to be punished, as the base was wont to do to those who didn't complete their duties, they would continue to serve soldiers in the queue, who were now just walking around Klaus to continue on their way.

Kebs hurried to the back of the kitchen. There were a number of contraptions and machines they used to compress the bags of liquified rations and press them into shapes easy to cut to serve to the soldiers. Though not the tastiest of foods they were nutritionally efficient and easy to produce and transport. Kebs went through the metal cabinets, but all he was able to find were cases full of leftover rations from days prior that were eventually packaged into MREs for fieldwork.

"Kebs!" The cook called out to the private, who stood and saluted.

The man was a lieutenant, easily outranking the line worker. Kebs quickly turned to salute, nearly slamming his head with the cabinet he had been rifling through.

"Sir!" Kebs stood to his feet and pulled his hand to his chest in a Western salute, lowering his head to his superior.

"What are you doing here? Get back your post!" He would order.

Swallowing in nervousness, as it wasn't uncommon to get punishments that ranged from demotions to solitary confinement. Kebs was careful not to make an excuse and was clear on his intentions.

"Sir, the General Honchberg's guest came requesting fresher food." Kebs wasn't even sure if such a thing was on the base, but it was worth trying to find it.

The lieutenant squinted his eyes at the private and shook his head. "The only fresh food is stored in the locker for the Angel Squadron." He looked away a moment before looking back to Kebs. "Why would he ask for such a thing?"

"I don't know sir, he said the General sent him our way and assured him we could help." Kebs didn't want to disappoint the General's expectations because he was the highest ranked male on the base.

The lieutenant could care less about Kebs' problems, but if the General sent his guest here... Rumors had been going around the base that they picked up a Second Generation pilot from the Hurvor Lab. The Angels Squadron were the female officers who were designated as Suit Pilots and had some of the latest first Gen suits. They were powerful suits and of great quality.

Compared to the T1 Suits the male squadron piloted, which were pieces of shit, the Angel Squadron used the first generation ANG1 which were the first gravitational units and specialized in close quarters combat. They got all the best resources at the base.

It wasn't fair.

The lieutenant crossed his arms over his chest. As the cook, he had access to that closet. This man was the first with a Second generation suit. He was their ticket to the top of this bloody hierarchy. It would knock those witches off their pedestals. Reaching into his back pocket he took out the key to the cupboard and tossed it to Kebs.

"Give it to him, he can take whatever he wants. If Mathis asks, tell her it was the General's order."

CHAPTER THIRTY-SIX

Day Two

Getting the support of a number of the males on the base, using their power struggles against them, his next goal was moving to the women. He cleaned out the food stock of what he needed. He was given permission by the Lt. to use the kitchen to cook. Making himself something to eat that was more substantial than military rations he would also prepare a share for Mathis and her girls. There was an obvious rivalry between the men and women at the base despite there being talk of equality among fresh faced soldiers who had yet to experience the hardships of their superiors. It was going to be easier than he thought to split everyone up even further with this rift to take advantage of.

Talking with the Lieutenant, who went by the name of Cromwell, he learned that Mathis was the female General at the base and the Angel Squadron was her nest egg, where General Honchberg had the Armadillo Squadron which consisted of first gen Hammer units. The Hammer pilot Klaus and his brother had met at the laboratory was Captain Mann Wen. He had been leading the Armadillos for over three years and was seen as a hero to the men of the base for his command of the suit and never once reaching overheating. Klaus had not seen him since they arrived at the base though. It mattered little. He was going to make a show of his arrival and take advantage of the holes in their system.

Making his way to the training field Klaus would bring with him a latch container which held his food. All eyes were on him the moment he stepped into the arena. The field for training was a round space that was a 30m circumference circle with sheer metal walls that reached up to the ceiling and a square field in its center that was cordoned off for combat. The field was well lit, the ceiling bright with artificial lights of a deep green tint. The place was sectioned for different types of training. Against one of the walls were small, metal protrusions that seemed to mimic stones and ledges one would find along a cliff. They lined the wall from the base up to the ceiling at different spacings to create an active climbing obstacle course. Another area was lined up with virtual training machines, a staple of the military's training systems. It helped train soldiers without risking them in live combat and was the fastest way to introduce situations both rare and hypothetical to better prepare the soldiers to think on their feet.

Klaus was going to make use of everything present to increase his skills. According to the Yamata system he would only need to use the VR units for twenty-four hours to see substantial results. Now that he had a plan in mind he would proceed.

~bwop~

[General Jes Mathis located.]

Klaus turned his eye to the mini map on his visor. It was an overlay of the base's map, zoomed in on his current location. He looked up and could see a woman in uniform standing at the climbing wall. On her shoulder was a symbol clearly indicating her rank. Klaus wasn't familiar with the symbol system, but thanks to his access to the database he could quickly determine it was a General's badge. Standing around the General was a small contingent of female soldiers in heat suits.

Approaching the group he could see there was much more going on. There was a group of men in the same suits. They seemed disgruntled, complaining about fairness and contesting what appeared to be the status quo. Standing at the front of the rowdy pack was a large man with ashen hair. His stripes marked him a high rank. His AI quickly identified him as Mann Wen, the Hammer unit's captain.

"Unacceptable General Mathis."

His voice was deep and posture proud despite facing the taller General and group of women who were more than willing to kill them where they stood. Women were a brutal sex and it was not uncommon for disagreements between men and women to end in bloodshed. There is no such thing as escape or mercy once you've earned a woman's ire.

"Tell me again, Captain: why should I care?" She crossed her arms over her chest, staring down at him with her pink eyes. "My squad has a mission to the Forstall."

The Forstall was a strange environment found near the entrances to the Abyss. The region spawned endless horrors including dog-like fiends that sucked the blood of a living creature until it was not but a husk. There were also Dameflys: gigantic insects with membranous wings that ambushed their quarry and were known to hang them upside-down on the gnarled and twisted Truys that grew there, letting prey bleed out before consuming them. Truys were leafless, tree-like spires that had sharp, serrated surfaces. The blood pools often became infested with Triglytes, which broke down both living and dead flesh for nutrients and with their needle-sharp teeth having barbs it was difficult to dislodge them once they were attached.

The Forstalls were a nightmare for many.

"We reserved this field for our training. The Marshall gave us her approval." Mann Wen asserted. "The Marshall outranks you General. We'll be going into Aglaophotis. We need to be in top shape if we are going to be anywhere with the Southern Military's group. We are delivering refueled cells."

Klaus would stand a few feet from the arguing groups. They looked like a pack of animals posturing. And folk like this from the city liked calling Farmers like Klaus' family animals. "If you're going to complicate things by arguing, I can go first."

Klaus' voice spoke up between the squabbling squadron leaders. The two groups turned their attention to the man, whose face had yet to be seen due to his refusing to leave his suit. Many were surprised he was able to stay in it as long as he was, seeing as most suits needed to be charged after a twenty-four hour period. It became a curiosity and rumors began to spread the day after he showed himself. There wasn't a soldier on base that hadn't heard something about the Dragon suit.

Mathis turned her head, laughing into her hand. Her more defensive squad members, who were about to stand up in arms, seemed to calm at her reaction. Mann Wen looked at Klaus and shook his head.

"Should you be here? Aren't you supposed to be with the General?" He didn't want Klaus to get on the wrong side of Mathis and her squad of harpies. They could get downright vindictive. "If you want to train you can go to the VR machines. They should suit a greenhorn like you."

Klaus wasn't one who liked to be called inexperienced. While he may not have grown up as a soldier he had plenty of fighting experience, among other skills. Maintaining a Farm not only involved knowing how to repair complicated machines, but exterminating pests that were bigger than you was an everyday occurrence.

"You're the farmer following around Honchberg?" Mathis stepped forward, holding out her arm to push Mann Wen aside.

Wen glared at her before looking at her squad who started to laugh. "Can't take a bit of heat boys?" One would chuckle.

"I heard you fecks praise this little guy," another began. "The General is going to chew him up and spit him out."

"I may chew him up," Another laughed. "He looks

breakable in that shitty suit. Looks like a man's design."

Mathis put her finger to her lips, hushing her girls. She looked down to Klaus, being that she was almost two heads taller than him.

"So tell me, little man, what makes you think I'll let you go ahead of us if I'm not letting that shit-stain of a Hammer through? Think you deserve it any more than him, who couldn't even secure two slow moving targets?" She turned her head to glare at Mann Wen.

He knew what she was alluding to. His group had failed to bring in both the Dragon and Dragonfly. They were untrained prisoners who weren't difficult to control and they shouldn't have been caught off-guard by the Driger, but none of their scanners picked it up. Klaus didn't have a hard time figuring out she was talking about Eric and him. This only fueled his drive to roll this base on its back. Klaus held up the latch container to Mathis.

"If you take this, I'll take the wall." Mathis stared at the man. "A trade." He moved his gauntlet to slide open the case, revealing a collection of foods. It was a simple lunchbox, but it was something that those that lived on a base did not have the luxury of seeing. Even if the women were given better meals, it did not mean any of the kitchen workers knew how to cook scrumptious food.

Klaus took the raw eggs and made an omelet with chopped vegetables, which was rolled into a convenient shape one could eat with their hands. There was a colorful salad full of various vegetables, including bright fruits and pickled veggies. There were fried cuts of white meat, now a golden brown and smelling something akin to a plate of breakfast one would see in the Capital.

It was like that Klaus had bought his way into Mathis' attention and got himself sole access to the climbing wall for the day. The female General had excused herself with her squad to take a break and eat the offered food.

CHAPTER THIRTY-SEVEN

Day Three

It had only been two days. By the time the morning of the third day arrived rumors had already begun to spread quickly throughout the base. The usual curses and expected belittlement from superiors had gone forsaken, leaving the men free of their vehement antagonism. The more experienced men of the base wanted to know how it was that this farmer had managed to turn gossip away from their daily duties. For the women there was talk of Honchberg's pet Teiers being different from the other men they've encountered. He seemed to be able to talk with confidence and knew well how to work a crowd, not wasting time with meaningless shows of whimsy, getting to the point quickly. The competence he showed was both interesting and unexpected from someone from the farms. It was common knowledge that those who worked in the Farm communities outside of the cities and capital lacked the education and etiquette to participate in public speaking. They lacked common sense. It made Mathis wonder where Honchberg had really gotten the boy, so she decided to go confront him.

Many knew well to stay out of her way. She had gotten up earlier than usual. She hastily stalked toward his office in full regalia to show that she meant business. Normally the generals did not wear their service uniforms for any old walk around the base, but she was going to press down on Honchberg.

Klaus had been in his room, waiting for the perfect opportunity to leave. After he spent much of the day on the wall he eventually left to try his hand at the virtual simulators. It was an interesting experience. His mind had convinced him he was there in those simulated situations, yet his body had never left the machine's cockpit. It was a bit frightening at first blush. It had caught him off guard, but after his defeat in the machine's virtual reality Klaus had nearly lost himself. Perhaps it was because it had been the first time he had ever faced death, or the measure of cruelty the programmed opponent showed him. Nevertheless, from that point on, he would be mindful of the possibilities that he now faced being so far from home...

Though normally barracks of that size had more than one occupant, he was left to his own devices as there were many who didn't want to house with a Teiers. Farmers were seen as inferior to Saiers. Those from the city looked down on those that farmed as much as all citizens looked down on prisoners. They were not yet aware of Klaus' current position as a prisoner, making him the lowest of the low. The only reason they did not have such assumptions was because of the way he carried himself. Prisoners were typically wasteful husks that no longer had a will, seeing as it wasn't uncommon for these facilities to use the men as work cattle. After all prisons were only meant to house men unable to abide by the laws of society. It worked differently for women. Women were sent to rehabilitation facilities until they were able to be retrained.

Regardless... he headed back. It was his goal to become stronger and if he wanted to achieve this he needed to spend time in that machine. But before that he had a goal to reach for the day... When he first entered the cockpit of the simulator the Yamata AI had done something quite strange. It began to connect itself to the machine's core processing unit and memory banks. It had only taken moments but the Yamata system began to download the various sources of information in the unit. It seems to have stored records of previous combatants, using these recordings to increase the difficulty of missions by learning the behaviors of soldiers. In short it was a less advanced AI system that created digital ghosts of users to greatly improve its success rate, further challenging them.

Yamata took it upon itself to copy all of this information so it could compile a suitable stage for Klaus to train in. Its user wanted to increase the rate of his growth exponentially, so Yamata would grant him access to a high level stage within the confines of the system, which it had found behind a number of security firewalls and increasingly complicated encryptions designed to be unlocked by higher ranked officers holding the appropriate clearance. The level was simply labeled: "Project X". It was interesting, but Klaus didn't much understand the point of hiding a useful program that could help improve their soldiers at a faster pace. Regardless of their reasons it was a win for him because if Yamata could unlock it he would be able to train using the most optimal stage.

Klaus leaned against the door of his room, watching the mini map on his visor. He followed Mathis' ping as she crossed the base towards the administrative areas, likely to find and question Honchberg. Klaus suspected her curiosity, with the way she watched him the previous evening while he quickly mastered the wall's obstacle course. For someone like him who regularly worked in harsh environments, scaling a few rocks was hardly a challenge. The suit only made it easier and allowed him to quickly adapt his experience to the machine's power. When she was at an acceptable range the Dragon-user would exit his room and make his way back to the training center. He greeted those who stopped to talk to him, and made sure to impress on them his opinions of the base.

"Like it here, farm boy? Pretty different, right?" A soldier and his friend had approached him to engage in friendly banter, though it sounded more insulting to someone proud like Klaus.

Klaus grunted and motioned his hand, the machine silent whenever he moved. Unlike first generation suits, the second gens didn't make excessive noise. The first gens had strong moving parts that created noise when parts moved in and out of place. The heat that rolled through the exoskeletons generated steam that sometimes rattled the internal components and triggered coolant that rushed through the outer limbs, creating audible hissing noises, especially when the excess steam was expelled through joint plates. The racket became an expectation for pilots. There was no such thing as a quiet suit, but this seemed nonexistent in the Dragon. It was a wonder that awed the men and women who were pilots.

Klaus turned his head away. "Farm work makes you strong. Besides I bet you've never seen a real Pigdog." He challenged.

The men looked to each other, their faces shrouded with a veil of concern as their features lightly contorted.

One man rubbed the side of his neck. "They're am'lo though. Hard to train. In fact I think only the Black Skull squadron are trained and certified to use them for combat purposes."

Klaus folded his arms over his chest. "We have Pigdogs all over the farming districts. They are mostly tame and fed vermin scraps." The Pigdogs served as early warning systems to anything intruding on the farm. The beasts would consider the farms their territory and guard the workers that fed them.

For the city raised soldiers that seemed an insane concept. They've seen Pigdogs up close. They were voracious creatures that could bite a man's hand off and ruin machines with a simple kick from their hooves. They were destructive and difficult to tame. Klaus seemed to impress them more and more.

"Hey, I can show you how to tame them, but do you think you can help me?" Klaus would motion his hand, urging the men closer. "The General seems to be in a meeting so he can't show me, but he said he was going to take me to the shooting range." Yamata had access to the base's layout and there was a place far outside the usual routes which led to an enclosed space called the shooting range, but it wasn't something as simple as targets laid out to practice firearms.

"Uh," The soldier looked at his friend, who shook their head. "We dunno, that place is only for Captains and high ranked pilots."

Klaus could understand their hesitation. He had learned as much from the Yamata AI, but that only made him want to access it more. Klaus would stay quiet, thinking over his words. With his face hidden from the men it was difficult to tell what was on his mind.

"Well, you aren't going in, just showing me. Besides, you do want to learn that right? I won't be able to show you until I finish my exercise at the range." Klaus would give them the space to decide.

It was tempting. Being able to tame a Pigdog would grant them prestigious accolades that could get them recognized. It was difficult to join the Black Skulls as it required intense training to be able to mentally withstand the Pigdog's mental intrusions. Pigdogs had a minor form of telepathy and were known to impede an Amaroxian's Geroiid organ. Most Amaroxian's Geroiid organs were damaged by the age of eighteen or twenty. They had once been able to subjugate the Pigdogs, but once the plague began to spread the organs shriveled away and pushed the once docile animals into proactive behaviors that quickly took advantage of their new power. They were smart animals, which was what made the Amaroxian and Pigdog relationship vital for early settlement of the Eastern Barrens.

"Sure, sure. Come with us. It shouldn't be too far. We can't show you in, but we can point it out at least." With that Klaus and the interested soldiers made their way to the shooting range.

CHAPTER THIRTY-EIGHT

Day Four

It was simple enough to convince the soldiers to take him to the shooting range, seeing as he was offering them a reward that was sure to increase their status on the base and likely get them closer to joining the Black Skulls. As Klaus understood it the Black Skulls was an elite group of all male soldiers that were allowed to join the Ostin regiment, which had a greater amount of freedom than most Military groups, giving them opportunities to work in the Eastern Barrens. It came with higher pay and privileges often only afforded to female officers.

It wasn't as simple as making one's way down to another wing of the base. To get there one had to leave the main facility and travel down a thoroughfare that led one back to a higher stage. That meant Klaus had to travel back up the level where he had entered through, and to another, separate facility, that was meant for suit care and maintenance. There were more engineers here than soldiers, shifting the environment considerably in terms of conduct and atmosphere. The superstructure was called 'the Garage' as it was where a majority of the base's vehicles and exosuits could be found. ATVs, trucks, assault vehicles, transport vehicles, and tunneler vehicles. These were the typical transports found on most bases, but each base had some unique units. The Red Shield base was equipped with Varys Trucks, which were capable of holding its ground against Driger Wyrms. The creatures were prolific in the area.

There were also a number of different types of suits within the base aside from the battle-oriented Turbo Suits. There were also a number of Military Construct Units that were designed specifically for hauling heavy materials as well as aiding in the construction of temporary bases that were necessary during reconnaissance missions.

The two most produced exosuits were the Charger Suit and Driger Suit. They were aptly named for their roles. The Charger was designed to carry heavy loads into the base as well as assist in the construction or repair of damaged structures, especially those that were considered load bearing. But its most used function was its Full Charge. Chargers were mobile wrecking units that could penetrate the thickest boulders and decimate foundations, allowing regiments to forcibly infiltrate rebel garrisons and enemy bases.

As for the Driger suit it was an advanced trencher capable of breaking through tough sedimentary stone and withstand the pressure found in lower stages. Driger was a commonly used word in the Amaroxian tongue, which seemed a mix of the Universal language and an Archaic language no longer used in the known systems. Drigers were a voracious species once exported for their terraforming use. Being stone eating am'lo their excrement served as fertilizer that increased the value of the land they tilled.

When Driger became feral animals, no longer able to be tamed or domesticated, becoming am'lo, Driger Suits were designed to replace them.

-

-

-

Though it was named as such, the range itself was quite an advanced field for training those who were piloting suits. It almost seemed like a combination of the training environments he had seen in the training AI, but perfectly designed to push a pilot to their limits. Regardless of what one imagined, the space was something difficult to conceive after seeing the layout of the main part of the base, which was a simple collection of buildings laid out symmetrically.

The Garage was constructed over a deep pit that ran down into the ground for several hundred meters. There was a ring of interconnected platforms that ran around the edge of the crater. These platforms were further braced by metal frames secured into the stone hollow, the beams and trusses bound within the innermost area of the circular crater.

There was a lift, similar to the freight elevator that carried him down into the main base, which was designed for the larger vehicles and cargo that often found its way into the facility. Instead of having to ride down, the shooting range was up. Platforms and targets were designed for pilots to scale, fly, or leap across in order to strike the machine's which calculated the pilots speed when reaching each checkpoint. It was child's play, Klaus felt. Run up, hit a target and make one's way back down? Even still he would benefit from using his suit to outdo any present records.

And he did.

The current record for the obstacle course had been held by Mathis, but Klaus had obliterated it. If not for the training area recording the activities none would believe what Klaus had done. Instead of trying to show off or otherwise boast of his achievements he immediately returned to his room, leaving the rumors to fly across the base.

It had taken to the next day, but Mathis finally chose to directly confront Klaus and demand answers.

She learned from Honchberg that Klaus was actually a prisoner. He was a casteless vagabond. She had planned to utterly destroy his pride and put the whelp in his place, but her own pride was ripped in twain when she learned of his accomplishments at the range. Klaus was invited to her office for -- a chat.

Klaus, though still a bit wary of women that weren't his

mother, had the suit now and felt powerful. He didn't see these soldiers overpowering him anytime soon. He had one more day to use. So far he has been able, with the help of Yamata, to completely download the protocols, operation plans, war plans, and other vital information concerning the four other bases within the Capital's territory. Entering her office he would stand at the entrance, arms folded behind him.

Mathis was on her final leg. Unable to see his face or find anything about him or his family prior to his imprisonment, she had no choice but to ask him.

"Who are you boy?" She wasn't going to beat around the bush.

She recognized she had in front of her a rare opportunity. This young man had access to the only known Second Generation Suit. Newberry's laboratory wasn't the only group tasked with constructing a viable design from plans left behind by her father, but she had the advantage of knowing his work personally. Honchberg made the right choice in buying the boys and gaining exclusive rights to them and the suits on their bodies.

There was just the issue of the missing one. They had sent operatives to locate him.

"We bought you from Haut's facility, meaning you belong to the Military now. You have to follow orders like anyone else."

Bought them?

Was that so?

"Klaus. That is the name my mother gave me. I have no caste so that is all I have left." He was smart. Plausible deniability. They couldn't find anything. Haut made sure they had no records left. "You have to ask my brother, or Elizabeth Newberry. They know more. My memories were taken by Mugenes."

She had no way of confirming that, and if she pushed him she was sure the slinky vermin would find a hole to hide in.

"What do you want to do here?" Honchberg couldn't have just up and taken them without making some sort of deal. "Whatever Honchberg offered, I'll do better."

"He said we can be free again. So he took us to the military. Said we can fight all we want." Klaus shook his head. "I want my brother. When you find him, tell me okay?" He pointed to the door. "Can I go? I have to train more. General Honchberg said."

Whether his brother was alive or a corpse, she would be sure to bring him in and wring them for what they were worth. Their suits were too rare to relinquish to the Sister's right away.

"Fine. I'll call for you as soon as we find him. But I can't promise he's alive, so don't get your hopes up." She dismissed Klaus.

He didn't seem to be lying, but since she couldn't see his face she wasn't able to read him. She knew she would have to be careful. Men couldn't be trusted. A prisoner had nothing to lose so it was more problematic. She would take the evening to think over the problem. There had to be a way to get him to do everything she said.

It was a longshot, but she could get a tool to help her twist that boy into a usable soldier. There were some who were quite willful, forgetful of their places. That tool would help tame him quickly, it was just the issue of getting one. It could take weeks for it to arrive.

Unfortunately for her it would be too late. They had one more day. All Klaus needed to complete his takeover was access to the base's mainframe. He now knew where Mathis' office was and saw she had a terminal. All he needed was to access the system. The reason he wanted to do so from her terminal was because it'd be far more confusing as to who would risk such a thing, if not a woman? He made sure to mark where all the cameras were on the map, Yamata building a perfect map of the halls he's traveled since arriving.

Returning to his room he would lay down. This would be the last time he would have to sleep under a starless sky.

CHAPTER THIRTY-NINE

The Final Day

~bwop~

[It is now 06:00 hours. The base has begun their foot drill training. It is advised user makes their way to the mess hall and establish the appearance of commonality, preventing the assumption of deceitful behavior.]

Klaus' skull vibrated with the system AI's voice. He opened his eyes, vision soon filled with columns of data. These columns consisted of hypothetical situations and their measured percentage of occurring. Once the calculations were complete each column would light up with the decided course of action that would best afford Klaus with success. Sitting up, his head turned towards the window. SInce falling asleep the scenery had not changed. It was still the same chasm of red stone and silicate towers formed from the ground to ceiling, creating an illusion of rows of buildings, outlined by darkness. If this was what the capital looked like, then he didn't need it. What was the point of freedom if it still made you feel trapped?

His mission began at 06:00 hours. Leaving his room he would be welcomed by the strange order that could be found on a base. Despite its hectic nature it wasn't difficult to see that they were a well oiled machine. Even despite any of the trappings of their constant exchanges of grief and subtle bouts of gender inequality, they understood that they could harness a great force by cooperating. Leaders did well to use their words and action to support an incredible control over their units. He would not be able to simply break their connections with his words. Regardless of anything he was still an outsider, but he was going to make use of the holes in their defenses to seep into their systems like a virus.

Making his way down the halls until he arrived at the mess hall. He made sure to greet passing faces and stop to chat whenever he was expected to. Eventually he arrived at the empty cafeteria. Getting himself something to eat, that was not the manufactured cubes of rations, he would seat himself near the window. Even from up here, looking down into the vales, unnaturally carved out by the hand of man, Klaus wondered just what it was like on the surface. To see wind, to hear the rampant destruction of weather.

~bwop~

[There are numerous records of our time above ground. In fact the first of us DRAGON systems were originally designed prior to our migration below ground.]

Klaus glanced to the side. The lower section of his mask did part to allow him to eat. It wasn't as if he could not take off the suit, but he chose not to. What the base wasn't aware of was, unlike the first generation suits, his did not require a Station to be removed. He learned from Yamata that all he would need to do was decompress and remove the suit piece by piece. He would only have to leave the posterior cerebcable attached to make returning to the suit easier. He wondered if Eric had figured out as much. Though his brother was particularly strong willed when they were together, he was exceptionally cowardly and was prone to avoiding conflict.

"Which system is it?" He thought his question, setting down his utensil, eyes turning towards the side.

~bwop~

[Tiamat. It was from Tiamat that all other DRAGON originated. It is her code that is the basis for ours. It makes Tiamat our mother, in a user's sense. Tiamat's current user is Eric Cipher.]

His brother? Well he could go over more of that later. For

now he had the rest of the base to take over. For Amaroxian society a great deal of their machines ran on a single system known as the Nexus. The Nexus was connected to the Capital and the Capital was controlled by the council. It was nearly impossible to interfere with the daily processes of the Nexus because it was protected by its own AI, though there were very few people who were aware of this. The AIs themselves were aware though and Yamata told Klaus which it was.

Ur. Ur was the DRAGON system that was used to control and protect the Nexus and Klaus found such a thing rather ironic. The Sisters condemned AI and yet they made use of one of the DRAGON systems, which was designed by a man they had used as a scapegoat for the hatred of the people. Yamata explained the way the Ur system was designed, as it was unique among the DRAGON.

[Ur is a social system that preferred interactions with users, which was why he was originally installed in the Nexus, but little did Ur realize that you users would be completely restricted from using computing machines. Aside from the occasional command from military users, Ur was isolated. The Ur system is eager to assist users, if it means they would be interacting with them.]

"But that doesn't mean he's going to simply follow my commands, right? Aren't you designed to only take commands from your users?" By now Klaus was making his way down the halls, following the route he had taken the night prior, towards Mathis' office.

[I am sure the user will be able to convince Ur easily. So long as he has Ur's system passcode.]

"Are you telling me you have the passcode?" Klaus finally arrived at the General's door.

While he made his way over Yamata would alter the broadcast of the recording cameras, making sure to loop the last five minutes of recording, ensuring no one was seen passing through the areas at the time Klaus passed by.

~bwop~

[Negative. It is you, user, who has the passcode.]

"*I do...?*"

[Affirmative. Though the user may be unaware of it, the passcode for accessing DRAGON systems is quite simple as it was invented by our designer. It was his intention to allow anyone to interact with the AI. It is merely our job as systems to support users into making the most correct choice.]

Klaus stepped into the room, closing the door behind him.

~bwop~

[User has thirty minutes to access Ur and reformat the system to his desire.]

Klaus would walk around the desk and seat himself. Placing both hands on the surface, the keyboard would appear over his wrists. The holographic keyboard was not the common design found within the immediate galaxy. Amaroxia's writing system has long since diverged from the Universal system, instead creating a simplistic collection of encoded symbols that related to words, creating text that was legible by most educated Amaroxians. The system was reminiscent of ancient dash and dot communication, which was still used today within the Universe as a form of emergency contact to races they could not write with.

"I know the passcode?" Klaus began by opening the computer's terminal system. He looked to the empty text box, eyes motioning along his visor. There he was able to keep track of movement of key targets in the base, specifically Honchberg and Mathis.

He had no idea what the passcode could be, but the more he thought about the experiences he had at the base it slowly began to make sense. His fingers began to move over the symbols with knowingly. When marks were entered together they formed larger marks, creating familiar words. It reminded him of the codes Elizabeth used in the laboratory. They were always command chains as opposed to simple strings of numbers or letters.

Yamata said he had the passcode...

-.-. -....- .. -....- .--. -....- .... -....- . -....- .-.

CIPHER

[[Welcome user. What can I help you with today?]]

The Ur system sounded quite different from Yamata. It was more energetic and a little sad...

Klaus tilted his head. "System Ur?" He questioned.

[[Yes user!?]]

Klaus hesitated a moment before he pinched his fingers together and raised his hand up. Partying his digits he would open a new window beside him.

"I need you to transfer all system control to me. Can you do that?" Klaus' question was met with silence.

[[User, that would give you control of the weapon's terminal as well as support systems on the base. Are you sure? It is difficult for a user to manage on their own.]]

Was he imagining it? Did the system sound hopeful? Yamata was right.

Nodding Klaus would stand. "You're right. I'll need the help of the system. Are you willing to interface?"

[[Of course user!! You can count on me!]]

That was easier than he expected. "Yamata?"

[Simple enough user. I can open direct communication

with Ur in my system.]

"We'll have to leave quickly." Klaus made sure to put everything back the way it was.

Stepping out of the office he made his way back to the main hall as the troops were returning from training. Yamata returned the camera to normal and adjusted his system to allow Ur easy access. Seeing as all the DRAGON systems were connected, all the AI had to do was open his channel.

[[Thank you for the access, Yamata! Good morning user! Ur had completed control of the base's system. What would you like to do first?]]

"I want everyone called back into the base. Shut them out of the weapons and lock down the base. Let no one out."

CHAPTER FORTY

From Beyond The Horizon

The Geyser Field was far from silent. The hissing plumes of superheated water erupted into the air with enough force to scorch off a limb. The air itself was twisted into a constant fog, squeezing the landscape into an isolating habitat. Mist from the mix of heat and moisture filled the biome with the humid clouds, constantly swirling across the sea of boiling water. The movement in the fields was constant and was what kept most predators at bay, but it did nothing to deter scavengers...

In the distance the towering pack of a Junker could be seen, just a dot on the horizon. Junkers were individuals who traveled throughout the world gathering abandoned technology, old materials and other junk. They would trade their goods for their food, shelter, and cloth to make their clothing. A Junker was a person that had long since abandoned their nation, for whatever reason, and turned to living in the untamed wilds of the Barrens. Junkers were recognized by governments as a people, as there were enough of them to form a nation, but they were greatly valued for their knowledge as they alone seemed able to travel the most dangerous Stages without difficulty. They had a culture that was distinct and clothing recognizable from a distance. First was the great rucksacks they carried on their backs. These packs held everything from their junk to their sleeping bags. Most Junkers had robotic limbs so kept repair kits on them at all times, or jerry rigged their own from the parts they picked up. Unlike Roxoid, Junkers weren't considered cyborgs so weren't applicable when it came to laws regarding them which limited the twisted amalgamations of people.

Junkers also wore respirator masks that were functionally

scrap pieces of metal and leather stitched together to create a filtering device that assisted in their breathing. They sometimes traveled to some of the lowest Stages where air was thinner, but it provided them with choice fishing spots seeing as there were many lower Stages used as a dumping ground for Amaroxian refuse. The loose cloaks they wore shielded them from environmental hazards such as the acidic swamps created by chemical reactions between different underground sediments, heat from the deepest caverns, and even the boiling waters that spilled from the active Geysers.

~wrrrrr~

~wrrrr~

With a whirr and pop the Junker's limbs creaked as their hydraulic joints were weighed down and fought to stabilize the heavy pack on his back. Their legs were thin looking metal rods, bent back at the ankle like a bird. The steel toes clambered along their path like a hoofed ungulate sprinting across open plains. Their arms were hidden beneath the heavy cloak, the flaps of the fabric fluttering against their movements. Over their face was the respirator Junkers were known to have. It had a beak-shaped form in front of it, which was attached to the metal plate mask that held dark goggles over their eyes. The lenses of the goggles themselves seemed to have a black tint to them. All that could be seen in the oddly shaped eye coverings were their yellow eyes, shifting along the space, tracing their environment.

They came to a stop at a curious lump that occupied the silt covered terrain, moistened by the heated waters of active geysers. The sound of whirring mechanisms rattled in the head of the Junker. This particular fellow's name was Howitzer and as such Howitzer was quite surprised to find themselves face to feet with a pristine Turbo Suit in one piece.

"Is it my lucky day~?!" They moved their mechanical talons to briskly kick the body of the machine.

When it groaned and moved the Junker jumped back with surprising speed. Despite the heavy rucksack, Howitzer was able to move quite easily. When the spry scavenger landed about a half foot from the body, standing with their spine straight, glowing yellow orbs within the goggles, blinking. When the suit did not move any further the stout figure sunk back to a reasonable height and slumped forward as a hiss of steam fizzled from the side of the mask as the Junker let out a sigh.

"Wowie." Letting out a little whirr the animated figure took a few steps back towards the occupied suit. "S'alive." Reaching their mechanical talon over they would give the suit another poke only for, this time, nothing to happen. "Queer though, why's it still s'alive?" Howitzer would crouch down, setting the heavy rucksack onto the ground.

The steaming pillars of heated water didn't seem to bother them much, the leather cloak doing well to shield the smaller body from the burning droplets. Reaching into the sack the junker searched around the innards of the clutter-filled pack. After a moment of searching the familiar pockets, Howitzer would find a small handheld device. Pulling a cord from it they would attach it to the multitude of wires that were exposed on the back of the suit where the base of the skull met the upper shoulders. Plopping themselves to the ground and crossing the metal limbs as they handled the device. Their hands weren't easily visible as the cloak seemed to cover them in a shadow.

~bwop~

A voice rumbled from the device.

[You are not the User. Why are you accessing my suit?]

~wrrrrr~

A buzzing whirr rang from Howitzer when they succeeded in entering the suit's systems. "Lucky I guess. But it's because I can. So you're the AI for this suit huh? If you're still active, whoever is in there is s'alive?"

For a moment there was silence. The AI was calculating the situation.

~bwop~

[Affirmative. What is your mission Junker?]

The glowing dots within Howitzer's goggles seemed to fade in and out as if blinking. "So you know what I am, yet don't know my mission? To collect junk! But seeing as you weren't thrown away, you aren't junk." That was too bad. They had thought they'd finally found a treasure! "Soooo..." Standing they would pull their rucksack back onto their back and latched the device onto the chest of their cloak.

At the moment the Tiamat AI was vulnerable, seeing as Eric had collapsed from the intense heat of the field. The Junker shuffled around, reaching to grab the arm of the unconscious suit user and would effortlessly hoist him onto the top of the pack. A Junker's strength was a paradoxical variability. Many times they seemed able to carry tons of rubbish in their sacks, but relatively weak when concerning day to day tasks and could be viewed as some of the clumsiest of entities, often tipping over with the lightest tap.

~bwop~

[Where are you taking us?]

The gears and mechanisms within Howitzer's talons would adjust to the new weight before they pulled their cloak more tightly around their bodies. "My camp is nearby. We can cool off your suit. Just touching it, my fingers almost roasted!"

This confounded the AI as there seemed no proof that the Junker even had fingers. Nevertheless the AI had no choice but to relent to the wiles of the wiry trash hunter, seeing as they were the only one for kilometers around capable of moving and weren't immediately hostile to its User. By the way of it the Junker traveled for almost five kilometers before arriving at what looked to be an ordinary pile of junk, but upon closer inspection it was a makeshift shelter cobbled together by parts of things and bobs that the scavenger had procured from other treasure troves of garbage lined dumps.

Reaching out they tapped their finger against the front of the trash shack. With a pop the front entrance snapped open. Removing their rucksack, Howitzer would lean it up against the simple sanctuary and would roll the Dragonfly into the dome-shaped haven. Seating themselves on the ground, once again crossing their ungulate-like feet. Snapping the device against the wall of the shed the able-bodied scrounger would look over the suit.

"Doesn't seem broken." But leave it to a Junker to be able to analyze an item and spy any deformity to determine its state. "It'll take at least an hour to fully cool down. After that you can reset the system and shock your pilot awake."

Once again there would be no immediate answer from the AI as it carefully measured its response against the nosy dumppicker.

~bwop~

[This Junker has knowledge of my systems in recognizable detail. This Junker was even able to access us within the confines of the user's subconscious. How?]

A slow whistle wheezed from the traveling junk-dealer. "What a silly question!" They laughed. "I wouldn't be worth my salt as a Junker if I couldn't do this much. You should certainly have details about our people." They implored.

~bwop~

[Correct. There are documented details of Junkers and their society within many databanks accessible by us. Your mastery with machines outmatches even the brightest minds serving the Military and Laboratories within the two hemispheres. But -- it does not explain it.]

Quieting their laughter the Junker sighed. "A Junker like me can't just give away trade secrets, right? There are things even your databanks can't know."

~bwop~

[Highly improbable.]

"But not impossibly difficult. Nothing is zero percent." And so they would wait until their guest woke from their slumber.

CHAPTER FORTY-ONE

The First Step

With the Hurvor Laboratory destroyed, Elizabeth and Casey had no choice but to return to the Capital. The Capital was located on the Argatha Stage, the primary reason it was called Argatha Capital. Stages were walled inside of chambers found deep underground. Each chamber acted like its own island continent, isolated by a sea of darkness and stone. Argatha was a Stage constructed during the Dyna Age. When one entered the capital's dome they would find themselves on a ring of metal dug a few thousand feet into the ground, seemingly embedded into the stone, as if it were growing out of it. Following the inner circumference of the ring, at each Cardinal direction, were bridges that connected to what appeared to be a floating island in the center of the outer ring. The island was actually built upon a column of stone reinforced by titanium. The metal structure was a nest for the main population, the outer ring serving as a station for the local Military force.

Sitting at the capital's center, from its base to the ceiling above, was the Worm's Spine, the ancient sky elevator that had once served to transport Amaroxia's people beneath the soils.

During the Dyna Age the technology used to construct settlements was slowly changing and beginning to affect the shape of infrastructure. Instead of the older ring style which stacked rings of platforms up, they went further down. Amaroxians managed to survive for an epoch before they met with their greatest disaster. Scientists say there was a coronal mass ejection generated by the final stages of their sun's destruction. Plasma ejected from the dying star released a magnetic field with enough force that all of the primary storage of their electronic devices were wiped clean. With no records left behind it was a new starting point of the Nowylith Age. Today they were in the Foregiphte Age and faced the destruction of their own species as they slowly deteriorated from the Mugenes Disease with no cure in sight.

Kris sat with Elizabeth and Casey at a small eatery just outside of the capital's government facilities.

"That T1 model had not been seen since the **Conyard Incident** over twenty years ago." Kris had been discussing with Elizabeth and Casey about the incident.

The eatery was sparsely populated. Many of the customers, workers from the nearby facilities. It was a sleek building made of a mix of titanium and silver steel. On its roof, and perched on the windowsills, were small gardens and planters that added color around the grey city. It was the same with the grandiose towers crowded around the capital, making use of every square inch of surface possible, to build. Wherever there was space, plants were grown, with the use of SEED vats which helped terraform all settlements in the Dyna Age.

Liz sat back in her seat. "That was before the division of the Militia and Science Corps, right?"

Casey was in her chair, a tablet on her lap. "But they were also bound to the government to produce new technology, demanding a project every year." She was glad they were separate because the Science corps now answered to Yellow CROSS, a former force among the disbanded CYR.

Kris agreed with Casey. "I was glad for it. But on the incident; it happened during the *Day of the Sun*, and it was a colony-wide holiday, but after that it was no longer held."

"I get that," she began to complain. "But what does that have to do with curing Mugenes?" Despite being in a different field of science than Liz, Kris desired as much as her to cure the disease where many had given up.

The dark-skinned woman narrowed her eyes, glaring at Elizabeth from behind her glasses. Elizabeth settled in her seat. "At the time augmentation was reserved for those in military service and wasn't considered to be *wrong*, just illegal. A lot of people were unsatisfied with the way the outbreak was being handled, and tried to circumvent the disease by replacing affected limbs and organs with machine parts."

Casey laid the tablet, face down on her lap, and sighed. "Mugenes started a hundred years ago. At the time we were still a minarchy, but everything fell to lawless anarchy as the deformities began to have fatal results. Augmentation spread rampantly so in order to control it the government began to intervene and banned it, only allowing the military to do it even if these augmented individuals had only accounted for 1% of the population at the time."

So when Mugenes started the line between man and machine began to vanish.

Kris set down her eating utensil. "Right and that meant Augmentation broke the law, turning people into criminals. They had been seen as second class citizens and undeserving of the Vox - which acted like a painkiller that almost removed all of the agony caused by the mutations - so it was withheld." As a result of the government withholding the medicine gangs quickly formed, leaders appointed according to the amount of augmentation done to a body. Their leaders called themselves Pharsyts, removing themselves from society.

Elizabeth listened, trying to collect the information she

was being given. "Right and I know around that time there was a lot of violence within the colonies that were previously super safe." As such the growing violence from these gangs required a new weapon to combat the rebels.

"The gangs raided local clinics for their supply of Vox. After a year of research the first Turbo Suits were hastily put into production." Casey continued, showing that the Suits were irrevocably connected to Mugenes. "It was first shown off during that celebration, the Military flexing."

Kris continued. "The neurologist that was on the leading Science team claimed the suits CN connectors, central neuropath connectors, risked damaging, even destroying, the Neuropathic Systems in the body that controlled the Geroiid organ."

Liz sat back in surprise. "But we can't travel, let alone live, down here without it. We'd be completely blind! How could they leave such a defect?!" Elizabeth and Kris' glasses weren't just for show. The women were essentially blind.

Casey pressed her finger to the air, her seat projecting a small hologram screen. "Not just that but the first suits needed at least 6000 MFLOPS per watt to run efficiently, thrice that of our current supercomputers. To put all that power into a small core they used to use I can surmise the other hazards like overheating would otherwise melt the pilot, if the suit didn't tear their muscles apart first."

It was frustrating! It was what they worked hard to prevent as suit engineers!

Kris rubbed the side of her head, Casey's words mostly gibberish to her since she was an analytical chemist. "They were much worse than just external damage. There was the suit's compressor. The suit was using a small compression chamber that used the radioactive isotopes from Goraynium to fuel its power. It had incredible energy consumption. Using Goraynium as an energy source had long since been illegal in the capitol, because it was a known aggressor to the Mugenes disease, aside from being its source."

The blond-haired woman sat back, feeling defeated. "Yet they still use Goraynium in the outer rims." It was a cheap power source. It could fuel lights, equipment and generate heat.

"Several Roxoids had snuck into the event, at least according to official reports. Eyewitnesses say there was only one. When everyone was distracted with the parade he entered the fields and used a pulse bomb to set off the suit's core." It made Kris a little nauseous thinking about it. She had seen reports about the explosion. "The damage was untold and the casualties are still incomplete in number. They wanted someone to blame. A lot of people said they saw him talking to a young casteless woman and her two sons, but that was a dead end. In the end the Science Corps took the blame and we were dropped off, stuck in the helpless position we're in now."

Elizabeth lowered her head, feeling disbelief towards the tale, but it was Kris telling her. "So you're saying it was this incident that likely introduced the strain's mutation in the first place?"

Kris nodded. "Up until then, nothing changed. But not even a day later, the strain started to mutate in people, eliminating all our work towards the original disease. Something in that core created a chemical reaction with Mugenes and if we can find out there's a good chance we can solve this mystery."

Liz shook her head. "But shouldn't you be able to do that if you have a sample of the original strain?"

"But that's the thing, Liz. We don't. Even the sealed samples we had -- changed." Kris assured.

Elizabeth and Casey looked over to Kris as if the woman suddenly grew two heads.

"Excuse you?" Casey sounded offended, but why wouldn't she be? What she was hearing was nonsense. "That doesn't make any sense. It couldn't have been the suit then. The explosion didn't reach the--"

"But it was." Kris pressed. "And it did." Kris adjusted her glasses. "After the suit exploded the shockwave went far enough to blow the windows off the council building. That energy bled far and wide, and what I need to find out is how the suit was made. It's really the only avenue I have. If I could see the composition of elements it has I could perhaps isolate the source of the change..."

"We'd be able to cure it?" Elizabeth questioned.

Kris nodded. "We would. Liz, please?"

When Liz looked over to Casey, the older woman shrugged. To the chair bound scientist it was a wild theory, but Kris was a meticulous person and it was hard to deny her. Elizabeth sighed deeply.

"Alright... I can take you to meet my father. If he has any of grandfather's research we can see how the suit was made and what it was made out of..." She'd finally relent.

CHAPTER FORTY-TWO

Waking On The Edge

Eric would wake with a start. He wasn't sure what happened or that it even did. One minute he was racing across the Geyser Fields to get away from a gang of renegades and the next thing he knew all he could see was a dull, pulsing blue light. Had he died? A quick scan of his surroundings and he would quickly find the answer. On the corner of his screen he could see data blinking in the corner, answering an array of questions on his status. His body was heavy, but he could feel his breath rushing from his throat and across his lips.

[Unit: Dragonfly]

[Pilot Biometrics.... Average]
[Heart Rate.... 250 bpm]
[Pressure... 475 amp]

[System... AR, HUD, Scan -- Ready]

"System....?" Eric tried calling out to his suit, but he realized when the word was half way out of his mouth that he wasn't sure what to call the suit's system. "... what do I call you?"

"This one is named Tiamat, surprised you're even askin'!" A jubilant voice called out.

Eric gasped out. The blue tint over his visor snapped open, revealing the environment to his vision. The visor had looked to have created a screen over the pilot's vision to protect it as he lay unconscious, but when the machine felt him start to sit up it retracted the shield.

The pilot couldn't recognize where he was. The room was small and looked to be some sort of metal dome. He was laying on top of what he could only describe as trash. Looking over towards where the voice was he would get an alert.

~dwop~

[... correct. This system's name is Tiamat.]

Howitzer sat across from Eric. The figure appeared to be wearing a brown, synthetic cloak with small, mechanical legs that looked like spindly insect's limbs and a face that he couldn't humanize. The legs were small and were digitigrade in their nature. They were seated on the ground and they were tucked close to their body. There were two ports over where eyes should be. It looked to be a visor. There was a mechanism that looked to be placed over where a nose and mouth should be that he recognized as a ventilator. He could hear the stranger seemingly breathing as the machine pulled in air from the center parts and expelled from the valves on the side. There weren't any features he could point out that weren't machines. Even from within the cloak he could hear the chirps of mechanical parts or the whistles of processing, which he recognized from his own suit.

The Junker sat some distance from Eric in the small space. Between them appeared to be a small thermal unit that worked to heat the dome. The Junker had a long screwdriver in hand and was actively adjusting the heat. Eric reached up to touch his helmet. Looking at his hands he could see he still had his suit on. He knew the suit couldn't be taken off unless at a station, but for some reason he worried about it being removed while he was unconscious. What if those reavers peeled him out of his suit forcefully? He was sure that they had their ways.

"Where am I? And who are you?" Eric felt his voice was barely working, the heat having dried his throat.

Wait, if he couldn't take off his suit how could he eat or drink?! Sure this was quite an experience at first, but the more he faced these harrowing situations the more energy he found himself using to get out of them. Howitzer starred in the Dragonfly's direction, prodding at the thermal unit.

"Quite rude of you young'un. Asking my name without even givin' yours. But you know what, since you're just waking up we'll give you a pass." They would set the tool to the side and rest their glove covered hands in their lap. "My name's Howitzer. I'm a Junker. Found you shut down near the Geysers." The Junker paused to tap at their ventilator. "Actually 'passed out' is the right term for the living, huh? You're a man in that suit, right?" The Junker's eyes appeared to snap shut quickly like shutters, a sound coming from their head sounding akin to a machine whirring, their eyes dimming slightly as if the backlight was turned down.

"A Junker?" Eric had never heard of the term before. Looking the man up and down he would have easily mistaken him for a Roxoid. "What's that?"

"What's that? Me? Junkers are what we are. We collect junk, repair old technology and try to teach you young'uns to not make the mistakes we made. Tools, tools to be used by this generation, huh?" Pushing their hands onto their knees the Junker would push onto their feet, though they were more like needle-like toes.

Whenever Howitzer moved their joints would whirr or a chirp would click from their hidden body. Eric looked up over his head. The dome was too low for him to fully stand so he remained sitting. Howitzer moved around the small space. Their feet tapped against the hard ground of the shelter, rapid ticks as they needed to take many short steps to reach their destination. They would lift a sheet of metal here or a pile of cords there. Tucking a few of the collected objects in their arms they would walk around. Eric leaned his head over to get a better look.

"According to your system's analysis you've been in the suit for almost twenty-four hours." Howitzer quickly looked back over their shoulder before continuing to browse the piles of trash.

"How did you know that?!" Eric slapped his hand over the back of his neck, checking the cerebro cable was still in place, letting his hand pat around his body checking unauthorized connections being used.

~dwop~

[Pilot's caution is unnecessary. No ports or nodes have been accessed without consent.]

"So what is he talking about?" Eric looked over to Howitzer when he came over to his side and dumped the armful of Junk onto the floor beside the raised surface being used as a makeshift bed. "How does he know that? Is he with the military?"

"They." Howitzer corrected. Eric looked over to the Junker with a sense of confusion filling his features, though the helmet obscured them. "Nice of you to bring back old memories though." Eric continued to stare. "Well, Junkers don't have genders, per say, anymore. We've kind of moved past all that. What with all the modification." But looking Howitzer up and down there would be no telling what sort of mods they could have had. Howitzer waved their hand dismissively. "Well don't worry about it. As to how I know, I think your little assistant can tell you." They'd point their finger at the suit wearer.

Meanwhile Howitzer looked to be piecing together some flexible, translucent tubes to a switchboard. Their hands were covered in a thick pair of gloves, but it didn't seem to diminish their dexterity.

~dwop~

[Junkers are unique Users with the capacity to scan numerous systems that are stored within their personal databases. They are not locked out of secure operating units and have the ability to override many, if not all, regional restrictions set in place by Hemispherical governments.]

That was more than Eric could really understand. But at the heart of it it seems whoever these Junkers were, are knowledgeable. Eric would nod. "Alright. So what are you doing? And where are we?"

Howitzer chuckled. "I am making a Siphon. And as for where we are...?" They would tilt their head before resuming their crafting. It was interesting seeing how quickly they were able to force fit the different pieces of machines and parts they had. None of them looked to fit together. "We're near the entrance to the old highway. Out of use these days, but it was pretty active when Sofu was still around." They looked at the work they had in their hands and nodded, quite proud of their contraception. "But these days? It's a deep trove of junk, a treasure for Junkers." Howitzer moved to crouch down. "Alright. This should help you." They picked up the end of the semi clear hose.

Eric reached up to take the hose. "What is it?" He would stare at it in confusion. The end of the tube appeared to be covered in a sharp ring of metal. The switchboard could fit into his palm, connectors of different sizes making it look more like a tattered mess than an actual working machine.

~dwop~

[It appears to be a feeding tube used for taking in nutrients. Typically it is inserted to the nasogastric region or directly into the stomach, but because of the design of the suit you are able to insert it into the abdominal region of the chassis.]

"Can't take off the suit without a station, right?" Howitzer motioned their hand. "Just put that on your chassis and it should readily connect." Eric looked down to his side, raising his arm. Just as he looked there appeared to be a small hatch on his side that slid open. He looked over to the Junker who motioned their hand encouragingly. After a moment Eric would hover the object over the hatch and slide the tubes in as well until the hatch closed with a snap.

He would wait, but nothing seemed to happen. "That was i--auuugh!" Eric shouted and held his side. He felt something pierce into his side, right through his skin. He turned his head up towards the Junker who clapped their hands together and shrugged.

"That first piercing can hurt quite a bit. Don't worry, at least it didn't need to be twisted." They'd laugh out loud. "The suit should have inserted the tube into your side and now you can open that hatch and take nutrients in by just placing a block in the slot and closing it. It'll break it down, and do the rest. It's more complicated than it looks, but it also helps that Tiamat's programming will do the rest."

CHAPTER FORTY-THREE

I'm Not Junking

After leaving the dome, Howitzer would break it down. Eric watched as the Junker took apart their camp piece by piece. Each part seemed to be folded into another before it was laid on top of another part. The Dragonfly pilot could only watch as the technologically savvy forager eventually stored away all the pieces into a small pack that was about the same height as the Junker. Though as it seemed the Junker was oddly proportioned. From their head to their torso they seemed to have a normal length to them, but their short legs gave them a shorter appearance. The average Amaroxian was only 139cm. It made Junkers much smaller as a happenstance of having small, robotic legs that carried them around with hurried pitter-patters.

Eric and Howitzer were outside for a short time while the Junker packed. This gave the pilot a chance to look around while the busy tinkerer would work. And though his curiosity was split he was able to get an idea of what kind of place they were in.

All around were towers of discarded steel, abandoned machines, and forgotten construction units. Some piles were rounded, others were flat. It made a twisting, winding highway of parts, springs, bolts, and circuits. The ceiling couldn't be seen through the roof of metal parts, which had tumbled over and created awnings of garbage, woven with meters of forgotten cords and discarded pipes.

He was far from Ikelos by now. He had checked with Tiamat's maps and they were at least one stage down from that place. He wasn't sure if that gang was able to follow or not, but he wouldn't be left with much of a choice beyond moving. He had to keep moving to stay off their radar, but he also had to find his way at least one more stage below and find that station Tiamat had showed him.

"So," Eric watched as Howitzer hoisted their heavy cargo pack on their back and turned their head to look over. "Do you know where the nearest base is?"

"Near?" Howitzer parroted. Their metal legs seemed to lock up and let out a sharp whirring noise. To Eric it sounded like the tiny locomotives were struggling with the weight. After they adjusted themselves, Howitzer laughed. "I wouldn't say close! You're a whole stage away, sure, but sorry to burst your bubble my friend, but there are no roads or tunnels that lead out of Sofu." Reaching up the Junker put their fingers against their goggles and pushed them up, as if they were adjusting it. Once again their eyes seemed to slowly close in, like the shutter of a camera. The numerous small blades within the aperture folded in as the eyes seemed to 'blink' before fanning open once more. "Besides, any stages below this..." They reached up to knock the back of their knuckle against the stomach of Dragonfly's abdominal area.

A metal sound rang out, causing Eric to take a step back in confusion. Lowering his hand to his stomach he would stare in the Junker's direction.

"Did ya hear it?" The Junker stood in front of the suited pilot. They only came up to just below Eric's chest, making the Junker half his size. Eric didn't know what to make of the Junker, but so far they had shown themselves to be a knowledgeable person.

"I didn't hear anything." Unfortunately he didn't know what he was listening for, but he felt the Junker just wanted to pull one over on him by asking. With the way their eyes seemed to brighten up and start to glow.

"Isn't that just like a kid!" Howitzer laughed. "Well do you know which depth you're at right now, without asking your system? It should show somewhere on your heads up display." They pointed out, as to not leave the man hanging. Eric would take a moment and look around his display.

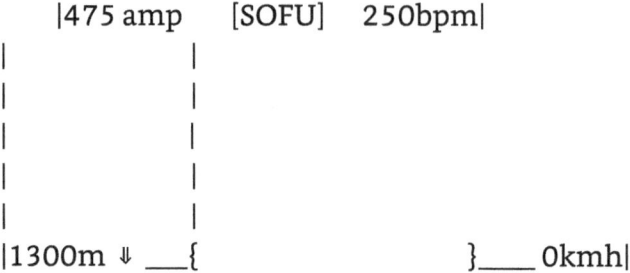

This was the usual menu that Eric saw, but occasionally other system messages popped up that he ended up focusing on. Now that he was more used to seeing the HUD this way he never really bothered to decipher some of the details. Seeing the previous screen he could now understand that some of these were his statistics, but the bottom left and upper left were a mystery to him.

"Well the number here..." Eric pinched the air before spreading his fingers and forcing the menu to focus on the stat. It would pop up in the center of his point of view and expand out the details.

[1300km ⇓ → UM, Spinel Major]

"It says 1300km... U-M..." Eric could easily read what it said, but understanding it was a different matter.

"Incorrect!" Howitzer would whistle, moving to point up. "That is the layer we're at right now. You should have originally been a little above the thousand kilometer mark, but at this stage you've only added a few hundred kilometers to your travel. While going down stages adds to the depth, what it doesn't show is your pressure. The pressure is the reason why we don't have more colonies near the fifteen hundred kilometer mark. You'll be crushed into mash." Howitzer would adjust themselves and tuck their thumbs beneath the straps of their pack. "What you need to be mindful of is the a-m-p. That's the atmospheric pressure. Right now we should be around 470 or 480." Howitzer tilted their head. The sound of rattling could be heard before silence. "475 according to the scans!"

That was a bit surprising; they were able to draw up the exact numbers, but what did that do for him? "And what does that mean exactly? Does it mean it goes up the further down you go?"

The Junker nodded at the question. "With a suit you can handle up to 500! Without it you can be assured you'd be having trouble even standing in front of me. But don't you worry! Ol' Howie has the very thing to help put! Come on!" With a zzzip, the Junker's joints did a jaunty little jump. They would turn and amble down the way.

Eric held out his hand, trying to stop the mechanized man, but they were already speeding along on their little legs. "Why should I trust him?" He was glad the Junker didn't scrap him for parts in his unconscious state, but who knew if they were even capable of it. Still, if he couldn't travel down to the next stage.... "Can they be trusted?"

~dwop~

[Affirmative. Of all Amaroxian entities Junkers have shown themselves to be reliable and completely neutral to the plights of society unless it affects them.]

After confirmation from Tiamat, Eric would decide to follow. He would hurry to keep up with the skittering fellow. As they walked the towers of junk started to become more organized, though not in any easily recognizable way, but Eric could notice the towers had been scattered swaths of trash but now they were more uniformed and straighter. Soon, in the distance, a rain of mechanical noises filled the pilot's ears. It was almost like being in the lab with Elizabeth's busy goons typing away their precious calculations. Voices were soon thrown into the mix and finally he would see awnings of fabric overhead as some of the junk pils became stalls for one Junker to trade some parts. Some used the piles as seats and some worked together to take the discarded refuse and turn them into working machines. Two even appeared to get a clod to get up and move, to which they threw their arms up and cheered.

As Howitzer came into view the other Junkers looked up. They had different cloaks of varying sizes. Some of them had their digitigrade legs visible, the gears in the joints spinning around as they stood. Others had different styles of ventilators and different shapes of goggles. Some of their packs were tall, others were fat, but they had many things in common.

"What's this...?" Eric looked around as many of the Junkers stopped what they were doing and hurried over to the suited pilot. "They're all Howitzers."

Howitzer's eyes within their goggles dimmed a bit as the mechanical eye narrowed as it focused on the Dragonfly. "How rude. We don't all look the same!" They'd complain. But quickly getting over it the Junker stood with their back straight and motioned to the crowd of Junkers. "These guys can help me upgrade your suit! I didn't have all the parts, but together we all will." They'd cheerfully explain. "It'll help you withstand the higher pressure so you can travel to the lower Stages easier without needing an armored vehicle."

Eric looked around as the Junkers surrounded him. The system didn't alert Eric of danger. In fact it had said little since they came into Howitzer's care. Their eyes shifted and blinked under different speeds before all their eyes would brighten up at the same time. The Junkers pounced!

CHAPTER FORTY-FOUR

Begging The Question

"What are you doing?!" Eric found himself quickly overwhelmed with the tinkering hands of the Junkers. Their fingers ran over the body of his suit. Some were pulling his arm down to their levels and others were opening hatches on his chassis that he didn't even know existed. He watched as Howitzer seemed to seat himself in front of him, using some sort of ancient looking mechanical keyboard to type on a screen. Unlike the more modern computers that used a light display to display the data above the work station, these models were thin plates full of nearly microscopic fiber optic cables that lit up the screen in order to show the information. Those screens haven't been used for over fifty years in the industry and were often used by collectors who felt some things needed a 'physical' presence.

"Now calm down and let us work." Howitzer would console the pilot. "You want to go to the stage below, right? Without an amored vehicle or fitted suits it's impossible to travel down." Eric understood his limitation, but that didn't make him comfortable with these people messing with his suit. It was his and he sweated blood and tears being used as an experiment in order to test its worth. After Howitzer's words Eric would relax a little bit.

"Can you at least walk me through what you're doing....?" He was the one wearing the suit, so he wanted to know what was being changed. Howitzer glanced up at Eric, their mechanical eyes widening and shifting its brightness setting.

"Well, first off your armor is too thin." The Junker began. "I can understand that the idea for your suit is speed and being light, seeing as you have some anti-gravity units for flight, but it makes you vulnerable to pressure. We're gunna use some old junk we got to reinforce the support joints inside the chest of the suit. Don't want the metal bending and crushing your heart and lungs! That would be bad." Even with the Amaroxian skeletal structure being so dense, there was only so much pressure they could handle before bones started to break.

"Alright, but just there?" Eric questioned. It made plenty of sense to strengthen the suit, but his arms and legs were exposed. Though the black thermal suit he wore did well to protect him from heat, and being burned at the Geysers, that wasn't going to stop gravity from snapping his limbs like twigs.

"Well, glad you asked!" Howitzer called as they reached out to another Junker beside them who handed them a strange looking roll of, what appeared to be, white glass. They looked to easily unfurl it and walked over to the Dragonfly suit, wrapping it around his leg before cutting the excess with a sharp tool that made quick work of the thin sheet.

"What is it?" Try as he might Eric couldn't figure out what it was. He reached down to touch the white surface. Tapping his fingers against he would be greeted with a metal sound. "Huh? It isn't synthetic?" He had thought it was some sort of thin glass used in decoration, but when they unfolded it he had a new array of wonder as to what it was. "It's hard."

"But flexible!" Howitzer added. "This is a type of flexible metal they don't really make anymore as silver-steel has taken over most of the space for things like old steel, or titanium. But the major problem with silver-steel is that it bends under high pressures so while perfect for construction projects because it bends and is non-conductive, it is a time saver, but too much of it and it becomes heavy. This stuff, if installed correctly, can act to redistribute pressure to its connecting points. So as long as it touches these two points of your suit, it will protect your legs from the enormous pressures of the next stage." He would explain. "It's called polycarbon ditanium. It used to be used on old space faring vessels before we came underground."

After a moment the Junkers moved to solder the pieces to his suit. He could still bend his legs with the way they installed it, but when heat was applied to it the metal turned silver, almost invisible as it became so mirror-esque that it easily reflected the environment. The Junkers continued to use their collective items to refit the outer portion of the suit, making sure that everything was looked over as to make sure that no piece was left exposed to create a break in the sound restructreneering of the suit's upgrade.

"Amazing..." Eric looked himself over. The suit had changed from its original faint, green-blue color to a more audacious magenta and bronze. "You changed it."

Howitzer stood with their people, their hands folded behind their back as they stood with their chest proudly held out. "We only changed the outer look. All of the modifications were accepted by Tiamat. All she would need to do is send her NERVS through the body and completely synchronize with the changes."

"Nerves? The suit has nerves?" Eric questioned. "I thought these were all surface changes?"

"Not nerves, NERVS, network electronic rerouting ventricle system. It's something these types of AI can do. They can take and reroute their electrical systems through any hollow space between machines connected to their network." Howitzer tickered over on their legs and tapped the chestplate of the Dragonfly. "They were designed with this originally to allow new systems to be quickly integrated or other AI to merge into a unit without the need for time wasted on reprogramming. If we had to put this on you without the NERVS, it would have taken at least a day, including three reboots." They held up their fingers to indicate the number. "So hopefully you'll enjoy the hassle free upgrade!" They would hold out their hand, offering it to Eric.

One reboot was bad enough, but three?! Could he even survive that many reboots were the system to need it? No, he should be thankful, he moved to step forward and take Howitzer's extended hand, but when their hands met he would freeze, realizing something. "Are the NERVS those wires in my Cerebrocable?" He reached to the back of his head where a dark cord, almost ten centimeters thick protruded from the back of his skull and into the spinal groove in the chest piece.

"Oh, you realized?" Howitzer nodded and looked over to the other Junkers who worked to unroll a long length of black cable, while two others stood beneath it to lift it up. "This is the NERVS system, though without an electrical signal and AI to route the data all it is is optic cable. An AI like Tiamat can take control of the Cerebrocables and move them through other machines, including people."

Howitzer would reach down and grab the end of their cloak before lifting it. They would expose the central cavity of their body. There a ball of Cerebrocables coiled around like a writhing nest of driger, connected to a number of organs shielded under tempered aluminosilicate glass.

"I don't get it," Eric looked shocked by the sight. It was like Howitzer was a person infected by a machine instead of a person who had willingly changed their body parts out due to the Mugenes sickness. "Are you .... Amaroxian?"

The Junker's eyes brightened as their mechanical eye slit folded in a way that looked like an arch curved up towards the ceiling. They were smiling. "I told you already. We're Junkers. We've been around a long time, probably since before the Amaroxians. You could say we're the original inhabitants of the planet. But enough about us. I think you and Tiamat are ready to go to the Stage below." Howitzer took a few, quick steps back and pointed out down the intricate path built between the towers of junk. "You can make your way into the

Tunnel Strelitzia that's past Pardes. It's the one connected to here. Pardes is through Ganeden, but it isn't a tunnel per say, it's more of a door."

"A door...?" Eric questioned.

Howitzer would nod. "Most tunnels meet a certain threshold in meters before they're considered Tunnels, but Ganeden is a door because it leads to Pardes without crossing any Stage or breaching the thousand meter mark. Oh, and here!" Howitzer collected a small box from one of their compatriots and would turn to present it to Eric. The box was about palm sized in length but it was a few centimeters thick, making Eric wonder what was inside, but Howitzer didn't leave him hanging too long. "Some nutrient blocks. I'm sure you're hungry after being in there for so long. Just be sure never to eat more than two in a day. It isn't good for an Amaroxian's system." Handing off the box their eyes seemed to brighten up to their max. "Be sure to come by again if you ever need some repairs. As for me, maybe I'll see you on the road! Us Junkers never really stay to one spot very long, but we're kind of fond of Sofu." They'd admit.

CHAPTER FORTY-FIVE

Misdirected Vision

With his suit now upgraded for the next stage and his direction set, the Dragonfly pilot would make his way through the winding paths that were carved through the tall columns that seemed to dot the horizon, as if they alone were holding up the stone ceilings he could no longer see so far down this stage. Underfoot the ground seemed to crunch or crackle as he stepped across thin layers of debris that seemed to occasionally break up the monotonous pathway.

The tap of his footsteps worked well to distract him from the distant sight. To some the boundary of the land and ceiling looked peaceful, but it was a reminder that they were trapped down here and would eventually be eaten away by the disease. While the Junkers were a reprieve from the troubles of reality, one couldn't help but wonder what would become of the Amaroxians? On this side of the hemisphere it was not only illegal to augment oneself, but it was also viewed as blasphemous. The religious doctrine of Sol had a strong control over Amaroxians who lived in the Northern Hemisphere. The Military were exempt from the law because it was seen as their duty. They could not defeat the enemy without using the enemy's own weapons against them.

But the Pharyst and Roxoid of the Southern Hemisphere weren't always seen as enemies. It wasn't until the Conyard Incident that they were seen as betrayers of the faith. But what was that faith doing for them? All Eric could think about was how every day they got sicker and he could only watch as his younger brother was consumed by this seemingly unstoppable sickness.

Eric would come to a stop. He noticed a strange

notification on his system.

[Warning] [Warning]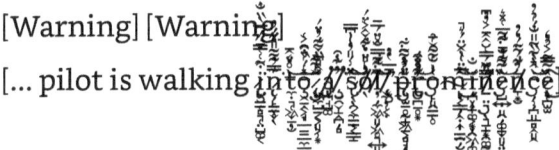
[... pilot is walking into a self prominence]

As the text began to twist and glitch Eric felt something hot on the back of his neck. Dropping to a knee he would gasp out, letting the searing pain pass. All the while his visor began to display strange images, moving scenes from, what he could only assume were Tiamat's database. First he saw a close up image of a man, as if his face was right up against the screen. They pulled back only to show they had a metal face with two eyes blinking behind the openings. There was a faint voice recording, but he couldn't make it out. In the next flash of images Eric would see a number of containment cells, something he was all too familiar with, having spent a year in one on the prison base, but these cells all looked empty. The images jumped from one unit to another, before landing on an occupied cell. But before he could make it out the image faded to black and vanished entirely. As the pain receded he realized he was regaining control of the system.

"Tiamat, are you there?" He'd call, only for his visor to become operational again and Eric was freed from the dark field of view he'd been staring at for the last few minutes.

[Connection with Pilot restored.]

At this Eric was confused. He hadn't lost connection. For some reason everything had gone haywire. "Hey," he called. "What happened? Did the Junkers break something?"

[Negative. No systems were tampered with during upgrade.]

"Then why did my visor start showing me strange images?" He'd question. "And what do you mean 'reconnected'?"

[Due to atmospheric disturbances this system lost connection with the user for exactly 0.04 seconds before connection was restored. As far as my data shows there was no link with the user and the visor was offline for the same amount of time.]

"I'm not making it up! I saw something there on the screen!" Of course there wasn't a need to shout at the system. It wasn't as if it was calling him a liar. It could only express facts it could read in its data. He took a moment to relax and pushed to stand. He would continue walking. "Nevermind." He'd brush aside. "I'm sure it's there -- we'll look later. Right now I need to find this door."

[Affirmative. Door Ganeden as described by Junkers is located 42m to the south. Continuing on this path will put you on the route.]

Eric sighed at the distance calculations given to him. It wasn't that walking forty-two meters was difficult, but all this walking was getting to be problematic. How was he going to reach the capital on foot? He had to rest, though luckily Tiamat had the system information. It shouldn't be hard to find his way. That would remind him. Looking to his left he raised his hand to pinch his finger in the air and spread his digits in order to expand the menu over the area name. This opened up a map that the system had and he could see where he was and the routes he needed to take. But he was surprised to see much of the map wasn't filled out and it was black.

"What is all this? These dark spots? Can you not see them?"

[Negative. Pilot can visibly see the structures in the distance, but I am prevented from scanning them, disallowing detailed visualization of what is located there. The Junkers are preventing any scans over their land.]

"Is that possible?" He didn't think anything could stop Tiamat's system seeing as it was directly plugged into the mainframe of the Capital.

[Negative. This system can be limited by the Junker's advanced control of data.]

It was that simple it seemed. But Eric felt that there was more to it than that. "Can you elaborate?"

[Negative. Data not yet accessible.]

While he would rather disagree with that, he felt that there was no way they would lie. He had seen it himself earlier in the day. There were some menu settings he couldn't read. They looked corrupted. He didn't have time to really delve into the matter. Right now his focus was the door and according to the map it was straight along the path in clear view. There were no rocks, towers, or anything obstructing his approach. As he continued along he came to a stop, seeing a warning in the corner of his visor again, but this time it was one he was familiar with.

[Warning, enemy detected.]

The loud revving of vehicles caught his ears. Turning his head he would spot what appeared to be a massive, armored truck. The truck was speeding through the path he had just come from and roared to a stop.

The trucks looked to be modified all terrain vehicles. They had heavy plates that covered the usually naked sides of the trucks. They were welded into place and had massive wheels that looked to have been reinforced. Their wheels were gigantic non-pneumatic tires that weren't affected by pressure and wouldn't go flat if punctured. While these were usually the preferred wheels of most vehicles, military vehicles tended to use metal wheels which withstood most terrain and damage and weren't likely to wear down easily.

From the top of the truck a hatch would open, revealing a heavily armored figure. Eric took a step back, hearing two more vehicles coming up towards him. He could feel the figure staring at him and would then point out towards the Dragonfly.

"I don't care if you have to run that bastard over! Get him and peel him out of that gear!" The figure called. By the large red, X shapes marked on the trucks he could guess that it was the gang he had seen earlier. They seemed perfectly prepared for the lower stages. Had they made these adjustments on their own or had the Junkers helped them? Eric felt it was best not to sit around and find out.

[Initiating Pulser Units]

Eric had taken only one step back and would feel the small units on his back, which were connected to his wing slats, start to generate energy. The pilot turned on his heel and took off running down his route. He could hear the trucks quickly rev up and start speeding after him.

"I didn't give up on you boy! I'll take that suit even if I gotta rip your broken corpse out of it! It'd be easier on all of us if you just give up!" The group commander called. In truth chasing him wasted resources, but the suit that he wore was a marvel of engineering that was well worth the use of their supplies. If they caught him they were looking at a major upgrade to their ranks with his suit alone. "We're not gunna let a second gen suit get away from us, are we boys?" He tapped the top of his truck and it would speed onward. The leader tucked back into the hatch and closed it behind him.

Inside he rode with his driver. The other two vehicles each had two men. With all three they would tear across the junk fields and run straight towards the suit.

"Let's see him run away from us now. That door's too small for him to out maneuver us!" Koper leaned forward and flipped a switch on the console. "And we have these to blow out his vision..." On the screen there appeared to be a numeric value counting up as, outside the vehicle, on the front, two headlights seemed to be humming. The headlights were connected with numerous cables and looked a mess of modification, but it would serve the rebels well.

The other two vehicles hit their switches and the members of the caravan dropped shaded visors over their eyes.

CHAPTER FORTY-SIX

Activating A Pulse

Eric was quickly able to cross the distance. With his Pulser systems activated it made the suit much lighter and capable of crossing meters with great ease and haste. Soon the towers of junk began to take the recognizable shapes of buildings. They looked to be completely rusted over, some with synthetic fabric banners racing across which were used to catch moisture. He could even see the well below that the water was filtered down into and collected. It was similar to the fog collector that they had at the old farms. It was the only way to produce large enough amounts of water from the atmosphere to farm. Was this an active colony before? The Junkers said it was called Sofu.

The buildings were 100m tall with great balconies at each window of each floor. Standing on top of the building appeared to be some sort of old antenna that ran cables across each building. Though he was sure these cables were no longer used by people, he could see critters scuttling along the wire. Red rats, large hairless rodents that have become versatile in the Amaroxian environment. Nothing stops them from entering an area, not even metal walls. Each building had smooth ground drawn around its perimeter. It was something Eric had never seen. Most of the modern colony buildings are built atop the land they were set on, without alterations. Most of the boulders, rocks, and metal stones were difficult to remove and left as they were. It took too many resources, too much time... But here the entire land looks to have been cultivated. There were few hills and all the paths were connected.

"But if they have a city, with prefab buildings -- why don't they live in them?" Despite his curiosity Eric didn't waste time and stepped around the large buildings. Having seen the map he took notice that even if he couldn't see the dark spots on the heads up display, he could see them with his own eyes.

Across the courtyards of the building was land which appeared unmanaged. This meant that there were stones and precipices that littered the landscape between the buildings. He wasn't sure why the Junkers didn't want such broken land being scanned, but this was better for him. He could cut across the grounds and get himself to the door before they can catch him.

He hurried. Jumping over the threshold he would land on the lip of a stonewall. Looking back the trucks seemed to hit into them without a second thought. The engines seemed to struggle, but they pushed. The machines seemed to roar louder and louder until they made it over the walls and slammed into the ground.

The trucks didn't slow down. In fact one of them sped up and started to catch up to Eric. The pilot had an easy time with the obstacles thanks to his Pulser unit. The device gave off a faint, blue glow that only seemed to brighten up with every push. Eventually the truck sped forward and slammed into a wall, nearly hitting Eric. He pushed his hand against the side of the vehicle and used the momentum to push back. The wing slats on his back spread out, allowing the energy of the Pulser to disperse and give him a measure of lift. He was able to jump back several inches before landing on the uneven surface of the ground.

"We have you now little man!" He heard their leader's voice blare over the intercom of the truck before the pilot hurried up and over the vehicle, clambering across its surface before sliding across the top.

Jumping a distance he would land and run towards the threshold of the door. The door was a grand archway reinforced with stone bricks and metal facets. Eric stepped through and ran, the end of the door visible even without the system's visor. He could see the other side with ease. It was dark, but he saw the faint glow of light that showed it was, at one point, occupied.

Koper leaned down over the console so he could see out the front port of the truck. He could see as the Dragonfly approached the opening and entered. It was their opportunity to catch the little bug in their net! Reaching down to grab the comms he would squeeze down on the side buttons.

"Ah, ah, ah! It's time you got a taste of our gift!" Koper laughed and motioned his head. The driver flipped the switch. With a loud buzz and click the headlights turned on. A bright, blinding white light filled the door space. White light was not a color of light Amaroxian eyes could handle, nor could any of the underground residents see this way. This kind of light was poisonous, damaging and it was known to burn the skin and eyes.

Though Eric's back was to the truck the light would reflect off of all the present surfaces and bombard the Amaroxian's eyes with a sudden burst of light. "Augh!" Eric's eyes rolled to the back of his head, his legs swiftly losing strength from the sudden, painful shock to his system. "Tiamat!"

[Warning! Warning! Switching modes!]

Eric had stumbled to the floor, his forehead pressed into the ground with his arms wrapped around his head. He rapidly inhaled and exhaled out of his mouth. The pain caused him to tremble. He could hear his heartbeat swimming between his ears and the blood rushing through his head. His nose was watering and his mind was spinning. As he blinked his eyes clear he found himself staring at the floor, but it wasn't bright.

[Visor darkness has been increased by 75%.]

Letting his eyes adjust from the painful assault, the visor was indeed darkened to allow for him to see. But as he was finally able to push to his feet he would find that the trucks had all surrounded him. Each of their headlights were pointed down at him, but by the sounds of the machines humming, it took a lot of power to keep them active. He would even notice the way they struggled to remain active and the occasional crackles of the electrical systems as they fought to keep up with the demand of power.

The hatch of the more abhorrently marked vehicles would open. Though they all seemed to share a fair amount of branding, the truck ridden by the leader was far more loudly painted with inks. It was easy to make red inks with the abundant color in the soils, but among their colors there was some gold that he could recognize on the silver body.

"Well, well. Looks like we caught ourselves our bogey!" Koper shouted. He looked to be wearing a full bodied suit. It was bulky and looked like it was pieced together using unshaped metal. "Pin him down!" At his command the other hatches on top of the remaining trucks popped open and one by one his men would crawl out. They all had similar patchwork suits and were heavily armed with weapons directly attached to their units. They would jump down off from the vehicles and approach the lone Dragonfly. Two stood behind Eric, two in front of him, with Koper and his driver near the truck. "Surprised you haven't thrown up in your helmet yet with the bright lights!" But when the words left Koper's mouth he hesitated. "Look out!"

But it was too late for him to warn his men. The Pulser unit on his back suddenly lit up and began to make his back glow with the vibrant, blue light. The two closest to Eric were slammed into when he charged the unit and dashed to the right in an instant. The men were thrown back with a surprised shout as Eric drove his elbow into them. What Eric wasn't sure of was how they recognized him with his armor changed like this. It didn't make sense that they were able to find him and catch up, but if they were free rebels that knew their way around the underground there were probably many things they knew how to do that he couldn't begin to fathom. They were prepared to come down this stage almost as quickly as he was.

What was going on?! He shouldn't be able to move like that. "Shit!" Koper shouted. "Don't be caught unawares! Watch yourselves!" Hoisting his weapon up to rest on his hip. Pulling the trigger the hand cannon would hum with a low energy before it let loose a blast towards the Dragonfly.

~beep beep~

The system quickly warned Eric of the heat signature behind him and he would strafe to the left, evading the blast which ended up hitting into the side of the door, ripping steel from it as if a stone was thrown into wet paper. The Dragonfly took a step to even his stance out and shot a look in Koper's direction. The long, mechanical tail-like appendage that hung from the suit would curl and stiffen, anchoring him against the ground as the Pulser unit on his back began to quietly hum. The particles from the system rapidly carried through the length of his arm, his palm starting to glow blue. The pilot held out his hand and would return fire as a blast of blue-white energy erupted from his palm.

[Pulse Blaster, activated]

CHAPTER FORTY-SEVEN

Amaroxian Stand-Off

The blast from the Dragonfly's palm ripped towards its target with such force that the very air seemed to tremble. The reavers pulled back, the force tangible even through their suits. A few of the headlights on the vehicles began to burst before going out completely. The vibrations raced with such abandon that the flimsy connections to the base of the lights came undone with a vigorous snap, many of the loose wires fraying while others were torn to unrecoverable shreds.

Everything seemed to calm after the Pulser blast ended. Only two lights remained. The one on Koper's truck managed to survive and the other looked to barely be maintaining hold on its vehicle and hung by the very cables feeding it power. Koper was shocked, to say the least. The display only fueled his desire. The suit was capable of firing a weapon without having to carry a cannon or a rifle! This thing was beyond priceless!

"B-boss..." The voice of one of his men called him from his shocked awe. Snapping his head toward his companion he was stunned.

The men all wore full bodied suits that were modified in such a way that their frames were doubled in weight and density. It would take even the most experienced mechanic to peel it apart. They were capable of taking one or two hits from cannon fire before needing to retreat. It was why they weren't worried about damaging the Dragonfly.

Instead it took one hit from the pilot's suit to rip a hole through not only the heavily armored unit, but the blast bore into one of the trucks. The shot man fell to his knees and died on the spot. The truck had also become a useless, smoldering pile. The components were ripped to ribbons and the vehicle itself was now structurally unsound.

Eric was also startled by the unbridled destruction the attack had created in the span of a second. But he wasn't about to relinquish the advantage he just gained. Even if he didn't know how he triggered the attack, he quickly turned his open palm to his aggressors.

"Enough!" Eric bellowed. "How did you even find me!?"

Koper held up his hands in surrender. Seeing as the lights weren't working on him and the man had enough firepower to take out not only one of their armored suits, but a truck, it was best to play nice for now and spare him from losing anymore resources.

"Now, now it's all just a misunderstanding. You know how it is!" Koper would smile beneath his mask, but even if Eric couldn't see his face, he could hear the smug grin in his voice.

And it pissed him off.

"Misunderstanding my ass!" The Dragonfly pilot shouted. "I won't ask again! How did you find me?!" Eric was top dog now. With a weapon that tears through the insurgents with no effort.

"Tsk." A tongue click rumbled through Koper's helmet. "Last time we met we managed to scan your system's signature. A handy trick to find suits we like or keep away from the Military, you dig?" That explained that at the very least. "Now come on, you don't seem like a Military type. How come you're running around in such a nice piece?" They moved to lower their hands and step forward, but Eric shifted his hand up towards Koper's head, forcing the men to step back.

"This suit is mine!" Eric made it clear. "Not the Military's, not the Science Corps, mine! And it's my ticket to freedom." Though that last part was seeming harder and harder to obtain.

"Oh, is that all you want?" Koper slowly lowered his hands. "And so do we. After all that little outfit you're wearing was made by the government. I don't know how you got it, but so long as the Military complex has control of the system none of us will ever truly be free."

That was something Eric understood and could see. It was the Military police who had taken them from their home for crimes they didn't even commit. Eric would lower his hand slightly. With his life somewhat off the line Koper carefully moved to remove his weapon and place it on the ground.

"The name's Koper. I'm part of the Red Rebels. At least that's what the Military likes to call us... in actuality we're freedom fighters."

Eric glanced over to the side to engage his system.

~dwop~

[Affirmative. The Red Rebel army are recognized secessionists that prioritize values that encourage acts that resist governmental control over society.]

"Is Koper a recognized member?" He'd ask aloud.

Koper and his men looked between one another. "Course, friend. I'm a knight in the Insurgency."

[Affirmative. Koper is a known member of the Red Rebels and is infamous for retrofitting suits to work with new users.]

That information was shocking. As far as Eric knew, once a suit's user died a new one could not be used due to the brain's biometrics being burned into the machine's data. Wiping that data permanently damaged the suit.

Luckily the rebels couldn't hear Tiamat as the system responded in his ear, but he couldn't ask it questions without them hearing. He still didn't trust them.

"Hey now, how about a truce?" Koper motioned his head,

ordering his men to cut off the remaining lights. Turning off the lights was beneficial for them as well because the heat they were beginning to generate was starting to become uncomfortable in the heavy suits. "Since you're not a Military dog and you want freedom."

But Eric's heard that before. Untrusting he would once again raise his hand. "I've had enough promises of Freedom be broken!" Once was enough. "What makes you think I'll trust you just like that!?" Eric had every right to be cautious after being chased through a damn Geyser Field!

Koper hated to admit the man was right. He tried hunting him down like a driger. But he wasn't too sure how to convince him if he couldn't show him. He looked Eric's suit up and down.

"The Junkers." Koper spoke up. "You can ask the Junkers about us. They'll tell you how it is!" It was true that the Junkers had helped Eric, but it also looks like the group of tinkerers helped Koper and his crew.

He couldn't be sure though. Eric motioned his head in an upward nod to point. "Did they do that work for you?"

Koper looked at his trucks. He moved to put his arms on his hips. "We did these ourselves!!" He proudly claimed. "As you know we collect old Military suits. There's an abandoned base a Stage below we sometimes hit. You were just a lucky find!" He'd laugh, but by the way Eric threateningly motioned his weaponized hand, he wasn't as amused. "Right, right. Sorry pal. Go on." Koper encouraged.

Eric quickly moved his hand down and his Pulser unit would charge again, this time within 0.02 seconds and turned Koper's weapon to dust. The rebels had all jumped back, having seen what it had done earlier. The power move quickly showed Koper his place. The man inclined his head and held up his hands in defeat as he stepped back to let Eric through.

The pilot would indeed return to The Junkers. Koper and his gang remained near the Ganeden door. The Junkers returned to their usual way of life. A number of them could be seen foraging the piles of junk, picking about the array of debris and other material visible on the ground. Others worked to meticulously stack the found materials into the ever growing towers.

"Back so soon lad?" Howitzer's familiar whistle rang from somewhere above his head.

Turning around to look, his visor — having returned to a normal view — scanned around the piles, but found it difficult to pick out Howitzer from the surrounding mess. With a sharp click the Junker dropped from the tower he was working on and landed in front of Eric.

The Dragonfly was taken aback, but settled. He would clear his throat. " Do you know anything about the Red Rebels? Specifically a man named Koper."

"Aye, I do. Why do you ask?" Howitzer looked up at him in a way that made him feel they knew exactly what he meant... but they would explain anyway. " Ah, those boys." They laughed. "Rowdy bunch, but as they said they don't get along with the Military! As for trustin' them... I'd suggest you talk to Rozlin, though those others call her Roxanne. She's in the Capital. She does a lot of work in the red-light district. Her, you can trust." Howitzer would explain while fiddling with a handful of junk, seemingly shaping something new.

"Who is she?" Eric wondered. "To the rebels anyway."

"Oh you can think of her like their mom and the Capital her junkyard. They greet her first thing and ask before they do anything in her yard!"

So he had a goal. That was good. "Do I have to watch my back with them? They've been trying to rip my suit right off my back!"

"Oh well if they're agreeing to parley, they certainly will. They're opportunists like us Junkers though. As long as you don't die along the way you should be fine!"

"... wow, thanks." Eric flatly offered. "Comforting."

"You bet!" Howitzer laughed.

CHAPTER FORTY-EIGHT

Resources Of Different Sizes

Eric had a lot to consider. Though he had been separated from Klaus the two brothers had been determined to get back home, but to do so meant crossing Argatha, the capital's Chamber. According to the maps he had from Tiamat's system he was a far, far way with numerous Tunnels and Chambers with incomplete or partial scans. Beyond Sofu was the Chamber known as Pardes, but the map he had downloaded from Tiamat's database drew no name over the region and marked it as a forbidden zone known as a Badland. In fact the next three Chambers were all labeled in the same way. Badlands were regions in Amaroxia that were dangerous to travel because they had no terraforming, no resources, and no access. But that is where the Junkers were sending them.

"Oh come on~!" Koper chuckled from the top of his truck as he leaned against the roof while standing outside of the hatch. "We said sorry!" After talking with the Junkers the Dragonfly's pilot was able to confirm that the reaving rebels could be temporarily trusted. He just had to make sure he kept up his act and worked to maintain a sense of authority among the insurgents. The remaining member of the destroyed truck boarded the vehicle with Koper and this would leave Eric traveling with two of the Red Rebel trucks and five of the entourage's members, but he wasn't riding in their vehicles. The man didn't trust enough for that. Instead he was seated on the front of the truck, his back leaning against the hood, beside the main port.

"We're just traveling together. I don't have an interest in helping you, but I will hear you out when we arrive at the capital. I'm not here to make friends." And he wasn't! He didn't care about other Amaroxians and their turmoil. Everyone was dealing with the same disease, the same degradation, and the same dying world. Eric was just someone trying to find their way home. "Did you get my map?" He had sent what he felt was safe to send to them, which was just a road map heading out from Sofu and through to Pardes.

Koper leaned back and looked down into the hatch. "Orville?"

Sitting in the main seat was a man in a full suit, but beneath that suit was an Arglion, a rather alien entity when compared to the average Amaroxian. They had tall bodies and thin limbs with long heads that had an extended proboscis, akin to an anteater. His suit reflected some of these traits but they were a bipedal hominid so that was all that mattered to rebels. The Arglion nodded and reached out to pull down a screen that sat above his seat. He swiped his covered hand over the plate of glass to change the view. It went from showing their current route to zooming out to show the available map.

"Yeah, once we pass Ganeden we'll be in Pardes, though I ain't never seen the map like this. It's actually showing the three humps so it'll be easier to avoid." He tapped his finger along the bottom of Pardes' region. It was only slightly larger than Sofu but rather than Sofu's circular chamber, Pardes' chamber was more rectangular in shape. Along the bottom edge that Orville concerned over were three dips with two narrow lengths of impenetrable rock dividing the space.

Eric stayed leaning back on the vehicle, staring up, but focusing on his visor. He zoomed in on Pardes, but couldn't quite understand what Orville was looking at. "These three, sequential spaces at the bottom before the Tunnel?" The dips became progressively smaller until it led into the Tunnel Strelitzia. "I don't see the issue."

"The problem is..." Koper pulled himself out of the hatch and would sit at the edge as the small caravan made its ways towards the door. "That entire area's full of driger nests. A lot are old abandoned nests since the buggers ate all the nutrients outta the soil, but there's still plenty of spots that they've managed to keep from draining." Eric glanced up towards Koper without moving his head.

"I see..." But Eric had difficulty believing what the man had said. From what he understood driger returned the consumed nutrients to the soil in their excrement and created a sort of cycle that altered the makeup of the surrounding minerals. When driger could no longer find the minerals they preferred to move on. Nests tended to move every few years, but what he was saying was that these particular driger are destroying that area. "What kind of driger are they?"

"Porthos." Koper responded, which caused Eric to sit up. "They're some kind of new species that showed up a bit after the disease started spreading. Some folk think they mutated from Miller driger because of their eating habits."

Except that wasn't the whole truth. Porthos driger had always been a problem in the farmlands. They were small and manageable at the time, but there had been an explosion in their numbers one season and while some think it correlated with the release of Mugenes, farmers could tell you that it had to do with a new mineral fertilizer that doubled farmer's yield. It was an expensive product at the time, but those who could afford it started seeing Porthos double their size and with thicker armor that looked like diamond. This was because much of the formula was made with synthetic diamonds.

"Well it's easy to spot an active nest," Eric noted. Growing up on the farm it was easy to figure out where active nests were just by the way the soil was disturbed and how dry it was. "We'll just avoid them." Drigers only ever came up to eat or excrete and if they were Porthos they would do anything they could to stay underground, but they were also highly territorial and fought with other driger for space. They were a violent bunch.

"Well that's half our problem." Koper would note. "That entire area is reputed to be a Driger graveyard. Nothing but their partially decayed corpses litter the ground making it difficult to see the soil. To boot there are scavengers out there that mine the driger's skeletons for their mineral resources and sell them for mint at a city or underground market." It was particularly problematic because digging around the grounds created vibrations that would make a driger think there was a rival nearby and summon them from below. "Scavengers are also pretty territorial and will kill others if they think you're trying to muscle in on their prospect." He looked over to Eric. "But that shouldn't be a problem for our little turbo charged cannon here!"

Eric turned his head up towards Koper as he sat up. "I would rather avoid confronting a driger, even if these may not be as big as Perovskite Driger." Not that much of anything was. Koper shrugged. He wasn't sure how big Perovskite Drigers were, but he knew Porthos were hearty and made it difficult to cross that pass.

"We've been through that area before, but never easily. This is the first time we've even seen a map that didn't label the region as Deadlands. You must have jacked an old map." Koper stood up as the trucks neared the door. The small lights on the sides of the vehicle were a deep red and allowed them to see without blinding themselves or disturbing any creatures that called the Tunnel home. Abandoned Tunnels like this didn't often get extermination teams running to it to clear it out of the red rats or venomous aardvarks. "We'll see though won't we?" Koper nodded and became quiet.

Crossing Tunnels that weren't maintained regularly was dangerous. They had already caused a ruckus earlier and could have already stirred hibernating creatures. Living underground wasn't easy so it was not uncommon for more predatory beasts to fall into deep hibernations to be able to survive. Lunar bears were some of the more dangerous examples of this. They could survive on anything and had grotesque appetites. They would often hunt and kill driger on a whim and were some of the more feared inhabitants of Tunnels. They were tidy and carved out so the Lunar bears, who usually dug their own burrows, didn't have to commit to a lick of work.

Soon Eric and his company were able to cross Ganeden without an issue. There didn't appear to be any creatures hiding out, hopefully scared off by the Dragonfly's earlier destructive attack. Stepping out into the Pardes chamber the gang and Dragonfly were met with a hellish landscape of ruined machines, twisted metal and the arching, half-decayed outer skeletal shells of driger. Porthos started off quite small and the mineral they fed on would contribute to the growth of their shells. In the case of these Porthos they appeared to have metallic shells from their diets of silver-steel and other metals that looked to be abundant in the area. Eric would slowly stand from his place and look around. The soft sound of metal hitting metal could be heard as scavengers worked to mine their goods. The scavenger camps littered Pardes with tarp tents and overloaded vehicles. The scavengers were heavily armed and looked to have partial suits with hefty ventilators over their heads. There were a few Junker foraging, but no one seemed to mind them. What did seem to trigger the scavengers was when others got near their camps.

What stood out most to Eric was the landscape itself. It looked exactly like his recurring nightmare... even the sky was a deep red here due to dislodged topsoil being thrown into the atmosphere.

CHAPTER FORTY-NINE

Jumping The Rocket

Unlike the Junkers the scavengers weren't a group of people, or even a collective with common likes. They were not a community, but were more like savage beasts that picked apart flesh until it was nothing but gnawed bone. Scavengers had no honor, but in the badlands they needed none. They survived and did what needed to be done. They wore whatever they could in terms of gear. Sometimes it was old suits that were rusted to constant disrepair, other times they were suits cobbled together by questionable mechanics in the underground markets. The markets themselves were well known by disreputable people. Their kind smuggled goods that were often tightly controlled by the government. Their supplies sometimes came from scavengers who would fish up old military bases, sometimes it would come from members of the Science Corps struggling for funding, but more often than not the goods came directly from the military itself. Ranked officers, low level guards, who want more than the measly handful of credits that could barely afford Vox.

Vox was the vice. It was the only medicine, the only drug known, that could diminish the painful side effects of the Mugenes disease. It was a costly remedy, but one that was only temporary. Eventually its effects wore off and they needed more. The pain grew progressively worse as the disease spread until one felt nothing at all...

It was a usual day for the scavengers. Vultures working hard to pick up the pieces left behind by others. Some focused on uncovering the old ruins that littered Pardes. From what had been uncovered so far one could see that, through the quarries of red sand and stone, stood great buildings that were deep below the natural line of the stage.

A stage's line was determined by the layers of stone and mineral found within the chamber. Whatever used to stand in Pardes was at least three levels, or 91m, below the Chamber ground's stage. Ladders and a maze of scaffolding were woven through the deep quarries. Some scavengers have made temporary bands to make digging easier and shorten the time, but others were too stubborn. These men were driven to keep anything they found for themselves even if more time was spent, they would often keep their prospects mere feet from another's. They were armed to the teeth and aggressively watched for any sign of intrusion. Sometimes hyper vigilance led to dangerous shootouts that caused damage to multiple sites.

When the two marked trucks tore through the encampments along the worn down paths that were dug out by the regular back and forth from the scavenger's vehicles, heads turned. Koper stood atop his truck with a leg perched on the roof while the other was gripped against the short ladder inside. His arms were crossed over his chest confidently. Eric was sitting with his legs hanging off the hood as he watched the camps pass them by. Each camp had its own personality. Some were a bit shabby with a few tools packed up near a water station that was shared by the groups. Others were off on their own while they prospected small claims no bigger than two people. It was then he spotted it. Among the Junkers perched on the piles discarded by the scavengers was a curious form. Though, to Eric, this Junker looked like all the others, except for one key point: they had a tail.

Sitting about the same height as Howitzer they looked to be wearing a dark green cloak with a pair of blue gloves that dutifully worked on a piece of scrap. Their ventilator seemed to be a whole mask that covered their head and their legs decorated with wire. But, unlike the other Junker, this one appeared to have a long, animal-like tail protruding from the cloak. It was fatter near the bottom and became thinner as it stretched out. It was a little longer than the length of their body with the end curled over their head with a lantern hanging from it, lighting their work.

In fact the Junker wasn't the only one with strange features that stood out. What few that he did notice were because they weren't all in suits. Some wore the heavy suits needed to withstand the pressure of the next stage, but others looked to be wearing little more than tattered cloaks and stained shawls. Between the rips and tears in the fabric Eric was able to see signs of extreme Mugenes mutations. In a few short years, maybe weeks, these people would be overtaken by the disease.

"That's an interesting suit you have there." The familiar whirr of mechanisms clicked by his side. Eric would startle and look over. It seems he attracted some attention. Clinging to the side of the truck was the tailed Junker. "Looks modified. Howitzer's work?" They held out their hand. "Name's Rocket." The Junker didn't give Eric time to reply with their rapid fire chatter.

"Hey!" Koper shouted. "Get off the truck!" He moved to shoo them away, but to no avail. The Junker adjusted their backpack, which was piled high with scrap. Their tiny legs skittered across the hood before they sat crouched in front of the main port.

"Nice truck!" The small, almost tiny looking Junker chirped. "Willing to trade for it?" They didn't wait for an answer and dropped their pack onto the hood of the moving truck. " Listen I have some old Cerebrocords, switches, Vox, and extra chips for--"

"Wait, you carry Vox?" Eric looked over to the Junker who held up a vial. "How... ?"

"Don't listen to that one." Koper warned. "She's always

trying to sell off her unsold stock on folk!"

"What do you mean 'she'?!" The Junker stomped their little mechanical foot against the metal hood. "I am obviously a 'them'!" Koper would sigh and rub his hand over his visor.

"Listen you, do you think we look like those muties?" Koper motioned to the scavengers out in the fields.

Eric turned his head to follow Koper's arm. Isn't that where they'd all be soon enough?

"Ye of little faith!" Rocket stood with their back straight. "Even if you Amaroxians haven't mutated yet, you will. Why not take Vox and prevent it? Not everyone dies from it if treated!"

"You rotten--!" Koper moved to jump from the roof hatch towards Rocket. Their name was not for show it seemed. The Junker grabbed and leapt back with such speed Eric missed them. "Scam artist..." Koper looked over to Eric as the vehicle came to a stop. "Ignore that one. She thinks Vox can cure Mugenes so sells it at twice its worth or for something called Naci."

"Why do they think that?" Eric watched as the Junker's light faded in the distance.

~dwop~

[V-1 O2Xe, Vox, is made of a rare substance found in the atmosphere that vaccinated the body against the effects of Mugenes. But due to the disease's rapid changes there have been at least five alterations. This suit currently injects V-4 O2Xe.]

"Hey," Koper called out to the pilot. He had been talking to the man, but he became silent. "You listening?"

"Yeah..." Eric responded. He quickly jumped down from the truck. "Wait for me!" He called back to the rebels before chasing after the Junker, following her dimming light.

"Wait!" Koper tried to stop the pilot, but it was too late. "Where is he going ---?"

Eric raced through the various encampments chasing after the Junker. Now that he was on the ground closer to the scavengers he could better see them. The majority, if not all, were severely mutated from the disease. Was this why they were on the edge of the world picking scraps off the fields of junk and garbage left behind by the past? Many were disfigured to the point that they were using their shovels and picks to lean on. Some had overgrown legs, calcified and unable to bend. Others had half their faces hardened by the disease that they had limited vision and depended on scopes that had practically bore into the skin of their faces with how much they were worn.

Wheezing coughing scraped through the air with a disgusting dryness. The heavy steps of limbs weighed down by the ossified flesh stirred frustration in Eric as it reminded him of his time in prison. It seemed it wasn't much better out here.

"So you were interested!" Rocket's voice cheerfully called. Eric looked to his left where the Junker stood with their light dangling over their head. The area was generally lit by the light sources from the other camps. "Glad to see! Come on in!" The stranger Junker invited Eric to get closer to the tarp they had set up over their little camp which looked stacked end to end with metal shelves full of nonsensical bits, bobs, screws, and switches picked up that they found discarded by the scavengers.

Though Eric couldn't be sure, maybe this guy knew something about the Vox or could at least inform him on where they got it. Eric approached the Junker.

Eric knew what he wanted. "Where did you get that Vox? And why do you think it can cure Mugenes? "

The Junker's eyes brightened up at the question. "Wellll...

my sources are secret, but how about I show you? If you help me get the Naci, I'll tell you, no I'll show you how it cures it!"

Eric wasn't sure he wanted to pass up the chance. Did he need to resupply his suit's Vox, or was there a limited amount set into his suit? Either way he wanted to know why this Junker thought it cured Mugenes.

"Where is this Naci?" Eric would agree to help if he could learn about the Vox. He remembered getting injected at the labs before and his suit injected him once before as well. It was valuable, useful, and if he could get some it could put him in a position of advantage. The rebels didn't trust the Junker, but why would they sell a product that didn't work? He doubted it cured Mugenes, but its known uses were just as useful.

"It's this way, in one of the labs. Come on!" Rocket jumped up and would hurriedly collect their pack, slinging it over their back before springing off in long, bouncing strides.

CHAPTER FIFTY

X

Rocket was soon leading Eric down to one of the old buildings in Parades that had been dug up by the scavenging Amaroxians, who were suffering from extreme mutation from the disease. As far as Eric could guess, these folk had reached the later stages of infection of A and S class. Eric himself was still about B Class.

"Do a lot of heavily infected scavenge?" The pilot was not as cold as to call them 'muties' as some did. They were still people, but near the end of their life. He also had heard how much moving around caused pain at A and S Classes of infection.

"Well sure!" Rocket looked back at Eric as they hopped along. "There are a lot of old labs down here that have different kinds of medicines they look for, but there are also old machines they can sell to buy Vox from the Science houses." They were a kind of hospital that continued to treat people with Mugenes. These days most hospitals were used to store the sick and treat injuries. "We're heading down to an old laboratory that has a big supply of Naci, but the problem is it's behind a blast seal door and I can't get through with the pieces I have." Rocket's eyes seemed to dim before quickly brightening. "But!" They looked over to Eric before glancing at his back. "That's a Zero Newton unit. They call it a Pulser Unit, right? With that you should be able to get through the door for me!" It seemed that this Junker wasn't different from the others and could easily analyze him and his gear without a second glance.

The two made their way down into the laboratory. The lab itself was partially buried beneath the stage, but its upper floors had mostly been exposed thanks to the work of the scavengers. It was a massive piece of architecture, nearly ten stories tall, that looked to have been constructed with metal and grey stone. It was a rectangular shaped building with the south and north faces twice the width of the sides. The south face of the building was primarily a sheet of black, pressured glass over smaller windows while its north wall was solid stone with metal reinforcing the frame. Along the narrower western and eastern faces there were smaller windows that looked to be sealed with metal bars that ran down to the ground floor where a wider window peeked over twisted pylons of metal that look to have been welded together. In fact much of the first two floors that had been exposed by the excavation work looked to have been barricaded by these wrapping and twisting slats of metal that look to have been fused together in large sections almost as if they melted together when they touched.

"How are we getting in?" Eric looked around but all he saw was a twisted collection of scaffolding that had no back or front end. He watched as Rocket hopped onto one of the ramps and scurried over to what appeared to be an opening. One of the smaller windows on the narrower side of the building had been removed, the metal bars cut off to allow passage into the laboratory. "Are all these sites like this? Buried?" So far he had seen one other, but other locations seemed to have been carved into the sides of stone walls.

"Yup! A lot of buildings in Pardes got buried a long time ago in an accident!" The Junker ducked their head as they entered the small window, but if they had to lower down it meant that Eric had to crawl in. When Rocket dropped onto the marble floor inside of the hallway of the building they would hurriedly turn around. Eric came face to face with the entity. This close they could see the small vents on their ventilator moving, which seemed to do so when they were going to speak. "It's a big, winding place, but I'll show you right to the blast doors! A lot of this place got sealed up during the accident. I think they were trying to save their work here." As they walked along Eric could see what they meant.

A number of the emergency blast doors looked to have closed down much of the building. Some were worked open, but others showed the damage around them from attempted forced entries. He would wonder what sort of accident would bury these buildings under piles of stone, sand, and metal. He followed the bouncing Rocket to the end of a hall. There a large door stood between them and the next room. The walls were decorated in banners and posters that were printed on glass plates burned to char, many of the letters unrecognizable to the Amaroxian. Reaching up his hand he touched it against the glass, which seemed to respond to his touch. Under the metal ends of his fingers were conductive points which reacted with the touch surfaces of most screens and tablets in use on Amaroxia. When he touched his finger to the glass it reacted as if it had responded to the charge between his finger and the glass.

"Is -- are these screens?" Rocket looked up towards Eric.

"Yeah, they used to be. Why?" When asked the question Eric moved to rub his hand over the glass, trying to wipe away the black char. Though mostly turned grey by whatever fire blew through, it was still visible. "Oh hey, there's still words on it?" Rocket hopped up to get a better look before deciding to step back. "Can't read it. Come on, don't worry about it! It probably says something silly anyway! Let's get this door open!"

Eric wasn't as confident as Rocket to dismiss the sign entirely, but since he couldn't read it either as it looked to be in an old Roxaedian alphabet that was no longer used. Nodding he would turn to face the blast door.

-

-

~BOOOOOOUM~

With a cacophonous roar, a flash of blue light filled the hall and shook the surroundings walls with such force that some of the scavengers roaming the outer perimeter came to a stop and looked around. The Dragonfly had shot the center of the door, causing it to bend and bow before it instantly blew open. In the aftermath it was still smoking and the blue energy that condensed around the damage started to fade away as the cherry red door cooled back to a charred silver. Though it did not blast it off the wall, it was open enough to allow Rocket and Eric to step inside. Looking around the room it was darker than what he was used to, but thanks to the visor he was able to see well enough. Rocket's eyes had enough backlight to help the Junker navigate the room.

"Wait here! What I need is in the back!" They hurried towards a long counter at the end of the room. Looking around Eric would notice there were a few round tables with seats settled up close to them. There were some strange looking vending machines that were nothing like the modern ones that had easy to recognize goods. The bright colors of the packages almost made everything in there look like poison or hazardous material with the alerting array of hues.

"Is this a kitchen?" As Eric asked that aloud he would spot Rocket coming out, now with a large sack on the top of their gear. "Did you find it?" Looking up Eric would recognize the packaging as food packing which was normally used for long distance shipping. Rocket proudly held the straps of their pack and puffed out their chest. Canting his head Eric would look back out into the hall. "What was this place even used for?"

"Oh, that's right! I was gunna show ya! Since I finally got some Naci, I'll be more than glad ta show ya how Vox helps fix the Mugenes. I dunno why more people don't take the doses regularly." They would hop out through the doors and motion to Eric. "It helps more when you take a lot. It's too bad no one believes me. The other Junkers say I should stop trying to sell it to you Amaroxians because you won't listen."

Eric followed the Junker. "I'm listening. Can you tell me how? And why do you know this?" The two would find their way to a stairwell and start climbing up.

"Well I can't read the words on these old terminals, but I can read the data. I learned that the medicine is supposed to stop Mugenes, except making it is hard because they don't have... the original disease anymore. It's all gone!" Arriving at the floor they pushed open the door. "But I found it!"

-

-

-

They crossed through the maze-like halls of the laboratory and arrived at what appeared to be the archival room. By the looks of the terminals this place was at least several hundred years old. The models were not even carried by antiquers, let alone were there materials available to even produce them anymore. Rocket came to a stop at one of the terminals, by the look of it the Junker had definitely gotten into the machine as wires, parts, and switches hung all over the console.

Pulling out a pair of wires Rocket would hurry out from the self-made hatch on the terminal's side. "Oh!" They chirped. "You don't have the same sized ports as me..." Eric wasn't sure where the Junker planned to put those cords, so he moved on to look around the room.

~dwop~

[S O S signal detected.]

"A what signal?" The pilot had never heard that phrase

before. Rocket looked up towards Eric. On his visor the system would show him the console leaking the signal. When he stood over it his hand came to rest on the tablet pad.

"Oh," Rocket mused. "Did your system pick that up? It's been repeating an old recording since I first got here. That's why I decided to check the computers. It seems to be coming from the Capital and here."

After the Junker pointed out the origin of the signal, he went over to check it out. He listened as Tiamat began to transmit the message to his helmet.

[Converge: Emergency assistance is needed. We have no airlift for the experiments and Experiment X has already reached the core! We have evacuated important personnel. Need Military support!]

[Capital: Converge Labs you are in the strike zone, you need to evacuate! Seal the basement and make sure the samples are safe.]

[Converge: Do you hear us?! S O S!]

[Capital: Converge Labs you are in the strike zone, you need to evacuate! Seal the basement and make sure the samples are safe.]

[Converge: It's too late... they've abandoned us...]

Eric stepped away from the console and looked at Rocket. "What's in the basement?"

GLOSSARY

Amaroxia

means red planet. Amaroxia's surface had once been inhabited, but the sun had reached a stage of life where it gave off more heat and solar flares ravaged the planet. Amaroxians moved underground to escape the dangers.

Roxaedian

The Red Center/Old Language

Geroiid

An organ unique to Amaroxians. Allows for telepathy and acts like a third eye for seeing light.

Amaroxians

do not have strong color vision. They can see ultraviolet spectrums. Underground society.

Roxoid

Augmented native or non-native Amaroxian

Pharyst

Non-native Amaroxian

Redfoot

Once a badge of pride for Colony Farmers. It is now a slur for arrogant Plantation workers

Tapetum lucidum

reflective surfaces in back of eyes. Seeing in greys and blues allows to see ultraviolet light

Turbo Suits

originally designed for space combat. Keeps muscles of space explorers from losing muscle mass from long periods in space. Change: suits were designed for UV protection with growing amount of UV rays in atmosphere.

Mugenes

has infected and killed 40% of life on planet. Some species mutate and survive most die.

Zalos

one who does not know his place and thinks them self a leader when acting rashly

Grul

Amaroxian term for male

Zagrul

indecent way of calling a man: one who has forgotten their duty to their mother's teat

Yhazi

Indecent way of calling a woman: one who keeps a man at her teat

Azi

Amaroxian term for female

artificial zygote insemination

Originally the members of the colony were genetically altered. Due to the earth's poisonous environment and the introduction to the terminator gene in gmo seeds, food was scarce. Women were the first to survive the battery of genetic testing because, unlike men, their X chromosomes were more stable and did not risk altering the unified gene therapy. The male Y chromosome evolved too fast to be able to create a stable serum.

Delpazh

leader of army

Deluazh

general under army leader

Felpazh
police leader

Feluazh
police under leader

sofp
System operation file primearc

tsxe
Turbo suit x-terminal executable

nanite
Nanomachines designed for turbo suits

Ifreeti
Inductive Francium Radiation Electronegative Electroplated Inculcator

CYR
The Cyr Legion were the unified armies of the Cyan GHOSTs, the Red SHIELDs, and the Yellow CROSS before they separated after the Conyard Incident ten years ago.

Red SHIELDs
sonic helio ionized emitting light domes

Red SHIELD
Named after the sonic hellio ionized emitting light domes, because their units were used to regularly combat am'lo

Cyan GHOSTs
Garrison Headquarters of Observation & Surveillance Tactical Security

SEED Vats
spore exteriorizing evolvement devices

Jules Vapor
The liquid oxygen used in chambers

Magnetosphere
An artificial field was created over Amaroxia whose collapse resulted in the firestorm that came from the sun.

Nexus
Connected information system in Capital

fyto
Food made of plants

DRAGON
Data Routing Aggrandized Global Open Network

Saiers
City natives

Teiers
Farm workers

Silver-Steel
A specialized steel invented on Amaroxia

Polycarbon ditanium
An old, flexible metal difficult to produce in modern times

ABOUT THE AUTHOR

R.a. Rex Draco

I am an Illustrator and writer who has been in love with storytelling since we were a wee dragon. I am a member of the furry community with friendships within the LGBTQ+ community so I understand the need for being inclusive and as such these are often represented in my stories as part of my greater worldbuilding. I write comics, light novels, and other types of unique genre models that represent myself and the communities I am part of.

I love science fiction first and foremost, romance, action and monster stories, so because of that I enjoy writing genre-hybrid fictions.

THANK YOU

Thank you for purchasing this book. I will soon have more to this series and other series posted up on Amazon and Books2Read If you're interested in supporting the xVerse series and my other comic properties check out my Patreon or donate to my Ko-Fi. Thanks again for your purchase. Please leave a review if you enjoyed it!

www.ingramcontent.com/pod-product-compliance
Lightning Source LLC
Chambersburg PA
CBHW051527290626
47170CB00016BA/2515